THE LOST ROAD
TO KEY WEST

Michael Reisig

As always, this book is dedicated to my wonderful lady, Bonnie Lee, who, through all these years, has always been there for me, even when I wasn't there for myself...

OTHER TITLES BY MICHAEL REISIG

Acknowledgments

I'm going to be a little repetitive here because sometimes the truth is worth repeating. Writers and editors are two different species. They are entirely different animals. Writers get most of the glory but without editors, most readers would be grossly disappointed and far fewer in number.

My readers would certainly be among "the disappointed" if it weren't for editors. My "first-eyes" editor, Tim Slauter, catches the brunt of my ramblings and makes them readable; then my incredibly talented final editor, Cris Wanzer (www.ManuscriptsToGo.com) steps in. She takes what has been collected and performs this "alchemy" that sculpts it all into a professional, accurate medium for publishing.

Thanks so much also to my beta readers: Virginia Williams, Bob Simpson, Steve Kittner, David Thatcher Wilson, and Nick Sullivan, who offer valuable suggestions and opinions.

And finally, I would be remiss not to mention Sandra Glassbrook, whose artistic talents have provided me with such a wonderful cover for this novel.

I owe the lion's share of my success to all these people and I am so grateful…

Once again, this book is also dedicated to all the wonderful writers of adventure and Caribbean tales, many of whom I'm proud to say are personal friends of mine. The support, insight, and friendship we offer each other are gifts beyond price.

Wayne Stinnett, John Cunningham, Nick Sullivan, Mike Pettit, Steven Becker, Ed Robinson, David Thatcher Wilson, Steve Kittner, Garrett Dennis, Julie Rogers, Charles Dougherty, Stanley McShane, Randy Wayne White, Bill H. Myers, Rodney Riesel, Cap Daniels, Dawn Lee McKenna, David Berens, Don Rich, and Gregory Dew.

— Michael Reisig

Introduction

The novel you're about to read is a work of fiction. But the premise of this story is taken from an actual incident. If you enjoy tales of lost treasure, wild adventures, ancient civilizations, and governments that sometimes bury truths...I think you'll like this one. Allow me to give you a small introduction to whet your appetite. The following is, to the best of my knowledge, a true accounting. However, you will find very little of it in any "official" documents anywhere.

On April 5, 1909, *The Phoenix Gazette* published a remarkable story. According to *The Gazette*, in the early part of that year, two explorers by the names of G.E. Kincaid and S.A. Jordan entered into an archaeological and photographic venture, paddling down the Colorado River in the Grand Canyon in a small craft. At the time, they were *supposedly* funded by and working with the Smithsonian Institution in Washington, D.C. (although this is apparently denied by government agencies now).

Among other items, *The Gazette* article told of the discovery by Kincaid and Jordan of *"a great underground citadel in the Grand Canyon, hewn from the walls by an ancient race, possibly from Egypt."*

The time that Kincaid and Jordan spent in transit on the Colorado River is somewhat unclear, although it appeared to be at least a number of weeks. When they returned to civilization, it seems that they, or someone affiliated with them, related the most remarkable tale through *The Phoenix Gazette*. The article told of the discovery of a lost colony of ancient Egyptians — early explorers driven by their imaginations and the edicts of their pharaoh, well over a thousand years ago. It was the tale of an advanced civilization, of bold statues, tablets containing hieroglyphics, high-quality metal weapons, golden vases, sarcophagi, advanced pottery and glassware, underground granaries, and more...all hidden in the walls of the Grand Canyon.

I will continue in a moment, but it bears mentioning that, while there is an earlier acknowledgment of G.E. Kincaid in *The Phoenix Gazette* on March 12 of the same year, I can't find any place where Kincaid and Jordan are actually proven to still be alive after the report of their discovery of the Egyptian colony in the Grand Canyon on April 5, 1909. Nor is there any mention of what happened to all the relics, scrolls, and precious artifacts they claimed to have brought back...for the Smithsonian.

Nothing happening here, folks... Just keep moving, eyes straight ahead...

But here's the real catch. A day after the article about the Grand Canyon Egyptians was printed in *The Phoenix Gazette,* it disappeared. *Poof.* Gone. Just like Kincaid and Jordan. Nothing left, no extra copies of the paper, no records in the newspaper archives, no proofs in the publisher's files, no nothing. No explanation from anyone.

In addition, the Smithsonian denied any knowledge of, or affiliation with, Kincaid and Jordan. *(Kincaid and Jordan? Weren't they a vaudeville comedy team? Nope, never heard of them...)*

The only good news here is the fact that thousands of people had read the original article in *The Gazette* and many of them still possessed copies of the paper, and there was no silencing them. But nonetheless, "the powers that be" did their best.

While still denying any knowledge of or contact with the two now-disappeared explorers, our government soon declared thirty-four miles of the Grand Canyon/Colorado River off-limits. Ironically enough, it just happened to be the same area Kincaid and Jordan described in their findings. It is said that American military were assigned to the area shortly thereafter — "to discourage private exploration on National Reserve property."

Nothing happening here, folks... Just keep moving, eyes straight ahead...

I know you think I'm making this up, but I'm not.

Prologue

Merneptah, the 13th son of Ramesses, was the fourth Pharaoh of the 19th Dynasty of Ancient Egypt. He ruled from the great city of Memphis, at the shores of what would become the Mediterranean Sea.

Memphis, Egypt
1207 BC

Merneptah stood at the parapets on the great walls of Memphis, near the apex of the Nile River Delta, surrounded by his immediate family, his soldiers, and his priests. The sun was just piercing the horizon in a blue-gray eastern sky, turning the thin line of stratus clouds that hugged the distant hills into a golden fleece.

Merneptah was a man of the hills and the valleys of Egypt, but most of all, he was ruler of the surrounding waters, having defeated and eventually incorporated the various "peoples of the sea" around the Egyptian Empire. He saw these waters, which would become known as the Mediterranean Sea, as a valuable entity for Egypt and he, more than any other Egyptian ruler of his era, saw the potential of expanding Egypt by sea more than by land. He was a visionary in the concept of distant exploration that might someday expand the power and wealth of the Egyptian Empire.

This day was the beginning of his dreams for an Egyptian rule "beyond the far horizon." Two of his greatest warships sat in the harbor below, their hulls filled with equipment, tools, food, seeds, and weapons. Their crews and captains were the best of the best, their soldiers the most experienced, and the women among them were of an equal fearless and adventurous nature. Their wombs would bear the sons of a new Egypt in places that no one had ever dreamed of. If this nation was to be remembered as the greatest civilization of its time, it had to expand beyond the parameters of simple man. Merneptah not only wanted to know what was over the most distant horizon, he wanted Egypt to own it.

The priests offered blessings. Fifty sheep were slaughtered in sacrifice on the parapets. Five hundred doves were released into the heavens as the anchors were pulled, and the sails of the two ships below billowed full. Twenty thousand people along the walls of the great city cheered, honoring the brave explorers, one and all, as the vessels moved out into the rising sun. But neither craft nor a single soul aboard them was ever seen again...

The Caribbean Sea
Navassa Island, thirty-five miles west of Haiti
July 1989

We had come back. But then, I knew we would. We had to...

That fiery yellow Caribbean sun was already leaning toward the mottled afternoon thunderheads on the horizon. We had to get a move on. There were things to do.

Three months ago, my partner Will and I had left a remarkable treasure cached inside the sliver of a limestone cave in the interior of this nondescript island. It was one of the last hoards taken by the pirate John Laffite — soon to be ours. But as I've said before, treasure never really belongs to anyone. We just hold it for a while, until someone takes it from us or we squander it like good pirates...

Our last experience on Navassa had been a heart-stopper. Our team (most of the Hole in the Coral Wall Gang) had parachuted from an aging Grumman Goose aircraft in the middle of the freaking night, with nothing more than this damned little dot of an island below us as our target. Surrounded by dark, totally unforgiving Caribbean waters, with bitter fingers of wind pulling at my face as I plummeted, I remember my blood pumping so hard I could feel the veins in my teeth.

That night we out-fought and out-thought a group of Haitian drug smugglers and their voodoo-spouting monster of a boss, and took back a treasure they had taken from us. Our attack successfully ended the plans of the mad underworld Haitian, Batife Detoure, who wanted to use Navassa Island as a midway fueling stop for Colombian drug smuggling.

All's well that ends well, they say...

But on this latest adventure, back on Navassa, Will and I had a new crew. With us were, of all people, our newly discovered children — my son, Tax, and Will's daughter, Jing. (A chance meeting in a New Orleans bar a few months earlier had led to the discovery that Will and I were parents. It's a long story that stretches back over twenty years.) Tax and Jing had shown up in Key West a month or so ago. They had decided to take a break from their newly formed investigative agency in Barbados to have a look at where their dads lived. They rented a duplex on Summerland Key, planning on staying for a few weeks, but they just hadn't left yet. I asked them about their detective agency and both of them sort of shrugged.

Tax offered a half-grin, his Colgate smile complementing a handsome, tanned face. He pushed the longish, sun-bleached hair back from his forehead. "It'll be there if or when we decide to go back," he said. "Given the nature of mankind, there is always someone cheating on, beating on, or thieving someone else."

I had to leave my remarkable dog, Shadow, at home with my neighbor. There just wasn't enough room in the plane and there was a weight and balance issue with another hundred pounds. But Shadow wasn't all that disappointed. My attractive neighbor had a large female Rottweiler that Shadow thought was the next best thing since red meat. Trish graciously allowed Shadow to stay with her and everyone got along famously.

We had come from Key West in my Cessna 182 floatplane. I made a quiet, high-glide approach in the dark gray, early morning hours, and anchored out a hundred yards offshore. After gearing up, we had taken a small Avon inflatable dinghy over to the tall, guano-splattered walls of Navassa and tied it off to a tenaciously surviving mangrove bush near the water's edge.

I tossed a tri-pronged rebar grappling hook up over the top of the cliff, slid it slowly back toward the edge until it caught, then set the hook with a solid yank. One after another, we climbed up, then began a cautious, hour-long hike through a stretch of bug-ridden mangroves and clutching, thorny jungle. We looked unanimously alike — boots, blue jeans, and heavy khaki shirts to ward off the mosquitoes, spiders, and other creatures. Will and I wore floppy Vietnam canvas hats, Tax had a baseball cap, and Jing simply bound her relatively long blond hair back with a rubber band, and carried a jungle hat tucked in her belt.

Our caution regarding the area came from two sources: First off, it was entirely possible that Navassa was still being used by secondary drug traffickers, and the last thing we needed was to run into a handful of glazed-eyed Colombian cocainers looking for a gunfight — just for fun. (Will and I had long since realized that there's no such thing as going out in "a blaze of glory." There is no glory in being "blazed." We were firm advocates of fancy footwork and heavy bullshit whenever possible.)

But that wasn't the least of the trauma this place offered. Batife Detoure, the previous but now very dead controller of this little paradise, had purchased a mated pair of spotted jaguars a couple of years back, when he first began designs on the isle. The two cats bred and they produced a third — a young, pure-black male. While the island had a good population of wild goats that kept them fairly well fed, they were still cats and they killed territorially — and for pleasure, as well. They were truly an unholy trinity for the unwary visitor. It didn't take long for the native fisherman of the area, who used to occasionally camp on the island, to avoid it entirely, given the tales of "night creatures" who dragged off the unwary...

Just thinking about those freaking cats brought back memories that made me shiver.

Finally, we found the cave we were looking for — still well hidden and undiscovered, thank God.

It was then that I heard the call. I glanced up through an opening in the canopy and for just a moment, I caught the flash of gray-and-white wings — an osprey. Then I heard the harsh shriek again. I couldn't help but smile.

"Easy, little brother," I whispered, a slight smile turning up the corners of my mouth. "We're not here to bother you."

Suddenly, I heard another loud call in the opposite direction, just as Will slowly, almost reverently, pulled away the heavy growth of sea grapes that disguised the entrance to the cave. For a moment, we all glanced at each other, bathed in excitement and trepidation, then, one by one, we squeezed through the narrow, vertical slit. As we stood in the eerie dimness of the small cavern, the shreds of light from the opening turned us into pale shadows. The fervor was almost palatable. Even though I knew the treasure had to be there, my pulse had ramped up to the point that I could feel that familiar little "tic" in my right temple.

Will hit the switch on his flashlight, breaking the spell. The rest of us followed suit. Slowly, in a solemn, dream-walking shuffle, we moved forward, the beams from our flashlights casting distorted shadows across the dusty floor and the rough gray walls. No one spoke. We were locked in the almost religious euphoria that exists between the present and the past — the amalgam that blends time and history with the thrill of discovery. It's a feeling only a handful of people ever get to experience, and it's damned near as good as sex.

I heard Will ease out a sigh of relief as he moved inward and the beam of his flashlight illuminated the four chests. They were all still there, against the gritty back wall, having waited over two hundred years for the opportunity to again share the glory of their contents with human vanity.

Will moved over and slowly, respectfully, knelt like a priest at confession. He pulled off his canvas hat and pushed his blond hair back out of his eyes, then carefully pried off the lock I had broken during our first experience here. He glanced up at the three of us, who stood silently, breathlessly next to him, and lifted the lid. Even seeing the contents for a second time, it still took my breath away. The whole scene was right out of a Robert Louis Stevenson novel.

Our flashlights lit the incredible array of gold and silver necklaces, chains, rings, pendants, and brooches, all exotically jeweled. Emeralds, sapphires, rubies, and diamonds sucked in the glow of the flashlight and lit up with a gleaming phosphorescence. The interspersed gold coins and remarkably intricate settings for the gems glowed with near-blinding luminescence. In this "assemblage," John Laffite had specifically gathered the most concise, valuable, and easily transferable collections of wealth that the rich and renowned possessed — at least those that had fallen under his control for a brief time at sea or on land. (Most he let continue on their way, after relieving them of their fortunes, but history tells us he was just as likely to gut a pompous or argumentative nobleman as let him scuttle off into a lifeboat.)

We glanced at each other, silently stunned. Then Jing giggled softly and knelt, her blond ponytail falling over her shoulder. She reached out, her blue eyes glistening brightly, and slowly ran a hand through the booty, coming up with a handful of rings and a gemmed necklace. Haltingly, she let it fall back into the box and her eyes lit with fire as the giggle rose to an incredulous laugh. A moment later, we were all laughing and hugging in the dark confines of that little cavern, our flashlights dancing across the walls as we embraced with tears born of glorious wealth and a sweet bonding beyond our wildest dreams.

Finally, when things settled down and our embraces reluctantly ended, Jing let out a breath, looked at Will and me, and spoke, a smile still turning the corners of her mouth. "You know, when you two first told us about this...this *find*...we thought you were great people but probably just two sandwiches short of a picnic, you know? Maybe too many dives with bad air..."

Will snorted quietly and I grinned.

Jing continued. "But son of a bitch! You were for real — *you are for real!*"

Tax spoke then, easing out a breath and running the fingers of one hand through his long, sun-bleached hair. "You see, the thing is, we've lived the better part of our lives having to sort the good guys from the hustlers, given Mom's penchant for company..." There was a quiet pause before he continued. "But we both thought it would be really freaking nice if you guys were for real because, truthfully, we're damned tired of all the sifting." He looked down at the chest of booty, then back up at us. "I'm thinking we might actually have a family here...and I'd like that."

"A rich family," muttered Jing with another smile.

Tax tossed a gold coin in the air and caught it adroitly, then got that little half-grin, which was a distinct characteristic of his. "And you being rich treasure hunters doesn't bother me at all." He held out a hand. "My dad and his buddy, the treasure hunters. That sounds like a lineage I could get into."

Will and I couldn't help but chuckle.

"He's definitely cut from my bark," I muttered.

Inside of fifteen minutes, we had the chests of Laffite's booty out of the cave and secured to the six-foot aluminum poles we had brought with us (two chests tied to each set of poles). Moments later, we were headed back to the plane. But we only managed to travel a couple hundred yards, our eyes darting left and right for hungry jaguars, when I heard the osprey call again. This time its voice was strident — filled with intensity. I knew the difference. I had spent time around hawks. A good friend of ours, Santino Roso, was a biologist in Belize. He and his lady, Talia, raised hawks and trained them to be their partners in hunting and exploration. (Hawks are considered to be among the smartest of birds.) I had learned much from him about these remarkable creatures. The effort is great but the reward is enormous — the companionship of a highly intelligent creature that becomes bonded to you for life. The truth is, almost all creatures, given the opportunity, will bond with humans if we treat them with the respect they deserve. The animal by your side can be an incredible friend and protector, or it can be "just a dawg." It's always up to you.

But the day's surprises were just beginning. As we moved out, we heard the deep cough of a big cat less than fifty yards to our right. I like domestic cats — they're smart, curious, independent, and yet remarkably affectionate when they want to be. But all cats, domestic or wild, carry that deeply ingrained hunter-killer instinct, and the wilder the animal, the greater the instinct.

I heard the scream of the osprey again, shrill and angry, coming from the same direction as the jaguar, and this time it was answered by another bird, undoubtedly its mate. There was angst in that voice — fear and outrage...

"Stop!" I whispered harshly.

Our little caravan came to a halt and we set the chests on the ground. I glanced around and sure enough, there was the male osprey, not seventy-five yards from us, shrieking and diving into the jungle. A moment later, the female burst from the foliage, soared out into the open crying angrily, then bent a wing and dove back. The male cut a quick circle and followed. Not five seconds later, we caught the angry hiss of a jaguar.

I knew in a heartbeat what was happening. I'd seen it with domestic cats and birds many times. It was a damned foolish thing to even consider, and I realized how easily this could go sideways. Will was already muttering something about the fine line between gallantry and stupidity.

I swung around to my friends. "There's a jaguar in there and he's found the osprey's nest. Dollars to donuts, man, they've got hatchlings and the damned cat is after them. The parents are trying to save their brood!"

Will shook his head and held up his hands, palms out, the late-afternoon sun silhouetting him. "Yeah, well, that's too bad, man, and I can feel the pain here but I'm not quite willing to get eaten in their place."

I looked at my son. "How about you? We gotta move quick!"

Tax shrugged with a slightly embarrassed demeanor. "I'm not

sure about this... I mean, it's sort of nature's way, man. I don't know that osprey. And that's an angry cat in there."

But before I could reply, Jing swung around and scrambled over to me. "Let's go!" she yelled as she pulled the .380 semi-automatic Smith and Wesson pistol from the holster at her side. "The clock's running!"

I couldn't help but grin.

"It is what it is," she added as we turned and dashed off into the sparse foliage. "The freaking weenies can stay there."

We had only just disappeared into the jungle when Will turned to Tax.

"I just hate being embarrassed into doing something," he muttered, shaking his head.

Tax huffed. "If you're gonna hang around that woman much," he replied, throwing a hand at his sister as she disappeared into the jungle, "you might as well get used to it." He exhaled hard. "C'mon. I gotta keep an eye on her. It's part of my job description."

By the time Jing and I reached the small clearing in the interior where the drama was playing out, the cat was moving up a large rubber tree and out along the heavy branch where the osprey nest was located. It was the young black jaguar. He heard us as we stumbled into the opening. Turning its thick head, the cat hissed angrily, then roared, shifting position slightly, trying to decide what was more important. The choice was the two large chicks in the nest (they appeared to be fledglings, almost ready to leave the nest, still downy, but their flight feathers were emerging), or the two intruders who were interfering with his feed. It roared at us again, its wide, pink mouth ringed with knife-like fangs and its velvety black coat rippling with antagonism.

The cat was wary of and bitterly angry with the human creatures, but he wanted the young creatures in the nest. Their screeching was ringing all of his primitive bells. It was too much. He couldn't resist. Without warning, the cat turned and leaped at the huge nest just as Will and Tax came stumbling through the morass of vines and boughs, practically under the tree. Shattering the nest, the jaguar snatched up one of the fledglings in his jaws and killed it, crushing the small body. Both Jing and I cried out in angst. Jing was bringing up her pistol but the cat was already moving toward the second chick, which was helplessly fluttering in terror against the remains of the broken nest. But at that moment, soaring out of the sky like a vengeful thunderbolt, came the mother osprey. She knew instinctively there was no chance she would survive but it didn't matter. She struck the animal in the face, ripping out one of its eyes with her razor-sharp talons, then rolling her blades across its face and jowls. The jaguar shrieked in anger and pain, rising up on its hind legs and instinctively grabbing the hawk with its claws — blindly ripping at and crushing the mother bird.

The nest was being shredded by the combat. The surviving fledgling screeched in mindless fear as it was bounced and thrown against the far side of the shattered aerie. I could see Jing aiming her pistol but even she knew it was too late, and even in her anger, a part of her understood that nothing would be accomplished by killing the jaguar. It was just doing what cats do and had already lost an eye this day to bad judgment.

At that moment, the jaguar lost its balance and both the cat and the female hawk went tumbling from the branch. Wings fluttering helplessly, the osprey was dead before she hit the ground, and a moment later, the cat was gone, a black streak disappearing into the jungle like a shadow.

Will and Tax had joined us and we all stood there, trembling, trying to recover from the trauma we'd just witnessed.

Jing slowly lowered her gun. "Shit!" she whispered vehemently. "Shit! Shit! Shit!"

Tax, next to me, exhaled a shaky breath, trying to absorb the carnage, when suddenly we heard it — the terrified chittering of the second baby osprey. With more luck than skill, the young bird had managed to spread his wings and perform a clumsy glide to the floor of the jungle, which probably saved its life. He had struggled to his feet and stood there. In two parts confusion and one-part defiance, the fledgling raised himself up and voiced a squeaky, singular statement of survival. I was damned impressed. But Jing was beside herself. Looking back, I guess I'd have to say that almost every woman is blessed with a degree of maternal instinct. But it generally takes the right situation to activate it. With some women, it requires little more than a cute puppy, or at the most, a drooling baby. But for Jing, who was not exactly your stereotypical woman, it was that motley, damned little gray-feathered creature.

Will's daughter slipped her pistol into its holster, then moved over and knelt on the ground next to the tiny hawk. We could still hear the male osprey calling fitfully and see him circling tightly above us through the trees. She carefully picked up the baby and put him in her jungle hat, closing it over the bird as if she intrinsically understood that the fledgling needed to be protected from outside stimuli right now. I knew this, from my experience with hawks, but I wasn't sure how she knew.

Jing looked up at us as we stared. "Quit gawking, you idiots. We gotta get this baby someplace quiet and safe."

After reaching the cliffs with our treasure, we lowered the chests down into our rubber raft with the rope we'd left, then paddled them over to the plane in a couple of trips. Then we refueled my 182 with a handful of ten-gallon plastic containers I had carried over with us in the cargo holds. But this time, with passengers as well as the small but heavy treasure chests, we were over-grossed. When we departed Navassa, my metal girl was like a fat goose lumbering in the somewhat calm waters below the lee of the cliffs. Finally, after a couple of attempts, I managed to "walk" one float off the water, alternating lift from one pontoon to the other and reducing the surface resistance. We bounced along, tilting back and forth precariously as I worked rudders against controls to trick the plane into lift. Eventually, both pontoons surrendered to the gift of wind, surging loose from the sea, and there was a mutual sigh of relief as we slowly rose into a peach-colored, late-afternoon sky.

Given the time it took to fly back to the Keys, we were trying to time our arrival for late evening/early morning — still dark enough to protect us but at a time when the senses of even those who are supposed to be paying attention are at the lowest ebb.

"Son of a bitch..." muttered Will gratefully as he eased back into the co-pilot's seat. "I wouldn't have put money on you getting us off the water."

I offered a small grin. "Never underestimate a desperate soul..."

We flew almost due north for a little over a hundred miles, then curved around the northern end of Cuba and headed west for another four hundred. We stayed well out of Cuban waters. The Cubans had fighter jets on constant standby, watching for anyone who strayed, accidentally or on purpose, into their waters. They had no humor regarding any sort of overflight. Will and I had friends who had made that mistake. Only some of them had lived to tell about it.

The moon was already reaching for the horizon, casting brilliant tendrils across the starry sky. That was my cue. I dropped us down, the floats on the plane just a few feet from the surface, practically skipping across the light sea beneath us. This was a method Crazy Eddie taught me — as long as you slow the plane to just above stall speed, your signal on radar is so close to the water it becomes indistinguishable from a boat.

It wasn't long before we could make out a few scattered mangrove islands just west of the main chain — Man Key, Barracouta Keys, and Joe Ingram Key. I took us up a few hundred feet for a moment and picked up my mike.

"Seaweed, Seaweed, this is Yellow Tang. Do you read me?" I kept my course, studying the horizon for any kind of plane or boat that looked…official. So far, so good…

The problem was, of course, that the government frowned on people bringing treasure into the country without clearing it through Customs. But once you did that, you could expect years of legal struggles with dozens of authorities, if they didn't just take it from you outright. This was especially true if you happened to have snatched it out of another country. So…we were doing it the "dancing with the devil" way, as Crazy Eddie, our infamous partner and primary pilot for the Hole in the Coral Wall Gang, would say.

"Seaweed, Seaweed, this is Tangfish… Five out. Running cool. Good time to hear from you."

Nothing…

"Where the hell are you, Bobby?" I muttered to myself. I looked over at Will.

He held out his hands. "Don't ask me. Remember, this is the same guy who got drunk and used a rocket grenade launcher to take out the sign on the top of Key West's only Vietnamese restaurant because he thought they were poisoning U.S. veterans' food."

Nonetheless, Bobby Branch was an old friend — an ex-Vietnam-vintage character who owned somewhat of an "off the charts" package store on Cudjoe Key for things that went bang. There was no question he was a wild man — okay, maybe a little crazy — and he'd done things in the past that his Uncle Sam wouldn't have been happy about. But at his core was the clean-burning fire of integrity that had never let us down. I was reminded of what our buddy, Travis Christian, once said about him — that real integrity was little more than a firm disposition not to violate your own identity. And Bobby Branch wore it well.

Our boy was supposed to be waiting in the mangroves in his twenty-one-foot Aquasport, just off of Man Key (about five or six miles west of Key West).

Just when I was starting to sweat a little, I saw a lantern blink three times from the mangroves dead ahead and my radio squelched.

"You're timing is freaking amazing," growled Bobby. "I'm waiting in these bloody bug-infested mangroves, serving dinner to these winged bastards for the last hour. I finally take a break to piss..."

"Sorry, man," I said with a smile.

"I didn't say it was your fault," Bobby hissed. "I'm just blaming you 'cause you're convenient. Now get your asses over here!"

During this whole time, Jing was doing all she could to keep her small osprey alive. Between shock and no food for over eight hours, the little creature was fading. I could see it in Jing's eyes. She was losing him.

"I found an eyedropper in the plane's medical kit and I've forced a little water into him," she whispered fretfully. "But it's just not enough. He's used to eating several times a day and I have nothing for him."

"Keep him covered," I replied. "The calmer he is, the more chance he has of surviving."

Moments later, I had us down on the water and taxiing into the protected, shallow bay between the three sections that make up Man Key. I had barely switched off the engine when a big, open fisherman roared out of the far side of the mangroves, skipping over the shallow waters, coming right at us.

"Whoooohh shit," muttered Will, echoing my thoughts.

Marine Patrol! Someone picked us up on radar!

But instead of being assaulted by spotlights and a bullhorn, the man at the helm of the open fisherman professionally reversed power and slid to a stop next to us. The fellow held up a flat box. "Did you guys order a pizza?" he called out.

Bobby! Bobby Branch! "That boy truly understands the value of an entrance," I said.

"What kind of pizza?" asked Will, deadpan, as he finished

opening the door of the plane and stepped out onto a pontoon.

"Pepperoni and mushroom," our old buddy shouted back, pushing back the brim of his weathered baseball cap.

Will shook his head. "Nope, wasn't us. But we'll take it for half price..."

Ten minutes later, we had offloaded the ancient treasure chests and all our weapons into Branch's Aquasport. Bobby covered them with a tarp and tossed a couple of lobster traps on them. He would run our find up to his place on Cudjoe and we'd meet later. While we all stood around on the plane's pontoons, gratefully munching on the pizza we hadn't ordered, our friend was idling away into the darkness, the moonlit silhouettes of the surrounding mangrove branches reaching out at him like something out of *Sleepy Hollow*.

"He's one of the good ones," I muttered.

"Yeah," agreed Will, nodding. "Crazy for sure but balls like cantaloupes."

Tax looked at both of us, a slice of pizza in his hand. "Is this any indication of what life is gonna be like with you two?"

I shrugged. "Yeah, possibly. But most of the time, it's a little more exciting..."

Will glanced around. "Where's Jing?"

In all the excitement of offloading, Jing had somehow disappeared. My first thought, as I saw her coming out of the high-ground mangroves, was she had gone for a call of nature, but she had something in her hand. We all stared as she held up a good-sized blue crab.

"Food for my boy," she said as she knelt, pulled out the small stiletto she carried in her boot, and deftly cut open the crab on the pontoon. In less time that it takes to describe it, she had a handful of firm white meat and entrails in the top half of the shell.

"Let's go!" I called. "He who lingers while unloading contraband often becomes a sad story."

As Will and I did a quick preflight, I glanced back and saw Jing peel back her jungle hat. Cooing softly, she carefully extended a small piece of crab between her thumb and forefinger. I shook my head sadly when nothing happened. She tried again, still with no success. I could hear her exhale in fear and disappointment.

Will looked at me. We'd seen this situation before. With the trauma the chick had endured, and the loss of its parents, it was unlikely that the small creature would ever eat again. My heart went out to him but we couldn't just sit there, waiting for the Marine Patrol or the Coast Guard to come for us.

"We gotta go," I whispered, knowing that the sound of the engine starting and the trembling of the plane would probably be the final straw. I reached for the ignition…

But at that moment, I heard Will's daughter exclaim softly, incredulously, "He took it! He ate it!"

"Son of a bitch," muttered Tax, who had been watching intently from the seat next to his sister. "The little guy snatched it and ate it! Give him another piece!"

Jing did, and this time the little hawk took it willingly, greedily…

We gave Jing five precious minutes…how could we not? In the strangest of fashions, that little hawk somehow, suddenly, represented all the impossible moments in our lives, where life and death had been balanced on a fulcrum of timing and luck, and the gods, for no good reason, had thrown us a piece of crab…

If it weren't for the knowledge I had accrued with Santino Roso, the fledgling probably wouldn't have made it, so I'll take a little credit. But as it was, that day a whole new chapter was beginning in our lives — one that would include ancient history and hawks, new and old friends, and life in the high currents.

CHAPTER ONE

The sun was just creeping over a misty pink horizon as I set us down in Newfound Harbor on Big Pine Key. Easing out a sigh of relief, I glanced at the last of the fading stars sprinkled against a hazy, dark-blue western sky. Then I taxied as quietly as possible into the mouth of the canal where my stilt home sat.

After a brief but joyous reunion with Shadow, Will and I got into my pickup and drove down to Cudjoe to meet with Bobby Branch at his house and pick up our booty. But that morning, before loading, we opened a chest and let Bobby pick out a few handfuls of shiny things to his liking. He'd earned it. Once again, our friend had slipped his 21-foot "Pegasus" through the moonlit channels and shallow passages like a backwaters wizard, transporting our goods safely to his canal home on the backside of Cudjoe.

Once everything was secured back at my place on Big Pine, we all took a couple of days off, just to relax. Will headed back down the Keys to his sailboat and the kids returned to their place on Summerland.

Jing and Tax had shown up in the Keys about a week or so after the gang's last adventure on Navassa Island and Barbados. They had come up in Tax's sailboat, *Windchild* — an older but well-preserved forty-one-foot Morgan. They found that they really liked the area, so they dug into their savings and rented both sides of an attractive duplex overlooking the ocean on Summerland Key, which put them a short drive from Will and his houseboat in Key West, and me on Big Pine. The duplex was for sale as well, and now that money was about to disappear from the list of problems in life, they were considering the possibilities of purchase. It wasn't every brother and sister who could deal with that kind of proximity, but they were close. They had spent a lot of time fending for each other as they grew up, and they'd come to see themselves as allies. As they settled into the Keys, they bought a couple of used vehicles — a well-maintained 1983 Harley XLH-61 for Tax, and a slightly older Volkswagen van for Jing, which seemed just right for the hippie that dwelled inside her.

It was true that they had just recently started a small detective agency in Barbados, but in the time that they had been in operation,

1

our offspring had learned that detective agencies were not quite as glamorous a profession as movies and television made them out to be. The profession vacillated between the mind-numbing boredom of dealing with cheating spouses to searching for missing persons, which could be equally mind-numbing but also carried a good deal of danger. There was a huge drug trade in the southern islands now, and people were killing each other for nickel bags. The folks who were doing the killing wanted the dead folks to stay disappeared. Just searching for a body could land you in the middle of a gang war. So, when the opportunity to visit with their dads came about, Tax and Jing jumped on it. Their mother, the indomitable, incredibly resilient Banyan McDaniel, had a list as long as her arm of suitors who would gladly help manage her bar, and any other needs she had.

Our kids had returned to their duplex and Jing was anxious to get her new "baby" into a secure location. Right now, she was fighting for the life of that bird. I knew that girl well already. She didn't like losing at anything, but she had taken up the gauntlet here, against the gods of timing and fate, and the odds weren't on her side. There was nothing anyone else could do. As our old Jamaican friend, Rufus, would sometimes say, *"It be up to da gods, mon. Dey make da sun and da rain..."*

After I had showered and fixed some breakfast, I called Ronald Landon, our remarkable antiquities dealer/friend in Miami. Landon had all the connections necessary to move the majority of our latest find. (We all would, of course, choose a few items to keep as mementos of the adventure.) We also took photos, to show the treasure to the other members of the Hole in the Coral Wall Gang. Will and I had informed Crazy Eddie and our team of our find well before we went back to get it...just in case things went south for some reason. No one was jealous that we hadn't included them. Cody and Eddie understood that this was "a family thing..." and Lord knows, none of them were overly anxious to go back to that godforsaken island.

Cody and the gang's latest addition, the tall, tawny-haired Venezuelan, Arturio, had more money than they could hide as it was, and Eddie was always complaining that he couldn't find a pair of socks that didn't have golden knickknacks falling out of them.

(Like socks mattered. I couldn't remember the last time I saw that old rapscallion in anything but wrinkled shorts, a T-shirt, sandals, and his precious ball cap, which he claimed was given to him by Jimmy Buffett.)

During this time, Jing was mostly preoccupied with the survival of her new charge. She purchased a good-sized cage and kept it on their screened porch, allowing the new arrival to get acclimated to life without the roar of civilization or the danger of cats or iguanas.

Most importantly, Will and I told Jing about our old friend, Santino Roso, in Belize. He and his lady had shared a remarkable adventure with us in Guatemala and Belize involving old Swiss coins and a handful of Nazis, but most importantly, he was an ornithologist for Belize Fish and Wildlife.

It seemed impossible that a "just out of the nest" fledgling could have survived such a terrible introduction to life. But that little one was a fighter. I was fairly certain it was a female because of the dark-brown streaks on the creature's throat, often referred to as a "necklace" on ospreys, but I recalled Santino saying that some males have the same streaks but lose them as they mature. It didn't matter — male or female, that was Jing's bird. Nonetheless, Will's daughter had a serious challenge in front of her.

As soon as Jing had the cage secured to a patio roof beam — out of the reach of cats and iguanas — she was on the phone to Santino. In a stroke of luck, she reached "Santi" at his office in the capital city of Belmopan. Jing introduced herself and listened patiently as Santi spoke briefly of the "remarkable journey" he had made through Guatemala and Belize with Will and me. (It truly was an adventure worthy of a novel...) Then, for the next twenty minutes, she took notes on nursing techniques and the care of her feathered child — invaluable information that would give her bird a fighting chance at survival. But Santino stressed that even then, survival was a roll of the dice, and the possibility of the bird accepting her as a surrogate parent was fairly slim.

For the next few days, Jing threw herself at this challenge — reading voraciously about birds of prey and the rearing and training of hawks while struggling to keep her bird alive. She discovered there were two lines of thought when it came to raising/owning a bird of this nature. The traditional philosophy for "hawking" (developed primarily for hunting and used as far back as 2000 BC) was to raise a young bird in captivity until it was capable of hunting, then train it to hunt and return with the prey it killed. The bird would soar out into the sky and seek out prey, or be shown a target by its handler and chase it down. But with this method, the bird was a tool. Being a consort to the handler came second.

A certain collection of hardware was necessary for training and hawking. Ironically, the equipment has changed very little up to the present day. First off, the handler needs at least one thick "gauntlet" — a heavy leather glove extending over the hand and forearm — to allow the bird to land and perch on the trainer's arm during training and hunting. The power of a big bird's talons is simply unimaginable — they are perfectly capable of breaking bone. The gauntlet prevents this. In addition, "jesses" (short leather or nylon straps) are attached to the hawk's ankles — for the handler's control on the ground and, in the old days, to secure the bird on its perch before and after a hunt. Finally, there is a "creance," which is a light leather or nylon line that is tied to the jesses on the bird's legs. The creance is an adjustable-length line used in the early stages of training the bird — long enough for the creature to experience the freedom of flight (as the handler guides it in somewhat of a circle around him/her) but not so long that the line can't be rewound on its spindle to bring the bird in and control it.

In the early days of falconry, the hunting bird was hooded most of the time and left on a perch in a caged facility called a "mew" when not hunting. While the hood was removed sometimes in its mew, primarily the creature remained caged until it was hooded and taken into the field for hunting. Training consisted of teaching the hawk to bring down a particular victim (a dove, duck, or rabbit) that the trainer had observed. After contact and a successful kill, the hawk returned with his prey and received a reward (generally, a piece of the immediate victim). While there was, without a doubt, some rapport between the person and the hawk with this method, it lacked any real bonding for the participants. However, Jing did realize that a hood could be invaluable at times — particularly when transporting the bird from place to place. She immediately ordered a calfskin hood from a falconer in Miami.

Santino also explained that the purpose of a hood is simply to calm the bird. Hawks are so visually oriented that they are not fearful of what they cannot see. If they cannot see it, then it must not be there. Santino said a freshly obtained wild hawk that has been hooded will often eat within hours of trapping, even standing on the fist of a person, simply because the bird cannot see anything alarming. Hoods protect the creature and allow ease of control in situations that would otherwise be startling.

Santino said that if she was fortunate, and the bird relaxed to humans, she might not need a hood except for while traveling and on hunting excursions. Jing began working with the bird while it was still in the cage, slipping her hands through the wide cage door. The idea of the hood frightened it at first but the bird soon relaxed once it was on, and there was a remarkable difference in the creature's demeanor.

Jing also discovered that not all hawks make good companions in this endeavor. Red-tailed and Harris's Hawks were probably the favorites, along with Peregrine Falcons, but ospreys were definitely one of the birds that were acceptable for human companionship and hawking. She read all the information available at the library in Key West and continually spent time with her new charge, who she had named *Cielo Niño* (Sky Child). But she often shortened that to just Cielo.

Her new friend remained in the large, four-by-four-foot cage inside the screened porch, and grew stronger every day. Cielo feasted on a diet of fresh fish and crab, and quarters of fresh mice, which provided the roughage hawks need to digest everything properly. Jing purchased a leather gauntlet and had taken to wearing it while feeding Cielo. At first, it frightened the bird and it retreated to the corner of the cage, but Jing's new companion soon became accustomed to it, even offering a few tentative pecks at it, and finally, actually standing on it for a few seconds, its young talons fiercely grasping the leather with surprising strength.

As Cielo's flight feathers filled in and the bird grew stronger, Jing was forced to break the back legs of live mice and put them in the cage so the hawk could develop her hunting skills. It was admittedly difficult for Will's daughter to have to cripple or kill mice to feed her bird, but there was no other way. Hawking of any sort is not for the faint of heart. Regardless of Jing's constant care, it was still somewhat of a small miracle that the young osprey survived, and when the dark-brown streaks on the neck of the creature disappeared, Jing accepted that it was a male.

In just three short weeks, Jing could see a bond forming between her and this remarkable creature. Cielo no longer hovered in the back of the cage. He perched on the stands and chirped contentedly when he saw his keeper, hopping over and taking food avidly, without fear, and hesitantly accepting an occasional, brief caress. In the process, Jing had cuffed the bird with a tiny, durable, red plastic anklet so that, God forbid, if she lost him, he might possibly be located and identified.

New, full flight feathers were filling in, covering the fluffy down on Cielo's body, and he was beginning to exercise his wings in mock flight. He would also boldly bounce onto Jing's leather-covered arm and sit there for a few moments, eyes staring intensely, then blinking in that sharp, hawk-like fashion, as if testing his own courage with this strange creature who had preserved him.

Jing gradually began to realize that she didn't want just a hunting relationship and she couldn't stand the thought of a creature of the sky like an osprey being cooped up in a cage for days at a time. Ultimately, the lady from Barbados, who loved the sea and the sky as much as her charge, decided on a compromise. She would train this bird and love it with the same passion that Santino in Belize had done with his first wild hawk. It would become a friend, not a pet, and ultimately, it would be set free — to make its choice. Santino had warned her that it was a gamble, and a painful one at that, because Jing had grown so attached and everyone knew she could easily lose her new companion. But she would raise it and train it to fend for itself, and use the jesses and the creance only long enough for Cielo to become comfortable with flight (and the concept of returning to his friend). Then she would set the bird free. If the hawk came back, it would be because he wanted to.

During this same time, Will and I were involved in a couple of secret meetings with our old friend in Miami. Ronald Landon III owned a small mansion near South Beach. He possessed an extraordinary eye for shiny antique baubles and an impressive list of filthy rich people. (Some were more filthy than others, but money was money.) As always, he would examine our latest find, appraise it, then store it in his extremely secure walk-in vault while he made some calls and set up a very exclusive showing.

While this was taking place, we arranged visits with our attorneys and the bankers we trusted. In the old days, we would have taken the money and run, hiding it in mattresses and closets, but given the times, we had grown more sophisticated. Offshore banking sophisticated. I remember our old Rastaman buddy, Rufus, saying that money was not the key to happiness, but if you had enough money, you could have a key made...

In the end, all was well. Hell, it was damned near whiz-bang perfect. Will and I had introduced our "protégées" to a rich adventure that would provide them with the finances to relax and enjoy life instead of chasing it. We set up offshore accounts for our offspring, and the Hole in the Coral Wall Gang (after a couple of introductory meetings) had gained two peripheral members.

Jing was enjoying the challenge that her new winged friend presented, and in the interim, Tax had decided to fly back to Barbados for a few days to get their affairs in order. They needed to inform the government of Barbados that their detective service would be unavailable for an indefinite amount of time. Tax would pack up and store all the things of importance from their places of residence, while paying their rents several months in advance. They would keep their rental homes/apartments because, at this point, nothing was written in stone. Most importantly, and by far the most difficult of the errands, was informing their mother that they would not be back for some time. The volatile Banyan McDaniel was not going to be happy about this.

For the rest of us, all was good. But then, I should have been reminded of Rufus and one of his sayings about the gods, and their penchant for entertainment. *"When da gods get bored, dey perform random acts of complications. You be jus' a goldfish in da bowl, mon. Cheap entertainment..."*

Sure enough, he was right.

CHAPTER TWO

The following afternoon, while on our way back from a two-day meeting in Miami with Ronald, our sophisticated fence, Will and I stopped at one of the "country" bars in Homestead. That area actually had an upscale country community with a number of small ranches and farms, and a fairly well-known rodeo arena. We were sitting in the outdoor tiki bar area, having a couple of beers and checking out the local talent, when a pickup with a horse trailer attached pulled in. The guy in the truck looked distantly familiar to me. But as soon as he opened the door and pulled those long, blue-jeaned legs from the cab, tipping back his weathered cowboy hat with a practiced flick of a finger and exposing that angular, suntanned face, I recognized him. Damn, it had been a long, long, time…

"Dax," I whispered, to no one in particular. "Dax Dryder."

Will looked up and eased out a soft expletive. "Damned if you aren't right!"

A moment later, a huge, gray-colored German shepherd jumped from the cab with practiced ease and stood beside the big guy. Both were calm and smooth, not a nervous bone between them.

As the fellow found a seat at a table near his truck, and the dog curled up by his feet, my buddy and I grabbed our drinks, slid off our barstools, and walked toward them. We got about halfway before Dax recognized us. The dog, of course, didn't, and he casually but purposely eased in front of his companion. No teeth showing yet but cautious…

"Tell him we're friends," I called out. "Old friends…"

Dax's face brightened in recognition. "Well, I'll be damned," he said as he reached down and laid a steadying hand on the animal's collar. "It's okay, Smoke," he whispered. "It's okay, boy…"

The animal appeared to agree with that as Dax stood and we all enthusiastically shook hands.

"You two still chasin' women and treasure?" he asked.

"Yep," said Will. "In no particular order."

Dax smiled, displaying his square, white teeth, then shifted his cowboy hat back and ran a hand through his longish blond hair. "Damn, man! You guys are like the original Harrison Fords!"

Will offered a caustic chuckle. "Buddy," he said, "Harrison Ford couldn't shine our freakin' shoes."

"Truth is," I added, "we don't always go looking for treasure or the accompanying trouble. Both just seem to have a way of finding us. By all rights, we should have been long gone to that palm-shaded island in the sun, where the drinks are free and the women never take no for an answer."

Will got that goofy grin of his. "And the jukebox in the corner of the bar plays nothing but seventies and eighties songs."

Dax had to grin again. He nodded to his table. "Sit a spell and swap some lies."

We moved over and sat down, the dog settling down at Dax's side. I ordered three beers from the bar.

The bartender, who was drying glasses, saw the dog. He moved over to the edge of the bar. "Hey man," he called to Dax. "No dogs in the bar area — regulations."

Dax (and Smoke) looked up. Smoke growled as if he understood every word.

"He's not 'my dog,'" Dax said. "He's my companion. You can try moving him if you want but I wouldn't recommend it."

The bartender took another look at the 150-pound black-and-gray shepherd.

The dog drew back his lips, exposing nearly inch-long canines, and rumbled low and heavy. His bodyweight shifted forward, just slightly, and the muscles in his huge shoulders tightened as he stared down the man. The bartender looked around, then glanced back at the dog and the cowboy. He shrugged in an aggravated but conciliatory fashion. "What the hell," he muttered. "I only work here." He nodded at Smoke. "And that's out of my pay grade."

I had to ask. "So, when did you hook up with your furry companion?"

Dax offered a reminiscent smile and exhaled softly. "Three years ago, I spent a summer in Montana breaking horses on a friend's ranch. My buddy, Ted, had an enormous female German shepherd. She was as intelligent and protective as an animal got but she had a wild streak in her, and she liked to wander. Sometimes she stayed gone for a week at a time, then she'd show up, tired, hungry, and occasionally scraped up. But she always came back." Dax took a swig of his beer and continued. "That summer though, she disappeared for over a month, and Ted was convinced she was gone for good. He felt she'd probably been mistaken for a wolf by one of the local ranchers and had been shot. Then one day, while we were working with a new pair of mares in the corral, I looked up and there, on the hill, was the dog. But she wasn't alone. Beside her stood a huge wolf — one of the largest I've ever seen."

Our friend paused for another sip of beer. "One of the cowhands reached for the Winchester that sat against the fencepost, but Ted stopped him. He shook his head at the ranch hand as the big German shepherd started down toward the corral. It was then that they noticed the small gray line of bobbing heads following her. The wolf stood on the crest and watched as she led her puppies back to the ranch. When she reached the outbuildings, she stopped and turned, looking back at her mate there on the rise. For a moment, they stared at each other, neither of them moving a muscle. Then, almost in unison, she turned toward the corral and he was gone."

Dax took another hit from his beer. "Ted shook his head and smiled as she trotted over, proud as could be, four gray-white furballs with legs following her as best they could. Ted and I stepped out of the corral and knelt to greet her and her new brood. She rubbed up against my buddy and he scratched her ears as the puppies spilled across our feet." Our friend couldn't help but ease out a soft sigh. "As I squatted down, one of the puppies, a smoke-colored fluff of fur with big gray eyes, broke from the group and stumbled its way over to me. It grabbed the tip of my boot with its nearly toothless maw and growled, looking up at me."

Dax stared at Will and me with distant recollection.

"It was love at first sight. I scooped him up, and as the pup squirmed and wiggled and tried to bite my fingers, I realized I needed a companion," he continued. "I'd been riding the rodeo circuit full-time again, for over a year, and life on the road got lonely. All the one-night stands in the world couldn't change that." Our friend eased out a breath. "It wasn't long and the puppies were weaned. There was never any question about me taking the little guy. From the very first moment the pup squirmed into my arms, he belonged to me. When he was old enough to leave his mother, I made him a little bed in the bunkhouse with me. From then on, anywhere I went, Smoke went."

Dax reached down and drew an affectionate hand across the animal's head. Smoke leaned into him. I wasn't sure, but I thought I saw the gleam of moisture in that tough cowboy's eyes. But I wasn't going to say anything.

"So, that's all you've been up to — just rodeo?" Will said. "The last time we ran into you — maybe three or four years ago, if I remember correctly — you were just getting out of a relationship."

Our friend nodded somberly and drew a breath. "Yeah, '84, '85. I'd just gone through probably the most bizarre time in my life."

Will nodded. "Yeah man, I remember. One of the wildest stories I've ever heard. You claimed you got abducted by aliens, right? Genuine little gray guys. But you got away...escaped..." Will shook his head. "Even with all that Kansas and I have been through, that particular story was hard to swallow. That was seriously 'whoa shit' wild."

Dax shrugged. "Doesn't really matter if you believe it or not. It happened."

"Yeah, now I remember," continued Will. "In the process of getting away, you stole a little handheld, golden device that gave you Svengali-like powers. No one could resist doing what you told them to do when you pressed the button on it."

Our friend nodded. "Yep. That's what happened. But unfortunately, I used it too much in the process of proving that my father, a significant politician, was innocent regarding charges of graft and the acceptance of illegal money, and I drew the attention of some bad people, who ended up wanting the 'Golden Persuader,' as I called it."

I didn't mention at the time that I had a similar gift — a stone we found in the Venezuelan crypt/cave a few months back that changed colors and warmed-up when a mental or physical threat was imminent. That particular "find" had virtually saved the lives of the Hole in the Coral Wall Gang, having warned me that we had been infiltrated by a Colombian hit-woman.

Dax took a breath and exhaled slowly. "Most of all, what that did for me was open my eyes to the mysteries of the universe, and the remarkable possibilities on this planet as well. It was a big step for a Methodist country boy."

"You sound a bit like Kansas and me," Will said with a wry smile. "So, what happened to it?"

Again our friend sighed. "As you know, I met a woman in the process of that particular adventure, and fell in love. But after it was all over, she wanted a house in the city and babies, and I still wanted to ride the rodeo circuit with my horse, Paint." He smiled somewhat sadly and looked down at the dog. "And my boy, Smoke." Again, he eased out a heavy breath. "We got married and there was no question that I loved her, but it just didn't work out. In the end, I gave her the Golden Persuader so that she would be safe on her own. We had ruffled the feathers of some important people during that time with my dad. I needed her to be protected..." He shook his head sadly. "Haven't seen her in over two years." Dax abruptly changed the subject. "So, what the hell have you two been up to?"

Will took a swig of his beer and grinned. "You know, the same old stuff — part-time treasure hunting and full-time trying to stay out of the trouble that the part-time treasure hunting brings." He paused and stared at Dax. "You really got abducted? I mean, the little gray men and everything?" There was still skepticism in his voice.

The big cowboy next to him just shrugged. "The whole shootin' match, man — lock, stock, and tomahawk." He offered a wry smile. "I can explain it to you again, amigo, but I can't understand it for you. I know you think I'm all hat and no cattle when it comes to this, but it doesn't matter. There are times in your life when you are simply forced to accept things that just twist your damn horns." He paused for a moment and grinned. "If I still had that little 'persuader' I could change your mind in the blink of a horsefly's eye."

I remembered why I liked this guy. He left you with a big, solid feeling. There was nothing fake or feigned with him. He was exactly what he was and you could like it or you could hit the road. There was integrity in his words and his actions and I had to believe, looking at him, that he would be a good man to have at your side in a tight spot. He reminded me a lot of Will but he wasn't as funny as my partner. Two or three drinks and a hit of weed, and Will could turn a room upside down.

I turned to Dax. "You just finished your rodeo in Homestead, right?"

Our friend nodded.

"Why don't you come down to the Keys with us for a little R&R?" I said. "We'll do Duval Street, turn it on its ear..."

Dax cocked his head and smiled.

"And the women right now..." Will added, holding out a hand. "Hot summer ladies with 'clothing optional' attitudes and little or no inhibitions..."

Our friend was still contemplating, his lips pursed. "Hmmm. I don't actually have another rodeo I have to attend for the better part of a month..."

"Then it's a done deal," cried Will, holding up his beer in salute. "There's a little dude ranch on Sugarloaf Key where you can keep your horse and trailer."

"You're right," said Dax. "Used it before." He offered that big, wide Texas grin, bright teeth contrasting his dark tan. He spat in the palm of his hand and slapped it on the tabletop. "Okay, boys, it's a bargain!"

Will got all excited at the thought of partying in Key West and reflexively reached down to rub Smoke. The dog growled and those canines appeared like bad magic. Will snatched back his hand in time to keep all his fingers.

Dax grinned. "Give him a couple of days and you not only get to keep your fingers, but you'll have a hard time getting rid of him."

CHAPTER THREE

During the couple of days Will and I had spent with Ronald in Miami, and during the next week while getting Dax settled into the Keys (and accompanying him on a bar-to-bar survey in Key West to determine what percentage of women were actually interested in frivolous, non-binding sexual encounters), Jing was still firmly dedicated to establishing a relationship with her new hawk.

Cielo had matured and grown significantly, and was definitely a "he." The bird was now a small but full-fledged osprey, with a wingspan that challenged his cage, hungry all the time, and restless in his narrow confinement. But there was, without a doubt, the beginning of a strong bond between him and his human companion. Jing, with the heavy leather gauntlet on her arm, had managed to attach the jesses to the hawk's ankles and acclimate Cielo to them. Holding the leather jesses, and keeping him tight to the gauntlet, she managed to take the bird from his cage and walk around with him inside the confines of the screened porch. It was an experience the first couple of times, not unlike breaking a horse, and both the trainer and the bird were exhausted at the end. But finally, Cielo started to accept the idea that the jesses held him to Jing's arm and began to relax. And he had come to accept, reluctantly, the hood, when it was necessary.

Finally, after a few more days of acclimation, Jing hooded her bird, attached the nylon creances to the leather jesses on Cielo's legs, and took him from the cage. It was time for a flight test. Tax had just gotten back from Barbados and decided he didn't want to miss this maiden flight. With the hawk grasping the gauntlet on her forearm, and her brother observing, Jing slowly moved outside and toward the open marl and mangrove lots a few houses from the duplex. The moment of truth had come. (At least, one of the moments of truth.)

It was a beautiful, early morning. The wind was slight and the sun warm, but not brutal yet. Jing quietly walked down the road, her hooded bird on her gauntleted arm. The only interruption was the large Rottweiler in the fenced yard at the last house before the marl lot, who barked and growled furiously, slamming himself against the fence as Jing walked past the house. Cielo trembled at the

14

sound, his head coming up in alertness, but the hood kept him from becoming unmanageable.

Once Jing reached the far side of the lot where marl boulders marked the boundary with the water, she removed the hood and let her hawk acclimate to the outdoors, while the jesses attached to the creances held the bird to her gauntleted forearm. The osprey blinked and his head snapped from side to side, taking in the sights and smells. A shiver ran down his back as Jing cautiously undid the leather jesses from her arm. Cielo's legs were still securely attached to the nylon creances that led to the spindle she held. Jing had barely dared a single breath when the hawk, without a hint of warning, suddenly surged up into the air, flapping wildly. The spindle hissed in her hand as the bird rose, the line screaming out, and for a moment it almost slipped from her hand. By the time she gained control, the small spindle was almost out of line and the bird was still flapping recklessly above her in wobbling circles, trying desperately for height and freedom.

When the spindle slipped from her hand, Jing lost all sense of protocol. She fell to her knees on the hard marl and grabbed the line, trying to pull the panicked, screeching bird back down, hand over hand. Finally, she managed to get Cielo down and onto her gauntlet, but the bird and the woman were both shaken. Jing quickly hooded the hawk and took him home, where she returned him to his cage. Then she mixed herself a drink and cussed furiously for a full five minutes. Tax said he had enjoyed the show and he'd like to come back for act two.

When we got into town, Dax had accepted the offer to bunk at my place. (Hell, I had three bedrooms and two of them never got used.) But the truth was, we were hardly home for the first few days.

After about a week of debauchery in Key West (with a day or two of recovery midway in between, which we spent diving and fishing), the three of us — Will, me, and Dax — were having a late breakfast at Island Jim's on Big Pine Key. We were telling stories over our coffees, trying, as usual, to out-yarn each other, when Dax leaned back in his chair and his eyes gathered a pensive gleam.

"I have a story I haven't told you," he said carefully. "About lost Egyptian cities, almost impossible ancient sea voyages, and of course, potential treasure, all tied together down in the Grand Canyon of Arizona." He paused and took a draw on one of the small, dark *cigarillos* he enjoyed on occasion, easing out the smoke like a weary, Stetson-donned dragon. "All of which has been suppressed by the U.S. government."

Will leaned forward. "I don't like the part about the government but I like the part about possible treasure..."

"Ancient Egyptians in the Grand Canyon, huh?" I asked. "That's a real conversation starter. Why did you suddenly decide to share this little tidbit of knowledge?"

Our friend shrugged and turned to us, eyes more serious for a moment. He held up a forefinger. "Liking somebody and trusting somebody are two different things. I've decided you're okay." He paused for a moment, as if gathering his thoughts. "I got this story from an old rascal — a prospector in Arizona with whom I became a drinkin' buddy. I knew Old Seth when he used to ride broncs, before he got 'the gold disease,' so we had a lot in common and we became good friends. One night in Amarillo, I ran into him. He came to me with some good news and some bad news. The bad news was, he was dying — cancer of the liver. There would be no more prospecting. The good news was real interesting, and he figured somebody ought to know about it because his time was running out." Those gray-blue eyes narrowed. "From the time I've spent with you, I know you guys enjoy chasing impossible stories..."

There was another pause. My partner and I shrugged in sync.

"Not a secret," said Will.

Dax continued. "Seth told me a fascinating tale about finding the remnants of a lost or maybe deliberately transposed race. About ancient Egyptians in the Grand Canyon. He said he found an entire Egyptian sailing ship inside a hidden cavern, and a collection of remarkable if not incredibly valuable artifacts...jewelry, weapons, tools, statues, and golden inlaid sarcophagi, all inside a cave just above the Colorado River."

"You certainly have our attention," said Will, leaning in.

Dax couldn't help but smile. "Actually, the first part of what I'm going to tell you happened quite a while back and isn't exactly a secret, but it was quickly denied and disclaimed by authorities, then buried deep, like a rabid dog. Then the area was suddenly declared off-limits by the government." Our friend took a breath, exhaled slowly, then began.

"There was a startling article that appeared in the April 5, 1909 edition of *The Phoenix Gazette,* out of Phoenix, Arizona. A couple of adventurers — a Professor S.A. Jordan, supposedly attached to the Smithsonian Institute, and an adventurer/professional photographer named G.E. Kinkaid — claimed to have found the remains of an ancient Egyptian city in the Grand Canyon. It was a front-page story but it got hushed-up really quickly, and shortly after the article appeared, it disappeared from the paper's files. Not long after, both of these cowboys sort of fell off the radar, then somehow disappeared..." Dax glanced at Will and me. "My buddy Seth had an original copy of the news article, and that helped pique my interest." Our friend paused for a moment and offered a bitter smile. "After the story appeared in *The Gazette*, the Smithsonian denied any knowledge of or association with either Kincaid or Jordan, and the artifacts they claimed to have brought back — from mummified bodies and weapons made with a strangely unique metal, to gold and silver artifacts — suddenly disappeared." He paused and looked at us. "This is a fact, my friends, and even though someone had the article pulled from the paper's archives, numerous copies were preserved by individuals and organizations. It's all easily verifiable."

Dax took a breath and continued. "Not long after that, the government declared about thirty miles of the Colorado River off-limits. The off-limits location just happened to coincide with the supposed area of Kincaid and Jordan's discovery — about forty miles west of El Tovar Crystal Canyon. There were supposedly American military patrols assigned to that section of the river for some time afterward. Anyone who managed to find their way into that part of the Rio Grande was 'discouraged' and removed."

He took a sip of his coffee, glanced around the fairly quiet restaurant, and leaned in toward us. "Over the years, there have been a few people who've gone looking for this particular situation. A couple of them produced similar accounts — about the possibility of a cave in the walls of the Grand Canyon that held strange artifacts. But none of them made the headlines. Then they, and their stories, quickly slipped off the public radar..." He exhaled softly. "I don't know exactly how much to believe but I do know this — the whole thing reminds me of the movie with Harrison Ford, where at the end, the story disappears from the news like a puff of smoke, every item of 'serious interest' ends up in the catacombs of the Smithsonian, and anyone who's anyone says, 'Just keep walking folks, nothing to be seen here...nothing of interest...'"

"Sounds like the Roswell incident in New Mexico in 1947," I said.

Dax nodded. "Yeah, much like that. Now, I can't say for sure what took place in Roswell, and thanks again to the government, it looks like none of us may ever know. But as information slowly surfaces, we're coming to realize that there may have been numerous 'Roswells' that the authorities suppressed." Dax huffed out a heavy expletive. "I don't cotton to the idea of someone making my decisions for me. They must think we're all as dumb as a barrel of hair." Our friend paused for a moment. "In addition, there have been a hatful of discoveries of really incredible items in North and Central America, from strange burial mounds that contain the skeletons of huge, ancient races, and the remains of remarkably complex temples, artifacts, and cities, to astrological and technological data that proves beyond a doubt that there were more than just primitive Indians settled throughout the Americas."

Will and I glanced at each other. With our experiences regarding unique devices from distant civilizations, we could seriously identify.

Our big friend shook his head with disgust. "The point that pulls my short hairs is, anytime something happens to be discovered that threatens the current status quo of history or religion, it has a tendency to disappear, and at the apex of the disappearance always seems to be either the Smithsonian Institute or the Vatican. It would appear that both of these organizations have a serious interest in maintaining a pure vanilla state of affairs on contemporary religious philosophy, and they like recorded history just the way it is. So the natives don't get restless." He took a breath and continued. "And, adding insult to injury to folks who have shared a firsthand experience like mine, there have been continuous, no longer deniable sightings of unique aircraft in our skies that possess flight characteristics beyond any technology we have developed." He gazed at us and his mouth twisted into a frown. "All of which ended up being declared weather balloons by our government."

"All I can say is, those government folks sure seem to be taken with the use of weather balloons," Will muttered. "And they're constantly losing them...or..."

"Somebody doesn't want to upset the historical/secular/technological status quo..." I said, finishing the sentence.

"No use riling the common folk by upsetting any of their major doctrines," said Will.

Dax offered a bitter smile. "Again, I don't like the idea of someone making my decisions for me..."

I had to ask, "Why didn't you go after this incredible find in the Grand Canyon before now?"

Our friend shrugged. "I wanted to but I didn't know anyone I could trust to go with me — someone with not just the knowledge of this type of operation and the equipment it would require, but somebody, most of all, who carried at least a little faith in something like this being possible." He sighed. "I'm partial to cowboys and their way of life but most of the rodeo folks I know are 'here and now' fellas. The idea of ancient Egyptians in Arizona would have been a stretch for them. I need folks like you, who have already had their imaginations stretched and have the proper equipment to pull it off — like floatplanes, two-way radios, metal detectors, and things that go bang." Then he smiled, somewhere between cagy and determined. "Besides, this is where my old buddy and his map come in."

"A map?" chirped Will and I in harmony.

Dax nodded, "Yeah, a map."

CHAPTER FOUR

During our R&R from debauchery and our introduction to Dax's intriguing tale, Will's daughter was still myopically dedicated to the training of, and a commitment from, her hawk. Jing's initial plan hadn't worked, exactly, but she wasn't discouraged. In the process, the young woman had learned from this and she would try again. And try again she did.

It took a few more days of the same process (a little less furious each day) before she finally had her bird lifting up into the air above her and accepting the limits of its flight capability. Along with my son, several of her neighbors had begun to watch, bringing lawn chairs out to observe the spectacle of hawk and woman. Gradually, Jing began to release more and more line on the spindle until Cielo was flying fifty feet above her in a wobbling circle, then grudgingly accepting the return to earth to the gauntlet on her arm (and a reward of raw fish) with manageable disappointment.

In the process, Jing was certain that a new dimension in their bond was forming — a new trust from both sides. The young hawk eagerly chirped when his mistress entered the porch where the cage was kept, and would bounce over toward the cage door. There was no urging required for the bird to step up onto Jing's gauntleted arm. He did it willingly, understanding that this meant a modicum of freedom — a chance to ride the wind. Cielo patiently waited for her to tie off the creances and even accepted a few strokes on his back from his mistress, then off the pair would go, to the marl yard for a ride, albeit limited, into the sky.

But regardless of her success, Will's daughter knew that there was a final step in this process she had to make if she was to live up to her concept of having a feathered companion and not a caged bird. She had to let Cielo go. She had to remove the jesses on the bird's ankles, and the creances that kept it from the freedom of the sky. She had to free the bird. And finally, after nearly three weeks of patience from Jing and her charge, today was the day.

Very carefully, if not reluctantly, Jing allowed her feathered friend to draw out all the line on the spool as the creature circled above her and she moved in synchronization with the hawk across the marl ground. Then she gradually brought the osprey back to her gauntleted arm and fed him generously. The young woman had proven herself to be calm and steady in a crisis numerous times, but now her hands trembled as the realization of what she was about to do set in. Once again, she threw Cielo into the air and allowed him all the line she had, and he cried out with pleasure as he circled above her. This time, however, as she drew him back in and he settled reluctantly but faithfully on her gauntlet, there were tears in her eyes. She gave him two handfuls of fish, because it might be the last time they shared this ritual, then she undid the jesses on his ankles and they, along with the creances, fell away to the ground. The suddenly freed hawk stood stock still, eyes blinking, head doing those sharp-angled turns as it sensed the change. It shifted slightly and stared at Jing. She drew a shaky breath and exhaled. "Go, Sky Child," she whispered as she slowly raised her arm. "Find your place in the sky, my friend, but don't forget me."

The bird stared at her for a moment, then raised those beautiful, gray-and-white wings and lifted off with a cry. Jing watched her friend soar up into the sky, free for the first time in his young life. The hawk circled her twice, the distance widening as he suddenly recognized (with what had to be unfettered joy) that he was no longer bound to anything. Then he swooped down toward the young woman on the ground, nearly touching her head. The bird cried out again, rose up into the clear blue sky, and circled her once more, crying out. Then he finally turned, it seemed almost reluctantly, toward the sea and sailed away.

Jing stood there like a forlorn lover, hands at her sides, breathing heavily, tears running down her cheeks. The die was cast now and the world was no longer in her hands. She watched as Cielo gradually faded away into the distance. She listened for one last call but heard only the heaviness of her breath and the pounding of her heart.

Suddenly, Tax was at her side. His arm slid over her shoulder and for the next half hour, they watched the horizon. But the hawk was gone. Finally, Jing sighed and instinctively Tax drew his arm down around her side. There were heavy cumulous clouds building on the western horizon, and their sonorous rumbling echoed sadly across the water of the nearby channel. Together, without a word, they reluctantly turned and walked back to the house. At the door to the porch, Jing couldn't help but glance back to the horizon. The emptiness and the silence taunted her.

It was a bird, just a bird, her mind told her. *But it was my bird,* her heart said...

Jing felt a richness inside her heart for what she had done, preserving the life of a creature whose entrance into this world had been so traumatic and tenuous, but all that was seared by the incredible pain of loss she felt. She hadn't realized how deep her affection ran for this creature. Somehow, it had touched notes of a maternal instinct the woman had never felt. In her mind, she had played the release scenario so many times before it happened. Always Cielo reached a point in his flight of freedom where he turned and came back to her. She just couldn't accept what had happened, emotionally or dynamically.

For the next few days, Jing found excuses to be outside. There was the garden that needed tending, and the vehicles needed washing, and long walks were good exercise. She had been inside more than normal for the last few weeks, tending to... She found it hard to say the name. Jing realized that most of the time, she was only going through the motions of whatever was required. Her eyes kept wandering to the horizon...

After several lonely days, in desperation, Jing called Santino in Belize. He sympathized but reminded her of what he had said at the beginning of her "project" — that some birds and some species of birds adapt to human companionship easier than others. Ospreys were not well-known for their rapport with humans.

"It is possible the bird will return," added Santino on a hopeful note. "He is experiencing his freedom at this moment and he is a very young bird, in the process of gaining his bearings in a world he knows little about." Then he sighed quietly and his honesty weighed in. "But you must be prepared to accept that the good you know you have done, in giving him a chance at life, is the only reward you'll receive."

It seemed like little damned compensation as far as Jing was concerned.

Over the course of the week, Tax had kept us informed. We all knew this was a really tough time for Jing, and I decided maybe a night on the town might be a good thing for all concerned. At first,

Will's daughter refused, but Tax and I talked her into it. In the end, we had everyone but Dax, who, while having sympathy for Jing, felt that this was a family thing and begged out.

The following night we dragged Will's reluctant daughter out of the house and down to the Half Shell Raw Bar in Key West. It turned out to be a good idea. The Half Shell was the perfect environment for the night — a casual place with picnic tables, good food, and great drinks, right on the docks. The sea air, the sound of laughter, and the smell of good food... By the second round of drinks the sun was setting and we were all relaxing — laughing, actually — even Jing.

The only thing that had begun to mar the evening were the folks at the table across from us. They were two large Haitians — not the working type — dressed too flamboyantly, with long-sleeved silk shirts, South Miami slacks, and Gucci shoes. Both of them were decorated in dreadlocks and gold chains. They weren't like the softer, earthy, generally warm-natured Bahamians the people of the Keys had grown up with and had so willingly come to appreciate as an integral part of the landscape. The two in the restaurant were a result of the 1980's Haitian boatlifts, when Haiti's government emptied a portion of their prisons, loaded them on boats, and conveniently dumped the dregs of their island nation on America. Sadly, that became a turning point in South Florida culture. These guys weren't the breezy, somewhat benign hippie pot dealers that everyone knew. On the contrary, they represented the practice of drugs and violence. They were everything that most people, everywhere, feared and disliked.

The truth was, I couldn't care less how they were dressed or who they were, or where they came from, as long as they left me alone, but as the evening progressed, they became louder and louder, their harsh Haitian *patois* crashing over the murmur of normal conversation around them like storm waves.

Jing was trying to tell us a story about her hawk, but it was nearly impossible to follow her with the volume rising off the table next to us. Finally, when she had finished as best she could, Will's daughter excused herself to use the restroom. But as she tried to squeeze past the Haitian's table, one of them tipped his chair back as he took a swallow of wine and Jing's arm bumped him. His wine splashed onto the arm of his shirt.

The man slapped his glass down on the table and forcefully grabbed Jing's arm, swinging her around. "Look what you do, woman!" he growled, holding the young girl in blue jeans and a T-shirt. "A hundred-dollar shirt, ruined because of your carelessness!"

"I'm sorry," Jing said. "But you're the one that pushed your seat back and bumped into me, not the other way around."

The big man turned in his seat and stared at her incredulously. "You stupid *blanc* bitch! You got de nerve..." He started to rise, still holding her arm. "You need a lesson in manners, woman."

At that point, Jing realized she'd had enough. She'd had all the bad news and bad attitude she could stand for one week. As the Haitian rose, she slapped his arm away and hammered him in the throat with the knuckles of her right fist. The guy's eyes took on a huge look of surprise, then concern (when he suddenly realized he wasn't breathing well anymore).

But when it comes to doing stupid things, some people need more corrective instruction than others. Still trying to stand, and now reaching out at Jing with his other hand, the man left his groin pretty well unprotected. Will's incredible daughter batted the man's hand away, stepped in, and kicked him solidly in the *cojones*. This time, the Haitian's eyes got that serious "oh shit!" bulge and he dropped to the floor, both hands holding his...pain...

But at this point, his friend was up and coming around the table. It was a hasty, terrible decision on his part. Tax, who was already standing near his sister, intercepted the guy. Until then, I had no idea how good Tax actually was at taking care of himself. Both the large islander and I found out almost immediately. As my son stepped in front of the man, the slightest of smiles turned his mouth. I thought that was odd.

The Haitian looked at the young man in Dockers shorts and a T-shirt standing in front of him. He huffed out a curse, grabbed his wine bottle out of its canister, and broke it on the table. Now he was coming at my son with jagged glass. I was getting up, and so was Will.

Tax didn't miss a beat. He was freaking amazing. As the man moved in at him, he threw up his hands and yelled. Instinctively, the guy in front of him brought up his arms. That was when my son spun and heel-kicked the guy in the solar plexus. You have to experience this once to appreciate it, but I can guarantee you, once is enough. The guy stumbled backward, his eyes suddenly going wide as he realized he could no longer breathe — all the air having been effectively hammered from his body. As he started to drop to his knees, Tax helped him along with a spinning kick to the head. That was the end of that.

"Son of a bitch," muttered Will, next to me. "What a pair we've sired!" He exhaled softly. "They're not as much into diversions as you and I were in the old days. But they get the job done nicely."

There was a smattering of appreciative applause from the relieved, but well-entertained audience as the owner and a couple of his big cooks dragged the Haitians up and showed them to the door. Again, another smattering of applause... *Damn, I really liked it.*

By the time we were all sailing home on U.S. Highway 1 that night, I had a wonderful glow and a terrific feeling about this new tribe of ours. And I even felt good about this possible new adventure that Dax had presented. Maybe a family outing, so to speak...

CHAPTER FIVE

The following evening, we all sat around in my living room with maps of Arizona and the Grand Canyon spread out around us on the floor. With Dax's permission, I asked Tax to join us. My son had a lot of his dad in him. Anything that was old and gold had his immediate attention. It wasn't just the gold, it was "the old" that really pulled his chain. Jing was too preoccupied with her hawk at the moment, and I understood. She came from a family easily lost to their passions.

Shadow, my furry companion, lay beside my chair and Smoke lay contentedly at Dax's feet. The two dogs, both being males, had done a little "dancing" when they first met, before they decided they were okay with each other. They were a formidable pair — enough to steal the breath from the average person. But now they seemed to be getting along remarkably well. (The truth is, we all need a friend, regardless of the shape God gave us.)

At that point, our buddy slipped off his nearly ever-present cowboy hat and produced an old, slightly yellowed map, showing a course up the Colorado River with clearly defined landmarks. Nothing fancy, but it was accompanied by a topographical map as well. These were what his friend, Seth, had left him. As the physical map neared its charted destination along the walls of the Grand Canyon, distinct landmarks were defined and accompanied by notes and a handful of old black-and-white photos. There was a notebook as well, describing scenes of the trip and providing valuable insights. The whole thing was remarkably well done for someone who was an ex-bull rider and a relatively unsuccessful gold miner. However, there were other notations on the map that were particularly eye-catching. For instance, in the area of Ninetyfour Mile Creek and Trinity Creek of the Grand Canyon, there was a profusion of locations with Egyptian names (originally designated by the old mapmaking company) like Tower of Set, Tower of Ra, Horus Temple, Osiris Temple, and Isis Temple.

"My friend claimed that those aren't just names — that there are man-made edifices of significant size at those locations, but they have eroded and not all are as clearly or easily identified now," Dax said. "Seth was certain that this was all part of a major, transported civilization. Most importantly, he did this on the sly because no one is allowed into the Grand Canyon without prior authorization now, and it's a no-fly zone." He paused and looked around at us. "Can you figure? A no-fly zone in the middle of freaking nowhere. Somebody want to explain that?"

With a quick breath, our friend continued. "Moving back toward our present goal, in terms of the location of the entrance to the first or original cavern, which Seth claimed was about forty-one miles upriver from El Tovar Crystal Canyon, there were the words, 'very near a large deposit of sedimentary stains to be seen.' Old Seth claimed this was hard to miss."

Dax explained to us that he had done considerable research on this, and it turns out that his old friend's recollections echoed the statements of the 1909 explorers, Kincaid and Jordan — that the location to the original cavern would have been above a six-mile stretch of the Colorado River in Marble Canyon, near the border of the Navajo Nation boundary and the Kwagunt Rapids. In addition, both Seth and the original explorers (Kincaid and Jordan) agreed that the entrance they found to the original cavern was in the cliff wall, just a little under 1,500 feet straight down from the rim of the canyon. It was understood that while that location seemed inaccessible now, the Colorado River was probably that high in its ancient youth. After all, it was the powerful river that had cut the canyon.

But here was the kicker. Dax explained that all this information was only important in terms of landmarks, because his old friend claimed he had found a second cavern that contained another complete city — and an entire, remarkably well-preserved Egyptian sailing ship. In addition, at this second site, there was a huge chamber that broke into passageways, like the spokes of a wheel. All the passageways supposedly contained equally fascinating archaeological elements, such as tools, weapons, precious-metal jewelry, precious stones, vases, urns of copper and gold, remarkable statues, and even golden sarcophagi. He claimed that carved over the doorways, on all the urns, and on tablets of stone were hieroglyphs. There were numerous mummies everywhere, and an incredible statue that appeared to be of almost Tibetan origin sat cross-legged against one wall.

Yet for all the remarkable finds that defined this as a significant colony, it almost seemed as though something had struck them unexpectedly. Oddly enough, it was also noted by Jordan and Kincaid that there was an extraordinary number of mummies, wrapped, ready for burial, and stacked in piles, and numerous sarcophagi as well.

Will sat back in his chair and exhaled heavily. "That is strange," he admitted, then my friend shook his head. "Lord! This would certainly blow the lid off all the smoke and mirrors the Smithsonian has thrown up."

"Wouldn't it though?" I whispered. "It might be the straw that broke the deceptive camel's back. Imagine irrefutable proof that North America was settled by Egyptians hundreds, maybe thousands of years before the first European explorer set foot on its soil." I drew a breath. "We know for certain that the surrounding seas and waterways were much higher then. If this were true, it would radically change the current view that all the Indians of the Americas were descended from Ice Age explorers that came across the Bering Strait."

"And if there was interbreeding, this could very well lend some credence to the difference in features among many Southwestern Indian tribes," Will, our historian, added. "Beyond that, there are a number of lineage questions regarding American Indians. The Cherokee show distinct haplogroup Egyptian bloodlines." He looked around. "Somebody want to explain that? Then there are the Southwest Hopi Indians, whose ancestral legends tell of them originally living underground, then eventually emerging from a huge cave..." He sighed. "I just wish we had a scrap of tangible truth before we set out on this wild gold chase."

Dax smiled. "Seth said that would be one of the things someone would mention." He shrugged. "I mean, who wouldn't?"

As he spoke, he began pulling something out of an old cotton cloth bag. As the light hit the object, it gleamed. It was a magnificent, short-bladed Egyptian sword with a golden handle. He handed it to Will and my friend hefted it with care as he studied it.

"There's an inscription on the handle," he said.

"Yep," said Dax. "Sure as fire..."

"Do you know what it says?" I asked.

"Yep," our cowboy friend replied with that Cheshire Cat smile. "It's the name of a tenth-century commander for Merneptah, the fourth king of the 19th dynasty of ancient Egypt, who ruled from 1213 BC until 1203 BC."

"Whoa shit!" Will exclaimed. "I mean, *whoa shit!*"

"Unbelievable," I said. "It's like a science-fiction movie."

"That's some damned serious proof!" hissed Will.

"All this will also verify Kincaid and Jordan's writings, and certainly throw some culpability on the Smithsonian regarding the disappearance of both men," said Dax. "If we could actually find this second cavern and that ship, and get the information to the right people, we could possibly expose the Smithsonian and its desire to maintain a continuous status quo...in any fashion necessary."

"You're right," Will added. "This isn't the early 1900s. There are a lot of people out there now who want the truth about the history of the Americas, and this planet! Imagine what the world might get to see if we could force open the doors of that institution."

Dax shook his head. "If you stayed alive long enough to do it, partner." He exhaled like an old bull and his eyes were hard. "Here's where it all gets sticky, and you need to know before you commit to this..." There was a pregnant pause and Dax began quietly. "My buddy Seth didn't die of his liver cancer. The 'official report' was that he committed suicide by jumping off a bridge over the Gila River, outside Tempe, Arizona, in the middle of the night."

I knew that look on our friend's face. "And I'm betting you don't think it happened like that."

Again the cowboy exhaled heavily. "We could be stepping on some big toes..."

"Now you tell us," muttered Will.

Dax shrugged. "You never get a mule into the barn by right off yellin' at him."

There was silence for a moment.

"Okay, tell us what you know," said Will. "So us mules can make some relatively intelligent decisions."

Our big friend glanced from Will to me, then over to Tax, who was obviously enthralled by all this. "First, I'll tell you what I know. Then I'll tell you what I think." He offered a final glance around and began. "Seth drank a bit and he liked tellin' stories. I woulda liked to have thought he kept all this to himself but I doubt it now. He told me that one day, after a night of heavy drinking and story-tellin', he was getting into his pickup when two men appeared. They were dressed too well for dusty Arizona and they produced a card saying they worked for a company called Tritan Enterprises in the District of Columbia. They wanted to inform him that certain sections of the Grand Canyon were off-limits and owned by the government, and there were severe penalties for failing to comply. The two fellas wanted to ask him some questions about his time in the canyon. Seth told them they could go to hell, got into his truck, and drove away." Our friend sighed. "I shoulda been payin' attention when he told me this tale but I was gearing up for a big rodeo in New Mexico, and I let it slide." He shoved out a bitter breath. "I shoulda been there for him."

"Not good..." I said.

"It gets worse," said the big cowboy. "The next day, my buddy came to me with all the information I've shown you — the maps, speculation, and artifacts. He said he wanted me to hang on to them for him, just in case the cancer caught up with him faster than he expected or something happened to him..."

"Oh, shit..." breathed Tax in anticipation.

"Two days later, his body was found in the Gila River," Dax continued. "The official verdict was suicide by drowning." Our friend sucked in a breath. "But I wasn't sure of that. I spent some time with the medical examiner involved in this. I asked him what had happened to my friend. He said he wasn't at liberty to say. I asked him where Seth was found. Again, he said he wasn't at liberty to say." Dax's eyes got that steely gray look. "So I threw him against the wall and took out my skinnin' knife. I'm not all that proud of it but a couple of minutes later, he got religion." He sighed again. "And I learned the truth."

We all glanced at each other as Dax continued.

"Apparently, a couple of fellows came in ahead of me and had words with him, and some money exchanged hands. The examiner wrote it up as an off-the-bridge suicide, but aside from the alcohol in his blood, there were traces of scopolamine, a truth serum of sorts." Dax shook his head angrily. "And, under a little duress, he said it looked like Seth's hands had been bound while he was drowned. That's an ugly way to die. He was already dead when they threw him off the bridge." Our friend paused. "My ol' buddy was murdered because of what he found in the Grand Canyon and I think it was our own government that did him — the folks from an invisible branch of the Smithsonian Institution, the watchdogs for any historical anomaly that don't fit the current story."

"Tritan Enterprises," Will whispered.

Admittedly, there was a bit of a pall in the room for the rest of the evening as we studied the maps that old Seth had given Dax. But we weren't ready to tuck our tails between our legs. Dax's friend had been killed for the ugliness of greed and the propagation of lies, and that just didn't set well, regardless of the risks. And, truth be known, we were damned well sure now that some kind of absolutely amazing treasure lay buried in the walls of the Grand Canyon. Hell, it might as well be us that found it.

As we studied the information, we realized that the landmarks to the first cave were there and an estimate on the second location. We were to watch for the sedimentary stain on the cliffs on the west side of the river, which marked the location of the first cavern that the explorers Kincaid and Jordan had found, then move upriver, supposedly about a mile. It was there that the river turned slightly and the steady current had cut into the base of the cliffs, shadowing the flow of water in the afternoon. Seth said that apparently, in ancient times, there was an entrance that was approximately 1,400 feet below the ridge of the canyon (at the high-water level of the river), with a large opening that led into the second cavern.

But Seth had added that apparently the residents of the cavern had blocked it off for some reason. The ancient, hidden entrance was impossible to discern from the canyon floor unless you knew exactly what you were looking for. He guessed that the opening had once been easily wide enough to bring in a small ship (when the level of the river in the canyon was much higher — as high as the cave). But again, this particular entryway had been sealed and it would be twice as difficult to spot now, with the water level having fallen a couple thousand feet over the past few centuries. Anyone wanting to gain access from the river, at the floor of the canyon, would have to be part lizard.

But there was more. According to Seth, he found several small wooden boats along the sandstone shore of a small, nearly dry, underground lake. The people who lived in the second canyon settlement had apparently sailed their boats along the main river, then in and out of their cavern via a narrow waterway around which they had built a city. We all realized that, given the time frame of the sword's original owner, it was doubtful they continued to sail the same/first ship with all the centuries that had passed. It seemed most likely that the "first" ship might well have become a monument to their heritage. But he was certain the one he saw was an Egyptian ship with a displacement of perhaps fifty to sixty tons. The water level of the small, underground lake was, in the early days, the same height as the river. Most Egyptian sea-going vessels were not that large, most had fairly shallow drafts and masts that could be dismantled, and all were equipped with oar ports. It all worked. It all made sense.

In addition, it was Seth's suspicion that they had to have developed some sort of illumination in their cavern, possibly openings in the ceiling to the outside or something more exotic. Who knew, at this point? Will reminded us that these people were the descendants of those who built the Great Pyramid, so anything was possible. And from the writings of Kincaid and Jordan, it seemed clear that the original explorers had brought women with them. This was a bold attempt at expanding the Egyptian civilization and it was entirely possible that more than one ship had set out on this quest.

But eventually, something happened in their new home, and as the water of what would become the Colorado River gradually receded, their ship and their small boats were left in a perpetual dry dock, and so was the city around it. Still, the question hanging in the air was, how did Seth find this?

Dax took a breath and explained. His friend hadn't originally found the entrance over the river. He was an old prospector and water travel didn't appeal to him. He had discovered the cavern through a back entrance, which led out into the desert. It was there, apparently, where the inhabitants grew crops and hunted. It was the perfect situation — a river for fish and waterfowl, and relatively fertile land (at that time) for carefully selected crops. When Seth came upon it, he thought he'd found an old mine entrance because it was deliberately small and innocuous. He was wrong in that respect, but he had certainly struck gold...

Nonetheless, if the explorers Kincaid and Jordan were right in their observations, something happened that changed the status quo of the two cities in a very short time. A thriving, miniature civilization had collapsed almost overnight. These people had turned a couple of mountain caverns into extensive cities. They had mined gold and silver, developed the art of smelting, and produced quality weapons and utensils. They created mosaics and tapestries, developed the art of kilns, and produced exotic pottery as well as glassware. According to Seth, the artwork painted on some of the interior walls showed that they had apparently captured wild horses and raised them outside the cavern, and maintained a small military force, which appeared to control their region. They were, for all intents and purposes, a new civilization on the rise. These people could have very easily become a definitive force in the development of the Americas.

But something happened — something dramatic and immediate.

Regardless of all the remarkable information that old Seth and Dax had gathered, I felt we were missing a piece. Will, our historian, was headed into Miami and the largest library in Florida the following day to learn what he could about the history of the Grand Canyon and the southwest territory that surrounded it — and ancient Egypt. Dax and I, along with my son, Tax, would spend some time going over the information Seth had presented, once again reviewing the original article in the 1909 *Phoenix Gazette*. (Yes, the coincidence in names — Tax and Dax — hadn't escaped us. I told them what our old Rastaman buddy Rufus used to say: *"I don' write da play of life, mon. I just be a member of da cast."*) It was going to take a while to pull all the logistics together but it was beginning to look like we were on the edge of another adventure.

On the periphery of all this was the indisputable fact that we were attempting to disturb the status quo created by at least one of the two major historical institutions in the world — the Smithsonian or the Vatican — which was dangerous at best. The only way we would know for certain about any of this was to make a journey into the Grand Canyon and step into the past.

However, there was one last thing Dax mentioned that thickened the air a bit.

"When we were speculating about the final chapters of this ancient society," our cowboy buddy explained, "Seth paused and his eyes darkened. He said he found one other thing — a strange situation that made him damned uncomfortable." Our friend glanced around at us. "There were thousands of pieces of what appeared to be nearly fossilized bone spread out in the desert, from the back entrance of the cave that led into the cavern." He sighed and shook his head, as if trying to dislodge the memory. "Human bones, Seth said. Something strange happened there. Something bad…"

CHAPTER SIX

Throughout most of my adult life I had been, on occasion, subject to oddly significant dreams and sensations — precognitive experiences that had literally preserved my immediate health at times. This was difficult for me to understand or accept at first. It left me confused and concerned. I thought maybe I was slipping gears. I mean, why me? And who was doing this? But a friend once explained to me that we are all "watched over" by "Spirit," if you will. Every society seems to understand this and calls the experience by a different name.

"The ones who listen best have been called a number of things: shamans, soothsayers, clairvoyants, priests, and sometimes, just extraordinarily lucky."

And the more you practiced this "listening" the more it came to you.

"What you call it doesn't matter," my friend told me. "The only important thing is that you open yourself to this process and accept the gift graciously."

She was right. And eventually, I learned to do just that.

That night I had a remarkable dream. It wasn't consistent, like regular dreams. It came in flashes. But for abrupt, remarkable moments I could see the inside of the ancient cavern in the Grand Canyon. In brief visions, I saw a reddish-colored people moving about — fathers, mothers, and children. There were mosaics, tapestries, statues, and gold and silver artifacts, which appeared commonplace. Domesticated burros carried goods about. There were peacekeepers, shopkeepers, and sandal makers, and there was a large waterway outside, in the canyon, which flowed into a recessed lake basin inside the cavern.

The whole experience was incredible, beyond fascinating. I was a frozen spectator viewing the day-to-day processes of a civilization that appeared to have existed thousands of years before the first white man set foot in America. When I awoke, I stared at the ceiling, desperately trying to capture all that I had seen. It was so real, so poignant, and I knew at that moment it was more than a dream. But there was a nagging sensation that I hadn't witnessed the important part. In the back of my mind, I could see a large cat's face, painted on a wall…and there was a strange sense of peace and conformity, and a desire to be a valuable part of…the hive…

The next day, while we collectively gathered information for what was beginning to look like our next quest, Will checked in on his daughter, then headed for the library in Miami. He stopped by my place on the way out and offered an interesting story.

Jing had been suffering terribly with the loss of her hawk. For an entire week she was in mourning. She might as well have worn black. The woman barely ate, she struggled with sleep, and the empty cage on the screened-in porch taunted her horribly. But she couldn't bring herself to remove it.

It was as if she had lost a child — and maybe, in essence, she had. Every day, just after sunup, Jing would rise and throw on a T-shirt and a pair of shorts. She rarely wore a bra (to the absolute delight of all the males in the area, and some women, I imagine). She had full, pear-shaped breasts (which she got from her mother) and she allowed them free rein to amaze and bedazzle gawkers of all ages. But right now, that distinct, mutual pleasure was lost to the agony of bereavement. Now, each morning, Jing slipped on her leather gauntlet (in a ritual of hope) and walked out onto the main road and down to the large marl lot where she had released Cielo. As time passed, this exercise edged closer to futility but she couldn't help herself. She had to do it…

By and large, it was a quiet, peaceful stroll, regardless, and the morning sun with the breeze off the sea helped relax her. The only impediment to this affair was the dog inside the chain-link-fenced yard at the end of the walk, just before the large, empty lot where she had released her hawk. It was a big Rottweiler, with a heavy chest and large head, probably weighing in at 150 pounds. I happen to like Rotts. I was blessed with one when I was younger. He was a huge animal, as intelligent as many people I had known, and blessed with a gentle personality. But then, I've always said, "There's no such thing as a bad dog, only bad owners."

This particular animal had bad owners. The dog wasn't just loud, he was ugly fierce and he carried a sense of violence about him, even in the calmest of moments.

As Jing walked by cautiously on this particular morning, the dog began barking, then throwing himself against the chain-link fence, snarling and growling like a lion. Jing kept moving, avoiding any eye contact with the animal. Nonetheless, she couldn't help but notice that one of the metal fence posts had bent slightly at the bottom, and as the dog hammered the fence in a rage, the post began to give.

The fence was folding down, outward...

The Rottweiler, recognizing the surrender, began to throw his weight against the bending post, and, with a final wrench, it gave.

Jing was backing up now, her face twisted with a good deal of terror. There was no escaping the slavering creature as it bounded over the downed chain-link. To run would invite an attack for certain. She held her ground for a moment and shouted at the animal, trying to stand it down. The dog had cleared the fence and stood with his legs spread in that typical, aggressive Rottweiler stance. Saliva was running down its jaws and being flung into the air as it shook its massive head and roared again. Jing backed up a couple more steps, hands out submissively. She retreated a little more, still yelling at the dog, but the animal saw her backward movement as weakness, and all its primitive instincts and bad rearing bubbled to the top. As it charged, Jing tripped and stumbled to the ground.

At that moment, as the dog growled menacingly and charged at her, Jing caught sight of a shadow racing across the hot, marl rock. She glanced up just in time to see an osprey streaking down, screaming in defiance, its legs out, claws flared. The bird hit the Rottweiler in the head, talons ripping through fur and flesh above the dog's eyes like razor blades. The dog bellowed in pain as the winged defender flared and pulled away, climbing quickly and rolling over again like an avenging angel.

Jing had regained her footing and resumed backing up, hands still out, as the dog lost its balance from the attack and tumbled. But the hawk wasn't done. It came down again, swooping in just as the animal scrambled to its feet. With those deadly barbs splayed, it slashed the dog on the back of the head, between its ears, ripping out a chunk of fur and flesh.

That was enough for the surprised and battered animal. Without so much as another look at the woman, the Rott turned tail and ran, bounding over the downed fence and dashing for the safety of his master's covered carport.

Jing sat there on the ancient, hard coral in the sun, somewhere between joy and complete disbelief. There, in the sky above, circled her Cielo, calling to her stridently. The hawk swooped down close to Jing, then rose again. With absolute impossible clarity, she understood completely what the bird wanted. She slowly raised herself off the hot marl rock and stood shakily, then she looked up at her feathered companion through tear-filled eyes and held out her gauntleted arm.

The magnificent osprey spiraled downward, calling again, and without hesitation, flared its beautiful, almost silver-colored wings, and dropped onto Jing's outstretched arm. The bird fluttered for balance for a second (even through the gauntlet, Jing felt the incredible power of those talons), then it turned to the woman, eye to eye, and offered a soft, shrill *chwirk*. Jing slowly reached up and gently stroked its back and the bird relaxed.

It was magical — something so extraordinary that it alters perceptions and draws emotion from the depths of the fertile soil within the heart. At that moment, it was as if the very angels in Heaven had struck a chorus. It was just that impossibly perfect.

Although Jing was ecstatic, she was stunned by the turn of events. Her boy was back, perched on her arm, but she wasn't quite sure what to do. She knew, however, that the next few minutes could well decide this relationship. The young woman realized now that she could not control the hawk, but she wanted the bond to grow. Jing eased out a breath and caressed Cielo's back again, whispering affection and leaning in, her cheek brushing the bird, then slowly (and it was one of the most difficult things she had ever done), she raised her arm high — the signal for release. There was a moment of absolute silence, as if the world stopped around her. Then, with a soft chirp, the hawk almost reluctantly threw up his wings and lifted off.

Now there were tears in Jing's eyes and regret was already hammering her. Her thoughts raced. *You let him go! You had him back and you let him go!* But in the back of her mind, the woman knew she had no choice. This had to be a mutual relationship or no relationship at all.

As Jing began to return home, she realized the hawk hadn't headed for the horizon and the sea as he had before. He stayed close, circling above her as she walked, easing down on occasion to offer a rich and rasping call. Nonetheless, when she was about halfway back to the duplex, the bird turned toward a stand of Australian pines in the distance and disappeared out of sight.

The young woman's stomach flip-flopped. She waited for five minutes but there was no sign of her friend. The moment of truth had come and passed. *He is a free soul, for God's sake. What did you expect?* Jing thought. A stratum of cirrus clouds was moving in, heralding some weather behind them, and the wind was rising. There was no point in standing there and waiting.

By the time she reached the house, Jing had seen no more of her hawk. Her insides knotted. *Why would he want to come back here, anyway?* She stood outside by the low wooden fence that surrounded the duplex and whistled, like one would for a dog. She wasn't sure why, she just did. Jing waited, then called, but there was still no sign of her feathered friend.

She sat in a lawn chair outside the screened porch for the next half hour. Unfortunately, the weather was closing in. The wind was rising and it began to look like rain. She got up and headed for the porch. She had recently built a six-foot-tall, freestanding perch out of a heavy buttonwood branch, simply in hopes… It sat just outside the door. Jing had reached the screen door when she heard the flutter of powerful wings and felt their wind. She turned quickly and there, at the top of the new perch she had built, was Cielo. He fluffed his feathers for a moment, then settled and cocked his head, staring at her.

Jing had to chuckle. It was if he was saying as nonchalantly as possible, "Okay, I'm back. So, what's for lunch?"

Five minutes later, as she watched the hawk take food from her hand as he relaxed on the new perch, Jing suddenly knew that this was a relationship based on new parameters. She realized that her friend would come and go as he pleased, but a new, incredibly powerful bond was forming — one that might only be discovered in the rarest of circumstances. She knew that jesses and creances were a thing of the past, and a hood would only be applied when the well-being of the bird was critical. They were two creatures of the earth now, who had found each other and had bonded, and they showed the world that faith and love can transcend species; that these elements may well be the glue that advances an understanding that can be found in no other fashion.

Over the next week, their relationship grew so fast it was astounding. Although Cielo was now an independent creature, he became quite comfortable with entering Jing's screened-in porch whenever he felt like it. She just left the door open. He would even, on occasion, swoop into his old cage and sit on the perch as if he owned the place, although the cage was becoming a little small for him. Their relationship was quickly becoming that of two equals, rather than a bird and a woman. It was very strange. Even Santino in Belize found it remarkable.

CHAPTER SEVEN

While Will was in Miami, Dax took a little time off to check on his horse, which he had stabled at the little dude ranch on Sugarloaf Key. Tax and I had begun arranging equipment lists and finding the items we would need for this next adventure, from weapons and ammunition to communication equipment and salt tablets. Neither Will or I were really wild-eyed, "veins in the teeth" gun guys but we both had an "affection" for weapons, and a fairly good knowledge of what to do with them and when. Dax, on the other hand, was raised in the country and had been given an "all expenses paid" one-year stint in Vietnam. If it made noise when you pulled the trigger, he knew how to use it.

While all seemed to be progressing well and life appeared fairly entertaining for all concerned, we might have been less pleased had we been able to see the big picture...

The only thing that was missing was our buddies, Travis Christian and William Cody. They would normally be part of an affair like this. But this wasn't our show, it was Dax's, and it seemed like we already had all the players we needed. I did, however, give both of them a call, letting them know we were striking out on an "affair" for a friend and would be in touch when we got back.

A phone rang in the small back room of an innocuous office on a side street off Maryland Avenue in downtown Washington, D.C. The large man in a slightly weathered suit straightened up at his desk, snubbed out his cigarette, and picked up the receiver. "Overview Office," he answered, calmly, politely.

"We have a situational breach," said the voice at the other end. "Has to do with the Grand Canyon thing. You understand?"

The man nodded, running a hand over the stubble of his crew cut. His blue eyes tightened. "Yeah, I understand. What can we do for you?"

"Seems the canyon thing hasn't gone away entirely. Somebody is asking questions. We thought it was taken care of but the doctor who handled the postmortem got talkative. Looks like someone else may have the same info that the old prospector had. We're following the new primary now. Should have names and places inside of twenty-four hours."

The man holding the phone nodded again. "Okay, what do you want us to do?"

"The usual," said the voice. "When we've got the information that you need..." There was a pause. "We want to tighten this down as soon as possible. The basic info package is already en route to you. This comes from the basement. They want to know what these people know, beforehand. You understand?"

"Yeah, I understand," replied the fellow in the chair, his hand instinctively brushing the firm hardness under his armpit, against his ribs. "I understand..."

I headed down to Key West. It was time to chat with Crazy Eddie to see if he was up for another adventure. I had a floatplane but it was nowhere large enough to take the crew for this new enterprise, let alone gear and supplies. We needed Eddie's Grumman Goose, and in truth, we needed Eddie's expertise and experience. We were going into an area with tricky up and downdrafts, and we'd have to come into it on the deck. And if my charts were correct, we'd have to run just above the river most of the way in to stay off any radar that might exist. All the information we could come up with said there was a solid, albeit subtly disguised law enforcement/military presence in the area. We also needed the Goose's capacity for at least six people and two dogs (who could hear and sense things way ahead of us). There were no Holiday Inns where we were going.

While driving toward Key West, I decided to check on Jing at Summerland Key. There was no question in my mind that a project like this would ring her chimes, but I knew she'd been incredibly busy with the osprey she was training.

I pulled up in front of the duplex she and Tax were buying, and had barely closed the car door when Jing stepped out from the door on her side of the building. She came out with that long-legged gait and gave me a hug, and I noticed the leather gauntlet on her forearm. We were still hugging when I felt a gust of wind ruffle my hair and a shadow passed over us. I ducked instinctively.

Jing grinned. "Not to worry, that's just Cielo, making sure everything's cool."

I glanced up and watched the good-sized osprey climb and make a sharp bank, then circle us.

"He's a little protective," Jing added proudly as she, too, watched her feathered companion. She straightened her light blouse and tucked it into her khaki shorts. "C'mon, let's go around back, by the pool, and sit in the shade."

We had barely managed to take our seats in a couple of lawn chairs when Cielo swept in and landed at the top of a tall buttonwood perch next to us. The bird fluffed its feathers and chirped, then settled with his bright, hard eyes on me.

I looked at the hawk and had to smile. "Something tells me it's a good thing he sees me as a friend."

"You're damned right there," replied Jing with a hard grin. "So," she said. "What brings you to my humble abode? Tax tells me you're into an exciting project but he's been too busy to offer much in the way of details — and we've only spoken in passing."

I nodded. "Yeah, somehow another one of those strange adventures has found us, or vice versa." I looked at my friend's daughter. "You want to hear about it?"

"Hell yes!" she said, moving forward in her seat and pushing back her blond hair with the fingers of one hand. "If you left me out, I would have been seriously pissed. So, Kansas...tell me the story."

I nodded and began, and for the next fifteen minutes, we were both amazed at what a tale it was. Finally, when I was done, Jing exhaled slowly.

"Damn, that's a hell of a story," she whispered, pushing her longish blond hair away from her forehead once more. "It has the makings of a great movie." Then she turned her chair a little and leaned into me, those blue eyes narrowing. "Given what happened to Dax's friend, I'm betting you have some big people after you. Nobody likes it when you tell their secrets."

She was a bright girl...

"Yeah, it's likely to be dangerous," I replied, suddenly a little concerned about her and Tax being in this, wishing I hadn't been so hasty. "It's okay if you want to pass," I said. "I really just wanted to mention it because we're likely to be gone for a while, and really your dad should be the one — "

"Save it," she said, waving me off. "When do we leave?"

Crazy Eddie's Bar and Swill in downtown Key West was doing a solid business for mid-afternoon. Eddie, in blue jeans and one of his favorite, albeit wrinkled tropical shirts (a relatively clean one), was drinking a beer and overseeing from "his table" in the corner. When he saw us, he casually adjusted the black patch over his right eye, ran a hand through his hair, and smiled. While he was now the legitimate owner of a Key West saloon, he had, in the past, been a gallant participant in late-night flights and the delivery of burlap-wrapped packages. The man was an odd amalgam of courage, integrity, and a large indifference to government edicts.

We shook hands and he stole a hug from Jing (simply because it made him the envy of the male crowd), then he offered us seats. "*Qué pasa,* amigo?" he said enthusiastically. "What brings you to the Swill?" He leaned into me and spoke earnestly. "Tell me, man, tell me you're here because you got a righteous gig for us. Come on, dude, tell me that." He threw up his hands. "Eddie likes his place, don't get me wrong. But he needs to get out and chase some naked-ass life again, you know, brother?"

Both Jing and I couldn't help but smile. He was such a character — the patch on one eye, his precious Jimmy Buffett ball cap perched on his head, long sun-bleached hair struggling to reach his shoulders.

"It just so happens that's exactly why we're here," I said with a grin. "We're looking for a crazy pilot and a fat, battered airplane for an interesting gig. Do you know where I could find that combination?"

My friend's eye lit up and I thought he was going to hug me, then he pulled back. "Don' jive Eddie now, man. He be too fragile…"

I held out my hands, palms up. "No, man. I'm for real. We gotta gig for you."

After he finished hugging me, Eddie pulled back again and I straightened my shirt.

"What kind of gig, dude?" he asked. He threw out his hands.

"Not that Eddie really cares. Just curious…"

I leaned in. "A lost Egyptian civilization in the Grand Canyon with possibly more treasure than you can fit in that fat bird of yours. But this is about proving it exists as much as anything else." My eyes narrowed. "It's become a little personal…"

He moved forward again. "You're not jiving Eddie, right? Egyptian dudes in the canyon?" My buddy paused and cocked his head. "And there's shiny stuff, too, isn't there? I know you dudes too well."

"Yeah, man, very possibly. That's the gig."

My friend got that same look a puppy gets when you scratch its back. "Eddie loves you, man. You know that, right?"

I smiled. "I know, buddy. I know. Get that bird of yours ready. We're looking at a couple to three days before liftoff."

On the way back, we stopped by Bobby Branch's place on Cudjoe and picked up a few items of indiscriminate destruction — a dozen sticks of dynamite and some timed fuses as well as a handful of grenades. My buddy, Cody Joe, once said, "There's no such thing as having too many grenades…"

I was tempted to go by Cody's sailboat, in the bight, to see if he was interested in going. I was fairly certain that he and the newest member of the Hole in the Coral Wall Gang, our South American buddy, Arturio, would be up for this as well. Then there was the indomitable Travis Christian, the highly decorated Vietnam helicopter pilot and all-around good guy/bad-assed son of a bitch. (Depending on whose side he was on.) But, first off, extra members and gear would over-gross Eddie's aircraft; and secondly, it might be nice to have a team in reserve, in case we got in the weeds inside the canyon. I did a quick check and made sure all of them were in the Keys, just in case.

After dropping Jing off, I was back home in my living room, making lists and checking them twice, when the phone rang. It was Will, calling from a payphone. He was unusually curt, saying that he was on his way back from Miami with some pertinent information. There was an angst in his voice that I couldn't place. He said it would be good if I could call Dax and have him join us at my home. After we hung up, I did.

Twenty minutes later, Dax arrived. He was as curious as I was but I had nothing for him.

An hour later, I heard Will's Mustang pull up under my Keys-style stilt home. My friend knocked, then marched in.

Dax and I looked up from the dining room table.

"You're back already?" I said. "So...either your investigation was very successful or not so good."

My old buddy grinned but there wasn't a lot of humor in his smile. "I'll let you make the call." He came over and pulled up a seat at the wicker-and-glass table.

"You want a beer?" I asked.

He nodded. "Yeah."

I looked at Dax. He nodded an affirmative.

"Okay," I said. I grabbed the beers, sat them down, and plopped back into my chair. "Let's hear it."

Will sighed, then pulled a sleeve of paperwork from his briefcase and spread out its contents on the tabletop. "Here's the good, the bad, and the ugly," he said. "The good news is, the Miami-Dade Public Library is one of the largest in the United States. In addition, because Florida was a hub for numerous New World explorers, the library has an excellent collection of historical reference books. In addition, it has a large microfilm division, which carries a good deal of what is available in the archives of Spain." He took a breath. "Long story short, I spent the entire day there, lost to microfilm and the early exploration of Central America and the Southwest United States."

"And..." I said.

"There are some remarkably good records of the Spanish invasion and conquest of the Americas," Will explained. "But I had to dig to find exactly what I was looking for."

"But you found it...right?" said Dax, hands out.

Will exhaled, somewhere between proud and dismayed. "Yeah, I think I found a small footnote that changed America." My friend pulled out a handful of papers, all hastily written in longhand. Then he began his incredible story.

"In September of 1540, conquistador Francisco Vásquez de Coronado led a large expedition from Mexico through parts of what would become the southwestern United States," he began. "History says that Captain García López de Cárdenas, under the orders of Coronado, took a party of Spanish soldiers with Hopi guides into what is now the Grand Canyon." He paused for a moment and looked at us. "This is all fact. Most of this comes right from the archives of Spain. Cárdenas's commanding officer had provided him orders to find the fabled Cities of Cibola — the Seven Cities of Gold. It was a tall order, and ultimately it failed, but in a footnote not mentioned in general recollection, Cárdenas speaks of the encounter and capture of two unusual 'Indians' near the rim of what is now the Grand Canyon. These Indians are described as having golden skin, slightly different than that of the other tribes he encountered, with black, slanted eyes and wide mouths."

He added that their hair was remarkably clean, silky black, and cut with bangs in the front, then fell to their shoulders — significantly different than the area tribes. They wore loincloths, similar to other cultures, but they were longer — to the knees and made of what appeared to be white cloth embroidered with a high-quality thread. These rather strange people carried metal swords and metal-tipped arrows, unlike the other tribes in the area, who were limited to stone arrowheads and obsidian or flint knives. And oddly enough, they had what appeared to be golden rings on their fingers, which was not a common practice of the "primitives" Cárdenas had previously encountered.

"The officer had great hopes that this connection might be his lead to the fabled golden cities but his captives spoke a language he and his guides had never heard before. He fed the strangers well, offered them wine, of which they partook, and was hoping to find an interpreter. Nonetheless, he did bind them as night fell."

Will paused and leaned in, adding that Cárdenas's notes following this episode say the officer was certain he had discovered not just a new tribe, but perhaps a significant race. Unfortunately, that night, as everyone slept around the fire, the strange Indians somehow cut their bonds and slipped into the darkness." Will paused. "They were never seen again."

My friend sighed.

"Unfortunately, there is an additional footnote to this expedition. A handful of soldiers on this same foray later began to exhibit signs of smallpox infection. All three had recently come in with the latest expeditionary forces from Spain." Will took a breath and it ended in another sigh. "It's probably not a bad guess that during the sharing of the food, water, and wine, the Spanish quite possibly shared something else — their most common gift to the indigenous societies of North and South America. The physician/priest who traveled with them recognized the disease among his people early on, and probably saved the lives of the majority of the expeditionary force. Cárdenas and what was left of his soldiers were forced to return to the main command in Vera Cruz. And, much to the disappointment of the conquistador, they were held in isolation for better than three weeks, where they lost several people to smallpox, but contained what might have been an epidemic."

Again my friend took a breath, then offered a bitter sigh. "I'm speculating, but I'll bet that in that one fateful meeting in the desert, the fate of the first Egyptian society in the Americas was sealed."

There was a cold silence for a moment. I felt Shadow pull himself closer to me under the table, as if he felt it too. I shook my head. "They — the people in the caves — would have had no more resistance to that disease than any other indigenous people. Probably less."

"And they certainly weren't the first society to be wiped out by it," Will added. "If that's what happened." He took a breath. "These people, the displaced Egyptians, having lived in such a confined society, were particularly vulnerable. They hadn't developed any natural antibodies." My friend stared at us. "They wouldn't have had a chance. Even worse. They wouldn't have known what was happening until the disease had overwhelmed them."

"My God," I whispered, dumbstruck by the incredulousness of it all. "The plague — smallpox. That would explain all the bodies stacked in the first cave that the explorers Kincaid and Jordan discovered, and the numerous sarcophagi and mummies ready for burial. They were a people that ran out of time. They were destroyed by a disease."

Dax nodded. "Yeah. It probably spread so fast, given their containment, that they were overwhelmed by it before they figured out what was happening. A society that might have changed history, that could have supplied firsthand information about the ancient

48

Egyptians and rewritten the history books…"

Will let out a breath. "And right there is where our present problem may lie. We're in this situation now because certain political and secular powers don't want their pat version of history to be changed." He threw out his hands. "Ancient Egyptians in America! No sir! No point in confusing the masses — damaging 'land-bridge' theories, disturbing the 'indigenous cultures development' thesis.'"

"The real issue for the historical and religious powers now is containment," Dax added. "The problem for them is, they took out the first people who tried to bring this to the surface — the 1909 explorers Kincaid and Jordan. It looks damned near obvious that somebody killed them, and probably a few others who became too...*interested.* Then they gathered together all the hard evidence and buried it — probably in the bowels of the Smithsonian. Finally, they leaned on *The Phoenix Gazette* newspaper and the article disappeared from its archives. In 1909, that was a lot easier than it would be now."

"The problem was, the newspaper had printed the article and there was no getting it back," I added. "So, before a rush to discover new history and the treasures it contained got going, a 'major Institution' in Washington with a desire to maintain the status quo got together with the government and made thirty-four miles of the Grand Canyon off-limits for a while. Then they apparently had the military send in soldiers to keep it that way. Then, later, they declared specific areas no-fly zones…" I exhaled hard. "Do you realize how deep and wide this conspiracy is?"

"Do you know how freaking dangerous this little expedition of ours is now?" Will added, his voice rising. "There are those in our current society who have graduated to killing in order to safeguard antiquated philosophy and maintain this status quo, so that science, history, and present archaeological/ecclesiastical theories are left intact."

"And you're just figuring that out?" muttered Dax dryly.

About this same time, 1,200 miles away, three men sat in the small back room of that innocuous office on a Washington, D.C. side street. The large man at the desk snubbed out another cigarette, the smoke streaming from his nostrils giving him the appearance of a sullen, pockmarked dragon. He stared at his swarthy companions as they studied dossiers and photos. "Okay, boys," he growled. "Time to earn our keep..."

Later that day, we had the whole team assembled at my place. Tax and Jing sat on the couch. Eddie was sprawled out in an armchair, and the rest of us were sitting around the table. The dogs, who seemed to be getting along better than any of us would have expected, were sprawled out in the shade on the deck. Jing's hawk was somewhere outside, hunting, watching. All I knew for sure was when Jing whistled, he'd be there.

"What makes you think we'll be more successful at finding this elusive treasure than all the other people who tried?" asked Jing.

"Remember, we got a map, darlin'," said Dax, as he sat his cowboy hat on the table and instinctively brushed down his blue jeans. "And if old Seth's map is right, we're coming into the cavern from the high backside. Nobody's having to drop down or scale up thousands of feet of canyon walls."

"That's providing we can find a place to set Eddie's girl in," said our pilot. "Eddie already changed out to heavy terrain tires — to be in the cool," he added.

"Old Seth said it was pretty desolate up top," Dax explained. "So we should be able to find a spot. We just have to avoid the larger mesquite and maybe desert ironwood trees. They're hard on propellers."

"We'll come in belly-scraping low," said Eddie. "Then, soon as we can, we'll slide into the canyon itself and run along the river. That'll keep us out of any radar and away from most eyeballs. At about the right place, we'll roll up and run the ridge." Eddie looked over at our big cowboy. "I'll put Dax up front with me, so he can watch for landmarks."

"Sounds like a plan," I said.

"We're on the hunt again," said Will, with that goofy grin of his.

CHAPTER EIGHT

The following day was pretty much a whirlwind of preparation — making checklists, then confirming everything from food and medical supplies to the caliber of necessary ammo. Dax and I made sure our dogs were up-to-date on all their shots. We didn't want to lose an animal to a miscellaneous disease or an overaggressive Customs person. By the end of the day, when everyone went their own way, my friend and I were ready for a beer or two.

We were storing some of the canned goods in the garage under my stilt house. The sun was being sucked into the western horizon, everything was starting to gray, and my first beer was just coming home when Dax tapped me on the shoulder and motioned me closer with a forefinger.

"There's a car that's been parked at the end of your road, near the highway, for the past twenty minutes," he said quietly. "It's a good ways away but I'm pretty sure I can see a guy at the wheel."

"Could be tourists," I said. "Maybe they've got car trouble."

"Here's the problem," he said evenly. "There were three people in that car before..." He took a breath. "Why don't you go upstairs and get that pistol you told me about."

I eased back a little. "What about you?"

Dax pulled back his T-shirt just enough so I could see a short-barreled revolver stuck in his waistband.

"Lucky you," I muttered.

He smiled but it wasn't necessarily a nice smile. "Luck favors the prepared." Dax pointed up to the deck. "Go."

As I moved around toward the front of the house and the stairs, facing the canal, I heard him whistle softly. I also noticed that the car that had been on the highway was moving slowly down the marl drive toward us. I had just made it up the stairs and across the deck, and was reaching for the door handle, when I sensed a shadow coming up quickly behind me. The muzzle of a gun buried itself in my ribs and a large hand grasped my shoulder.

"Don't move," rasped the man's voice. "Don't even breathe hard."

The fellow quickly and professionally patted me for weapons, then turned me toward the stairs. But as we went back down, I saw

51

an outline moving at the periphery of the mangroves across from the house — low and deadly silent, like a graveyard wraith. We had just reached the bottom of the stairway and were turning toward the garage under the house when I thought I saw another shadow flit across the marl from the direction of the seawall and my boat. I looked again, squinting in the light of a half moon, but it was gone.

The gun in my ribs brought me back to the present. Now I could see Dax, facing away from me, studying the car as it rumbled slowly toward us. Another man was coming out of the shadows behind him, raising a pistol. I took a breath to yell a warning. My captor's gun was coming up to my head. I knew I'd only get one shout before I was dead...

But at that moment, a dark specter streaked out from the mangroves on the east side of the house. It was a good fifty feet from us but it was moving so fast it seemed to be airborne. The guy about to shoot Dax barely had time to grunt out a surprised breath before Smoke, Dax's wolf-dog, hit him. They all rolled over in a ball of arms and legs, and I heard a gun discharge. Then I heard the assailant start to scream. A moment later, it ended in a gurgle.

The guy holding me got caught in the drama and I took advantage. Turning sharply, I slapped his pistol away from my head just as he fired. The barrel was close enough to my face for the discharge to sear my cheek. I staggered back and again the guy brought up his weapon. But at that moment, Shadow swept out of the darkness behind my assailant and leapt. I swear the damned dog appeared to be flying — all he needed was a freaking red cape. The incredible momentum of that charge slammed the man into one of the concrete house pilings in front of him. The guy's head caught the hard, concrete edge of the piling and there was a sickening *crack*. He had barely dropped to his knees, a surprised, definitely disappointed look in his eyes when Shadow had his throat. It was overkill...

At that moment, whoever was in the car had seen enough to encourage a hasty retreat. The car swung around in a spray of marl and gravel and was gone before we could do anything about it. A moment later, we watched it turn north on U.S. 1 toward Miami.

At this point, several of our neighbors on the canal were out of their homes, particularly the big "naturalist" blond who lived next door. She had thrown on a sheer robe which might have well as been a shower curtain. Everyone was vacillating between yelling back and forth and staring at our practically naked neighbor. I could hear police sirens in the distance.

Dax walked over to me. He stared out at the road, then back at me. "You mentioned you knew some people in authority around here. Now would be a good time to call them."

It was true. For guys who danced on the edge of illegality quite a bit, we had a pretty good rapport with an ex-DEA commander, the Keys Customs people, and the Key West police chief, who had a grudging admiration for the way we had handled a South American cocaine drug boss and his female assassin about a year ago. I nodded an affirmative. I couldn't help but recall an expression from our old Rastaman buddy, Rufus.

"You're not dead until they can touch your eyeballs and you don't flinch," I muttered with a smile.

We spent most of the next day filling out police reports and giving statements. We were as honest as we could be without mentioning anything about our plans for the Grand Canyon and probably a particular institution in Washington, D.C. Hell, if we opened up that can of worms...

There was really nothing they could charge us with. None of the entertainment last night had been our fault. Besides, it was our dogs who had protected us. They had handled most of the sticky business. Somehow, we managed to navigate around impoundment of the animals by providing blood samples that showed no rabies or other infections. Hell, there wasn't a guy on any of the investigative forces who wouldn't want to have dogs like ours.

———————

That same day, a phone rang in the small back room of the innocuous office on the side street off Maryland Avenue in downtown Washington, D.C. The large man at the desk snubbed out his cigarette and picked up the receiver. "Overview Office."

"We ran into serious problems," said the voice on the phone. "The mission went sideways. Decker and Johnsten are dead."

"What the hell do you mean, went sideways?" growled the big man. "This was a simple — "

"There was nothing simple about it. These guys are

professionals of some sort and they had some kind of animals protecting them — dogs, I think — that killed Decker, for sure." The fellow paused. "My cover wasn't blown so I'll dig in and watch."

"Son of a bitch!" muttered the man in the small office. "Stay on this. Pay attention. You got it?" The man eased out an ugly sigh as he sat the phone in its cradle. *The basement will want to know about this...*

The following day, we were back in "full ahead" mode, gathering gear and foodstuffs and loading them into Eddie's Grumman Goose in Key West. That plane was the consummate adventure craft — long-range fuel tanks, heavy gear and wheels, excellent dual navigational packages, reinforced wings and struts, and more hidden compartments than a magician's stage box. At present, we were loading everything we could get away with under the watchful eyes of the Key West tower. Actually, it hardly mattered. We boxed the weapons and miscellaneous items of painful distraction, and shuffled them aboard. Then Eddie hid them. It would take a freaking psychic to find them. Besides, we had a pretty good rapport with Customs in Key West, and as I mentioned earlier, over the years we had made a few friends with the local police and the DEA. They knew we weren't exactly the good guys but we definitely weren't the bad guys.

Finally, we were ready. Key West Customs did get curious near the end, when Jing prepared to load her now almost full-grown, hooded osprey onto the plane. But Jing was well ahead of the curve. She had all her permits in order.

Gill Harding, the head of Customs, was standing with Will and me as Tax and Jing headed for the Grumman Goose. Tax was enough to make a father proud — a dark tan, shoulder-length sun-lightened hair, bright hazel-green eyes, and a body like Adonis, all packed into a pair of blue jeans and a strained T-shirt.

Jing carried the very impressive hawk perched on her arm, her long blond hair ruffled by the wind, that dynamic figure of hers defined by a tight T-shirt and white cotton pants.

Harding turned to Will with a wry smile. "Your daughter,

right?" he said, motioning to Jing with his head. "Damn, that's impressive...all the way around..."

It was generally always the same — most people immediately gravitated to Jing and her remarkable looks and personality. Sometimes it seemed that Tax, with his laid-back attitude, was overlooked. But I'd been given a glimpse beyond the covers of the books. I had made a point to spend time with both of them, individually. Although it might not have always seemed so, Jing adored her brother. It was Tax who had saved her life, often a day at a time, when they were younger. It was a dark story that few people knew.

As Jing and Tax grew up, their mother, Banyan McDaniels, was hardly ever without a suitor. Sometimes the relationship lasted a few weeks, sometimes a couple of years. The real problem was that these men had no real genetic loyalty to the family, and when Jing hit puberty, she blossomed into a remarkably beautiful girl, her body developing well ahead of her sense of self-preservation. It was a recipe for disaster. Unfortunately, her mother was too busy with her own romances and her bar business to pay attention to the crisis.

Tax was young then and he was never one for the spotlight, but he carried a huge loyalty to his sister. More often than not, they were on their own in life — and that can carry a price. The first time, he was too late, and the damage, both physically and mentally, had been done, never to be repaired. Their mother had been out of town for about a week when one day, he found his sister in her room, brutalized without conscience by his mother's latest beau. It was then that he discovered a new level of savagery inside himself, and Tax, even at the age of fourteen, was a powerful and capable young man.

That evening, Tax had a girlfriend lure the man into a back alley on the waterfront docks with promises of a party. Without any introduction or conversation, he broke the man's arms and legs with a baseball bat. Then he paid two local fishermen to load the guy into the hold of a freighter headed for Canada. From then on, Tax developed his body, studied martial arts, and became his sister's guardian. While Jing may have appeared the more gregarious and motivated of the two, Tax was the ever-vigilant sentinel in the shadows. And he was okay with that.

But today, they and the rest of our team were the center of attention in more ways than one.

"They're like mercenaries of some sort," said the voice on the phone. "But they've got some support from the authorities. Don't ask me how that works. They're loading up a plane now with gear for extended travel — a Grumman Goose, N number 44558."

The big guy at the Maryland Avenue office scribbled down the numbers. He'd look into a flight plan but he doubted there'd be one. "Ask around about this plane and these people but don't be stupid. We need some background. I'll work the system from here."

CHAPTER NINE

We planned to shoot across the Gulf waters and into the New Orleans area, where we'd refuel. I needed to touch bases with our old buddy, Nick Crow, who had been part of our last adventure on Navassa Island off of Haiti. Nick owned a sizable piece of land at the mouth of a Louisiana bayou. A few years back, Crow had carved out an airstrip on his property, just outside the Pearl River Wildlife Management Area. He "rented it out" on occasion to late-night visitors who needed to drop things off or pick things up. Crow — tall and tan, with sandy colored hair and dark eyes — fancied himself as sort of the blue-jeaned John Lafitte of modern times. He wasn't without principles but he was a man who lived by his own set of rules.

I had contacted Nick about this well in advance. Our friend and his people didn't care for unannounced visits. But in this case, he was pleased to see us — especially considering that I had a suitcase of money for him.

It was a relatively short but mutually satisfying visit, and the following morning, after topping off our tanks, we were on our way again. We had places to be...

An hour or so later, we were sailing west across the rolling hills of southern Texas, the steady hum of the Goose's big Pratt and Whitney, nine-cylinder, air-cooled radials soothing out the tenseness of the last few days. Eddie was in the left seat, at the controls, of course. Dax was keeping him company in the second seat. Smoke, Dax's wolf-dog, lay sprawled out between the cockpit and the cabin, always the watchful sentinel. Tax and Jing had taken the last two seats in the rear of the aircraft. Jing had her hawk's covered cage next to her, in the aisle, so Cielo could sense her and she could calm him as much as possible.

Will and I had the seats just behind the cockpit partition. Shadow was stretched out in the aisle next to us.

We'd been in the air for about a half hour when Will eased out a breath, then turned to me. "Well, here we are again, off on another wild-haired adventure — another theme that, for all intents and purposes, seems freaking impossible." He paused. "Why us? I mean...*why us?*" He exhaled. "Hell, could Rufus be right? Do the gods just find some people more entertaining than others?"

I shrugged. "Yeah, we could be nothing more than a celestial version of late-night TV. But I'll tell you, if that's the case, it's been a very mutually satisfying experience. Time after time, you and I have discovered clear, unequivocal proof of an extraordinary universe — along with the depth and power of spirit. We're the lucky ones — to have witnessed pieces of this planet's history that have been lost or forgotten. And here we go again..."

"But *why?*" Will asked. "Why has this happened to us once again?"

I shook my head. "I don't know. But I think part of the answer is because we're 'receptive' to the extraordinary. Sometimes I think God, if you will, and the folks in His employ, give people like you and me a spiritual or intellectual nudge from time to time. We call it coincidence or extraordinary insight. In the past, it's been called everything from witchcraft to miracles, depending on whose side of the fence you were on."

"Then, if all this wasn't confusing enough, there is the 'other intelligent beings out there' theme dancing through all of this," said Will. "The more we explore the width and depth of this universe, the closer I come to realizing that it's just not likely we're alone." Will threw his hands up. "Scientists are estimating there are billions of solar systems in our galaxy alone. *Billions.* It defies logic and intellect to think that in a panorama that vast, there are no other intelligent creatures to be found. Worse, it seems like absolute theological and philosophical arrogance." Will paused and drew a breath. He wasn't done. "As much as I love my conventional faith in God, I'm also forced to recognize the possibility that we are not the only clay He shaped and Earth may not be the only place He had a potter's wheel."

I offered an affirmative nod. "The way I figure it, growth stops when you quit asking questions."

My friend exhaled hard and calmed himself. "It's entirely possible that mixed into this bag of miracles in the Bible, there may have been times when benign beings from far away, just a little more advanced than us, decided to throw us a bone to see if we would use it or bury it. And sometimes I think some of their efforts became recorded as miracles. For instance, there are numerous places in the Bible that tell of prophets and religious leaders coming into possession of devices like the Ark of the Covenant or the trumpet that blew down the walls of Jericho. There are magic swords, and arrows, and rings, etc. ensconced in legends across the globe — always presented at a critical time…"

"The more we research these things, the more we discover a consistent vein of convenience and timing," I added. "Maybe not all of these devices were spiritual in nature. Maybe some were simply the tools of advanced civilizations, placed in the hands of early cultures and briefly used for their benefit. Then probably retrieved."

My friend nodded slowly. "By the very grace of God, back in '82 you and I discovered that wand-like device in the mountains of Peru that could effortlessly raise monster blocks of stone. How freaking convenient was that for those early societies like the Egyptians, the Mayans, and the Incas, and their 10,000-pound building blocks? And you can't help but recall that the following year we stumbled across a remarkable gadget in a Cuban cave — the tool of an antediluvian culture that could bend the mental will of the strongest man." Will paused. "Again, I have to ask, why us?"

I threw up my hands. "Who knows? It's still totally possible it was all nothing but blind freaking luck. But I do know this. Here we are again, and we have, once more, been given a remarkable opportunity to grasp another unique piece of this planet and the workings of those who came before us."

Will couldn't help but offer a wistful smile. "That's exciting, man. I have to admit. However, it's my fervent hope that while we explore another chapter of this somewhat worthless but apparently entertaining species called humankind, we don't end up dirt-napping in a shallow hole somewhere…"

I shrugged. "We gotta roll the dice, man, regardless. At the core of every bizarre, nearly unexplainable circumstance is almost inevitably a grain of truth. If you ignore that seed, then you are limiting your understanding of the big picture."

"Who said that?" asked Will.

"I did," I said.

After my mind-stretching conversation with Will, I got up and took the second seat in the cockpit so I could spell Eddie at the controls. Dax moved back into the cabin. Smoke, of course, followed him, stretching out not a foot away from Shadow. My boy just leaned over and casually sniffed Smoke's hindquarters in recognition and acceptance. I would never have believed that those two dogs, with such powerful personalities, would have gotten along so well. But I was damned pleased. The alternative would have been hell on wheels.

After another four hours of droning along into the afternoon sun, Eddie announced that we were coming up on Flagstaff, which was about fifty miles south of the Grand Canyon. The great orb in the west was working its way downward and shadows were growing across the landscape below. After a quick consultation, we all agreed that we didn't want to "run the canyon" anywhere near dark, so I got on the horn and contacted the tower at Flagstaff Pulliam Airport while Eddie set up an approach.

After landing, we paid extra for a well-lit tie-down near the airport's primary fixed-base operator, then we rented a van for twenty-four hours. A half hour later, we were standing at the desk of the local Holiday Inn. The dogs and Jing's hawk were still outside in the rental, as there were no pets allowed overnight. (We had to work around that.) Will and I took a double room, as did Tax and Jing. Eddie and Dax took another. It was a weekday, and the motel wasn't full, so all our accommodations were in the same wing on the second floor. As soon as everyone was settled, we cautiously headed downstairs to sneak in our furred and feathered friends.

Dax and I ushered Shadow and Smoke from the van into the elevator without incident. Jing and Tax took Cielo, in his cage, and headed up the adjacent stairs.

When the elevator opened on the second floor, there was a young man standing at the entrance in front of Dax and me. He was dressed in a battered Jethro Tull T-shirt, wrinkled shorts, and weary leather sandals. His eyes were rimmed in red, and a waft of freshly smoked marijuana enveloped him. He took one look at the two huge animals, and those bloodshot eyes came up to mine. At that moment, Jing appeared at the stairway with her huge osprey. The guy glanced at her and Cielo flared his wings in nervousness. The fellow's jaw dropped, then he reluctantly returned his gaze to the two giant dogs in front of him.

"You didn't see anything," I said, quietly but firmly.

Shadow glared at him and offered a brief but ominous growl, as if he understood every word.

The young man took one final, nervous glance at the dogs, then looked over at the hawk, who again extended his wings and cried out angrily. Our Jethro-Tulled friend exhaled heavily and his eyes rolled to the ceiling. "I didn't see shit, man...I didn't see shit..." he whispered, hands hanging at his sides.

"Close your eyes and stand still for a minute," whispered Will conspiratorially. "And we'll disappear..."

As we moved around the man, I heard him saying to himself, "I gotta quit smokin' this shit...I gotta quit..."

That night, the team gathered around a table in Dax and Eddie's room. Dax explained that the Grand Canyon was over 250 miles long, up to eighteen miles wide, and up to a mile deep in some places. So it wasn't at all surprising that there were a number of geological and archaeological finds yet to be discovered in that region. But we had an advantage — we had old Seth's maps, and that offered a fairly clear trail and narrowed down the hunt considerably.

After studying the maps one last time, we decided that tomorrow we'd do a run upriver through the canyon, just above the cliffs. This way we could study the terrain on the outside of the canyon as well because this related to Seth's claim of an entrance on the backside of the canyon walls. Eddie decided that 500 feet above the cliffs should be low enough to stay out of any area radar, and that height would allow us to drop down into the canyon itself and wind with the river if we spotted any anomalies.

Obviously, there was a whole lot we didn't know yet but it wouldn't be fun any other way. We probably would have been less excited if we'd known how unpopular we'd become in certain places.

"There was nothing I could do," said the big man as he stood before a desk at the entrance to a part of a D.C. institute that tourists don't get to see. "These aren't your average Grand Canyon conspiracy junkies," he continued. "They're some sort of antiquities professionals — more like mercenaries. My man in Key West said they've got a reputation…and they're well-connected."

"I don't care about their reputation," said the blue-eyed, tall, thin man standing in the shadows behind the desk. His face was long, almost to the point of seeming like a caricature, his fingers so thin they seemed like claws. The Brooks Brothers suit he wore was carefully cut to add dimension but he still looked like a well-dressed scarecrow. Oddly out of place was his long but sparse blond hair. "The news is, they're headed into our playing field. The canyon is a dangerous place. I want them to become...*discouraged*...as soon as possible or I want them to become statistics. I don't care which." He eased out an angry breath. "There are people who generously 'encourage us' to maintain particular status quos. I don't want that to change because a handful of cowboys get a hair up their collective asses about ancient Egyptian history. Do I make myself clear?"

The big man nodded. "Perfectly, sir. As soon as we have a location, we'll drop in a team…"

———————

By eight the following morning, we were all buckled in and Eddie was pulling us into a brilliant blue-and-yellow sky. I was flying co-pilot. A few minutes later, what is considered to be one of the true wonders of the world was opening up below us. I really had no idea of the immensity of the Grand Canyon — the dramatic gorges and cliffs, the valleys and vistas, not to mention the indomitable, ever-winding Colorado River. It's a harsh but stunning tapestry — perhaps the greatest statement on earth to the dynamics and power of Mother Nature.

But it was also simply overwhelming, and without the prior knowledge we'd accumulated and the maps old Seth had left us, this whole affair would have been a pipe dream. We located El Tovar Lodge, and from there we estimated miles via landmarks left by those before us to the first cave. Or where we thought the first cave should be.

Still, this would have been near to a wild goose chase without the information from the original explorers — G.E. Kincaid and S.A. Jordon. We knew they said in their notes that the original entrance of the cave they found was approximately forty-two miles upriver from the El Tovar Crystal Canyon (and the El Tovar Hotel, which had opened in 1905), and just short of 1,500 feet down the sheer canyon wall. They said to watch for the sedimentary stains on the east wall, 2,000 feet above the riverbed prior to the original, designated "cavern." We also knew the original entrance found by Kincaid and Jordon had been apparently sealed since their find. Nonetheless, it was a place to start.

Then, supposedly, there was the second cave that Dax's friend, Seth, had discovered, but the old miner had admitted it was almost impossible to recognize from the river or the floor of the cavern, as it had apparently been sealed by the ancient residents. From the inside...

Two hours after leaving Flagstaff, we found the sedimentary stains on the east walls of the canyon, and that at least gave us a place to work from. But even with the hair-curling close passes to the canyon walls Eddie provided, there wasn't anything unusual to be seen. It was disappointing but nothing we hadn't expected. At that point, without much in the way of a warning, Eddie threw his bird up and we climbed over the great walls of the canyon and out into the desert behind them. The entire park is considered to be semi-arid, but the habitats change as you climb. Just above the river corridor there is a desert scrub community with a wide variety of cacti. Above that, there is a pinion pine and juniper forest. As you climb, the desert scrubs thin out and Ponderosa pines take over.

From all the information that Seth left Dax, it was obvious that he never really sought the higher altitudes and remained at the edges of the canyon itself. It was there, or in that area, that he claimed to have found the well-disguised back entrance to the cave system in the interior walls of the cliffs.

After a few minutes of investigation at about 1,500 feet, there appeared to be a relatively flat stretch just off the canyon where we could land. The trick to this was to put the Goose in somewhere close but not near the area we were to investigate. No point in advertising our location. But damn, even Eddie said this stretch looked a little rough. Staring down at the terrain below, I was glad our buddy had beefed up his struts and tires.

As we made a second pass above what we considered to be the most likely area for Seth to have found his entrance to the cave system, I looked out at the terrain, then across to Eddie, trying to bolster both our spirits. "It's not all that bad…"

My friend took a look at me sideways. "As opposed to what? Nailing your nuts to your knees?" He exhaled, then took another look around. "I've seen worse, I guess," he said with a shrug. Eddie sighed with a degree of finality. "Okay, dude, that tract straight ahead. That's it. We're gonna take out a couple of cactus but I think the old girl can handle it."

"Yeah…but we'll be running toward the edge of the cliff when we touch down," I mentioned quietly.

"Yep," said Eddie with an evil grin. "Talk about harshing your mellow! But we need to be landing into the wind, dude." He grinned. "Besides, if I call it wrong and we don't have enough distance to land, we got a 6,000-foot fall to get the old girl flying again before we hit the river below." He shrugged in a fatal fashion. "It's possible."

"Whoa shit…" muttered Will, definitely uncomfortable with the vision of our plane tumbling off 6,000 feet of cliff. "Call me crazy, but somehow that whole scenario doesn't sound comforting."

The usually reserved Tax even chimed in on that one. "I'm young. I'd like to stay that way for a while. As opposed to dead."

Eddie was right. It was an interesting landing. Once our pilot got us lined up a half-mile inland (aiming straight at the freaking cliffs), he tickled the power back a little and pulled up the nose, reducing our thrust as much as possible without stalling. Gradually, the fat Goose began to "float" lightly and drop. I was just starting to think things were okay when the first cactus hit the wing. I think I screamed a little but not as loud as Will. Even the generally inscrutable Dax was pulled back against his seat, his eyes uncomfortably wide. When we took out the second cactus and a small conifer, there was a chorus of yells (for which no one took credit afterward). It was a damned bouncy ride and I think we hit something else — maybe a deer or a coyote — but I was too busy making indelible imprints in the armrest to know for sure.

When the props finally jerked to a halt and the interior had gone silent, the nose of the plane was just at the edge of the cliff but we were still in one piece. As I sat there inhaling sweet breaths of life, I glanced out my window. Suddenly, I thought I saw an old man standing by a mule on the bluff to the side of the plane, maybe a couple hundred yards away. *A beat-up cowboy hat and sun-bleached, dusty blue jeans...* But before I could be sure, Eddie nudged me, asking about the starboard prop, wanting to make certain it wasn't damaged. When I turned back, the image was gone...

"That beats a mean Brahma on a hot Saturday anytime..." muttered a shaken Dax from the seats behind the cockpit partition.

I glanced out at the bluff again but there was nothing. No old man, no mule — just desert and pale-blue sky.

CHAPTER TEN

First things first. We all got up against the plane's fuselage and undercarriage, then pushed it back about twenty yards. (Hard work in that damned Arizona sun…) I kept watching the crests around me but there was no sign of the image I had seen earlier. When I told Will about it, he chuckled.

"You've been watching too many Westerns. What would an old guy be doing this far from anywhere?"

"Every desert Western has an old prospector," I muttered.

My friend chuckled again. "I think you need a beer and some shade…"

We secured the airplane with rebar tie-downs and rope. The sun was already becoming brutal and it wasn't even ten o'clock. Then we removed the gear we needed for a day hike — area maps, a couple of Vietnam-vintage two-way radios, two handheld metal detectors, water, weapons, compasses, some MREs (military quick-meal packages we got from our buddy, Bobby Branch), and a folding shovel or two. While we organized, the dogs checked out our perimeter as if they were trained for the job. Will and Eddie had binoculars, and most importantly, Dax had old Seth's notes and map. In the interim, Jing brought out her hawk and set his cage on a folding table we'd assembled. Her brother watched as she reluctantly slipped on her gauntlet, opened the cage door, and removed Cielo's hood. If there was an ultimate test, this was it. She whispered to her hawk and he came to her immediately, hopping up on her arm as she brought him from the cage. She eased out a tentative breath.

"The moment of truth…" she said.

Jing brought up her arm and her osprey launched himself at the desert sun. In just a few moments, he was nothing more than a dot rising high in the distance over the scattered pine and juniper forest.

Jing sighed. Tax, ever the protector, came over and put his arm around her shoulders.

"Faith," he said quietly. "Faith…"

But there was no confidence in this bird business for her yet. Every time she let that hawk go, she wondered if it would be the last.

While we did a final security check and made certain our gear was stored safely, Jing waited impatiently. Finally, we were as ready as we were going to be. Everyone kept glancing nervously at the distant bluffs.

Dax turned to Jing. "I'm sorry, hon, but we can't stand out here in this heat waiting for that bird to make up his mind. We gotta get a move on."

And so, reluctantly, we did.

Like Tax said, "It's a hawk. If he wants to find you, he will."

We moved toward the rim of the canyon, watching for the landmarks on old Seth's map. It made sense that the rear entrance to the lost underground Egyptian city would probably be as short a distance as possible from the desert. After all, it had to be used to transport crops and freshly killed game into the interior. Still, it was rough going. The land was hard and unforgiving, and after several hundred years, we realized there weren't many clues.

An hour later, as we entered the more jumbled terrain on the outside of the canyon ridge, Cielo still hadn't returned, although Jing was fairly sure she saw a bird of his size floating in the thermals about a quarter-mile behind us. We all offered hope — it was all we had to share. By now, we were into the collapsed buildup of broken granite and sandstone along the backside of the canyon. Shadow and Smoke were leading the way, cautiously examining the path and the surroundings as they moved along. It was tough terrain but it was an area that would more likely offer a fissure in the sandstone walls — and a way into ancient history…

We'd been moving slowly but continuously for about five hours. We were hot, tired, and had to pay attention to the water we carried. The sun was starting to move into the high walls of the canyon in the distance, throwing long shadows, and we were starting to look for a place to set up camp. That was when we heard it — someone singing, croaking out a song in what sounded like an Irish brogue. The melody was soft and melancholy but the light wind carried it well.

The Garden of Eden has vanished, they say.
But I know the lie of it still;
Just turn to the left at the bridge of Finea,

and stop halfway down to Cootehill.
Tis there that you will find it,
when fortune has come to yer call.
Oh, the grass, it is green around Ballyjamesduff,
and the sea is over it all.
Whispering over the sea they are.
Come home to Ballyjamesduff.

"What the hell?" I whispered.

Everyone had stopped.

Tax was standing next to me. He listened for a moment. "That's an invitation to dinner," he said. "No one sings out loud in a place as uncertain as this."

I looked at the others. They cautiously nodded in agreement with that assessment.

Five minutes later, we came over a jumbled rise of sandstone and there below us was a small, open expanse protected on two sides by rock walls. In the clearing was a fire, with a pot of something dangling above it on a metal tripod. It smelled pretty good. Smoke and Shadow, just in front of us, paused and sniffed, uncertain…

A large but older man (long, gray hair sprouting out from under a battered Western hat, forming a tattered halo around his face) squatted by the glowing coals, stirring dinner. He wore weary boots, weathered blue jeans, and a faded, long-sleeved khaki shirt. Off to the side, in the shade, stood a hobbled mule. But that wasn't the best of the image. On a boulder next to him sat what looked like a large squirrel monkey. Yeah, a monkey — brown and gray, about three feet tall, long curled tail, and intelligent, dark eyes.

"Howdy," Dax called as we moved out from our cover. "That stew smells damn good…"

The man looked up, not particularly startled, and waved us down. "Still plenty left," he called congenially.

As we cautiously worked our way down into the clearing, the monkey saw us and immediately began to chatter nervously and point. I swear, he started to point.

"Aye, Nugget, I see 'em," muttered the fellow. "Don't get your tail in a twit."

"A prospector, a mule, and a monkey," whispered Will. "Sounds like the beginning of a bad joke…"

A few moments later, we were all sitting around the fire making introductions. The old fellow's name was Connor O'Connor. He was an Irishman with a "yen for the horizon" as he put it, but he wasn't real anxious to talk about what he was doing there (and God knows our conversation had to be limited). But the old prospector broke the ice as he spooned out plates of his "desert stew."

"You're from the plane that came down today — in one piece?"

"Yeah," said Eddie between mouthfuls. "She's good."

"What brings you out this way?" the old guy asked. "A vacation? Engine failure?" He glanced around at us again and all our creatures. "Are ye a travelin' circus?"

"Sort of, at times," I said with a grin. Then I paused. "I bet we're not too much different than you, you know? We're just…looking around… How'd you manage to get into this area? I didn't see much in the way of roads as we flew in."

"Actually, lad, there is one route, an old mining road that will handle a tough four-wheels fairly well. I had a friend bring me in on that." He pointed at a southern rise in the hills. "Over there. You take Hermit Road out of the Grand Canyon Village, around to Pima Point. Then go north on the old mining road that leads out of there and head for Cathedral Stairs. The road will turn northwest there. Stay with it until it peters out. From that point, you can see this ridge."

"So," said Dax, attempting to break the ice a little more. He looked over at the simian, who was chittering somewhat unpleasantly to himself. "A monkey, huh?"

"Ahhh, you're obviously an astute fellow," replied O'Connor with a caustic grin. "Yes, a monkey, but he thinks he's bloody Richard Burton." He exhaled harshly. "Although he's considerably more talented than the British blighter." He leaned over and whispered to the monkey but the words were strange and ancient. The monkey chittered back. The guy looked at us again. "He likes Gaelic better than English and that's the language we speak…when we hunt…"

That caught our attention.

"He don't speak it worth a shit but he understands Gaelic as well as he does English." The old guy's eyes hooded. "He recognizes the change and knows immediately what to do." He smiled. "This way he and I are the only ones who know what we're doin'."

There was no good answer to any of that, and we obviously weren't going to get any more of the picture, so I switched tracks.

"How long have you been doing this?" I asked. "Whatever it is you do?"

O'Connor the Irishman glanced around at us again and something changed in his eyes, as if he'd come to a decision. Suddenly, his guard seemed to drop, his features lost some of their caution and for the first time, he offered a genuine smile. "Oohhh, laddie, for a long, long time I been doin' this. Me father was an Irish country vet and me mum was a teacher. But one day on a field trip to an ancient area castle, I found a gold ring buried against the wall of some old stone ruins." He paused and his eyes carried a strange light. "And it changed me forever. By the time I was in me mid-teens, I had wandered across most of Ireland and I had some fair booty to show for it. When my friends were heading off to college, I was stowing aboard a rusty freighter on my way to the gold fields in South Africa. From there, I bought a metal detector and headed into the Caribbean." He shrugged, the light in his eyes eerily bright with recollection. "I've seen things that you only see in the movies, the kind of dumb-shit stuff..." he paused, recalling, "...that the bloody American, Harrison Ford, plays in."

We all chuckled.

"We can identify," Will muttered.

"What are you up to now?" I asked. "What brings you out here?"

O'Connor looked at me. "You can ask but if I told you, I'd have to kill you." But his eyes sparkled, belying his seriousness. He huffed and lit a cigarette with a stick from the fire.

I continued. I had nothing to lose. "I mean, forgive me, but if you were really successful at finding things, it doesn't seem like you'd still be out here in the desert, scratching in the dirt with a mule and a monkey."

"This is me hobby, lad," O'Connor said, hands out. "And every good soul should have a hobby." Then he offered a cagey grin. "But

I also own a lovely little abode in West Palm Beach, Florida, and another on the shores of Northern Ireland. And I have a pilot at the airport down the river, with my airplane, waiting to take me home when I'm ready." He paused and ran an affectionate hand down the monkey's flank, and the little guy chittered comfortably. The fellow's eyes became... grateful. "And I owe most of it to this little fellow."

"A monkey, huh?" said Jing.

O'Connor smiled again. "The truth is, of the three most significant finds we've made, Nugget found two of them." He took a breath. "You can believe it or not, makes not a rat's ass bit a difference to me, but this little simian can smell gold. Don't ask me how it works — God don't give us mortals all the answers — but he's got a Midas nose and I'm a rich man because of him."

Now I was beginning to think the old fellow was a little...*touched*. Probably too much desert sun. But O'Connor saw me and he read my eyes. He bent down and spoke to Nugget again, in Gaelic, and pointed to me. The little creature uncurled his tail from around his body and raised up. With a quick mutter of understanding, he moved over to the Irishman's bags and reached inside one. He grabbed something and brought it over to me.

"Hold out your hand," said the Irishman.

I shrugged and looked at the others. What did I have to lose? I opened my hand and Nugget dropped something into it. I held it up to the firelight. It was a beautiful gold chain...*with a golden Egyptian cartouche attached to it.* As I held it up in awe, it glistened in the firelight.

Will, our historian, sitting next to me, sucked in a breath. "Good freaking God," he whispered. Slowly, he reached out and grasped the cartouche, raising it up in his palm and studying the inscription. My friend spoke quietly, in a hoarse fashion, almost as if in a trance. And maybe he was...

"In ancient Egypt, the kings, and sometimes powerful others, encircled their name with a design we now call a cartouche," Will said. "It's an oval ring that is a hieroglyphic representation of a length of rope folded and tied at one end. It symbolized everything that the sun encircled and was thus an indication of the king's rule of the cosmos." He took a quick breath, then continued. "The term *cartouche* was originally coined by Napoleon's soldiers, who thought the images looked like the ammo cartridges on their belts." He looked over at O'Connor with new respect in his eyes. "How long have you been doing this — whatever it is you do — out here?" He held up the cartouche. "And do you know who this belonged to?"

O'Connor stared at him for a moment, then glanced around at all of us, as if coming to a decision. "I've taken a couple 'vacations' here," replied O'Connor. "And aye, I do. A fellow named Merneptah — the fourth pharaoh of the 19th dynasty of ancient Egypt."

There was graveyard silence all around. No one even breathed. I was thinking, *This is totally freaking impossible!*

"You're looking for the Egyptians," Connor O'Connor said. "Aren't you?"

We were all knocked off our feet. No one knew what to say. The chances were near impossible that we would stumble upon someone looking for the same thing we were. I was dumbfounded, and so was everyone else. Everyone except Dax. He was on a mission. He wanted his friend's death to be vindicated. He didn't want old Seth to have crossed the Great Divide for nothing.

"And if we are?" said our cowboy. "Looking for the Egyptians…"

O'Connor paused. "Well, because I've been looking awhile meself." He drew a breath. "And you know something I don't, I think, or you wouldn't be here. But I know this area far beyond any understanding you might dream to have. I want ta make this 'little find' before they put me body on a barge at the River Nile…you understand?"

God, I guess we did. No one in the freaking world understood better than we did. Trying to find a single cave in the Grand Canyon was still the equivalent of "needle in a haystack" shit.

Our Irish friend paused, then offered a slight grin. "And Nugget's apt ta surprise ya. He has a knack fer gold…" He held out his hand and Will gave him back the golden cartouche.

At that moment, we heard Cielo's sharp shriek. Everyone snapped to attention and there was Jing's big osprey, flaring its wings a hundred yards away, coming out of the last of the sun like

72

something in an old Western. He was clutching an unlucky rabbit in his talons.

Nugget the monkey took one look at the incoming hawk and immediately freaked out. Flying hawks were a genetic message burned into his DNA. He dashed into O'Connor's arms. The old guy reached for the holstered pistol at his side. Jing began yelling, trying to wave Cielo off. The whole thing had all the elements of a bad ending.

But in the next second, Tax was headed across the small arroyo like a tight end with the winning touchdown. He cleared the cooking fire by a couple of feet, executed a roll, and came up with O'Connor's gun in hand before the man could do anything brave or stupid — whichever came first. All three of them, O'Connor, Tax, and the monkey, tumbled into a loose bundle as the osprey soared in, dropped the rabbit, and flared, settling on Jing's outstretched arm. (Thank God she had left her gauntlet on, just in case...) The bird fluffed its feathers, did its reflexive blink, and glanced around, impervious to the drama he'd just caused, but cautious.

The two men and the monkey on the other side of the fire gradually straightened up, still somewhat entangled and still sitting in the dirt.

"This is Cielo," Jing said calmly, as she took a tentative step forward and picked up the rabbit. He's part of our team." She offered a disarming smile. "Sorry for the dramatic entrance."

Tax came to his feet. O'Connor stood, bringing Nugget up to his shoulder. The monkey, still chattering nervously, wasn't quite ready to let his buddy go, given the dogs and the osprey.

"Not sure if it's for God's pleasure or the devil's entertainment," said the Irishman, dusting himself off. "But I'm thinkin' we got an unlikely union here." He glanced around apprehensively at all of us. "I suppose it can't hurt to try it for a few days..." He sighed. "Although it's a bit of a bloody circus."

"Have faith," I said. "We may surprise you."

"Faith," muttered the Irishman with a touch of disdain. "A casual stroll through any lunatic asylum will show you that faith don't prove anything, lad."

CHAPTER ELEVEN

The following morning, as we sat around a breakfast fire, we discussed a direction — both physically and figuratively. We, of course, had old Seth's map but we were unfamiliar with the landmarks it mentioned. O'Connor had no map but he knew the area well. Then, of course, there was the trust issue. We were incorporating the help of an old miner who had a monkey with whom he communicated in an ancient language, who supposedly could sense/smell gold. Jing said she was waiting for him to sell us a bridge somewhere. In the end, we compromised.

After a quick breakfast, Dax got out old Seth's map. The trouble with it was, it was hand-drawn and had only a few landmarks, and most of those were ones that Seth had created for himself. Having walked this godforsaken country for part of a day, I realized how difficult this challenge was. Even if and when we found one of the landmarks, there was no tight definition regarding the distance to the next.

Everyone was impatient to get on the move. The sun was well over the distant mountains now and it was already getting hot. Twice we had heard a helicopter but couldn't see it. That made me really uncomfortable.

O'Connor offered a couple of suggestions. It was obvious that he knew this area pretty well but he didn't have any answers, just ideas. I paused and glanced over at Dax, who had, more or less, become the leader of this band of scoundrels.

"What about the bones…"

The big cowboy sighed and looked at me. It was a long shot, and it meant giving away a key in our puzzle, but he decided to take the chance. Dax turned to the Irishman. "To this point, I been feeling like a blind man tryin' to put socks on a rooster," he said. "And you may be the only hope we've got, so I'm gonna roll the dice. We're looking for a place that has old bones on the surface — maybe fossilized bones. Lots of old bones. Have you come across anything like that?"

The aging prospector pulled on the brim of his hat for a moment, lost to reflection, then suddenly his eyes lit. "I'll be bloody well damned," he muttered. Then he looked up. "Yes, by the hairy tits of Richard bloody Burton, I have!" He paused and became more serious then. "But I didn't like that place. It carried a...sadness." His eyes went wary. "And an ugliness..."

"Can you find it again?" I asked.

Our Irish friend nodded. "I can find bloody well anything once I've been there." He straightened up. "It isn't that far from here — barely off the rim of the canyon. Maybe a day's hike."

"Off we go again," said Eddie. "Back to the ass crack of Mother Nature..."

But just about that time we felt the earth below our feet shudder slightly — everything trembled, just a touch, for a couple of breaths.

"What the hell was that about?" asked Will, as we all glanced around.

"Aaahhh, that was Mother Nature farting," said the Irishman. He drew a breath. "While it's not widely mentioned, it seems that Arizona has a number of active faults that run through the state. Mostly through an area called the Northern Arizona Seismic Belt, which has dozens of active faults, and runs from Flagstaff up into Utah. The largest one is right exactly where we are. It's called the Hurricane Fault, and they say, at some point, maybe anytime, it could produce an earthquake up to and around 7.5." He grinned. "Which would change the scenery considerably."

Dax exhaled and ran the fingers of one hand through his hair. He didn't particularly like the earth dancing below his feet. "It is what it is, lady and gentlemen. Let's be on the move."

"Chopper One to base," said the pilot over the steady roar of the blades above him. "Chopper One to base."

"Base here, Chopper One," replied a voice through the mild static of the radio. "Come back."

"We've located their airplane but there's no one in sight. We're doing one-mile circular perimeters now. Will keep you posted."

"Roger, Chopper One. Continue perimeters. We'll stand by."

It was farther than our Irish friend remembered and we had eaten up three-quarters of the day by the time we came to a heavy rise of sandstone and gypsum that ran along the backside of the canyon. O'Connor led Saluda, his mule, and the monkey sat on the mule or the Irishman's shoulders. The rest of us followed. Above us, Cielo spun a web of circles, watching for dinner.

We could faintly hear the whisper of the Colorado River rapids on the distant side of the cliff rise that led to the canyon. We were in the right place. All of this paralleled what old Seth had told Dax.

By the end of the day, just as our Irish pathfinder had promised, the terrain became rougher on the backside and took on a distinctly different feel. There were dots of small pinyon pines here and there now, along with spindly junipers, Freemont cottonwoods, and an occasional bevy of prickly pear cacti. But all these aided in disguising what we were looking for.

In addition, there was a composite apprehension rising in our little band, belying the excitement of the search. Twice we'd had to hide from helicopters flying search patterns, and they weren't military. Not a good sign...

CHAPTER TWELVE

Finally, as the sun was once again reaching for the rim of the jagged horizon, O'Connor found what he was looking for. The wind, or an ancient sea, had carved an overhang into the side of a sandstone rise that ran along the edge of the canyon for a little over a hundred yards. The overgrowth was heavier here, and I could see how a cave entrance might have been disguised hundreds of years ago during less arid times. Spindly but pretty Indian paintbrush grew on the sides of the abutment, along with the colorfully named western honey mesquite and catclaw acacia. There must have been water near here at one time because I could see the skeletons of old willows as well.

The sun was throwing long shadows now and the odd eeriness of the area was welcoming the night. At first, we were all excited about finding the place but it didn't take long for us to agree on a campsite well away from the shadows of those walls...and the bones...

Even in the shadows of evening, one could see the small pieces of bone — mostly fossilized, some obviously human — that littered the ground. It was ugly and eerie at the same time. Even the dogs seemed subdued.

"What the hell happened here?" muttered Will.

"I don't know for sure," replied Eddie. "But it makes me as nervous as a stick-teased lizard." He paused. "If there is still this much left after all these years, it borders on a mass extinction."

The weather was good — no rain clouds in sight — and the helicopters had disappeared, so we all opted for a campsite in the open desert.

We built a fire and warmed a few MREs. Dax and I fed our dogs, and Jing called her hawk in and tethered him for the night. No one felt the need to post sentries. The dogs and the mule would let us know if there was a problem. I wouldn't want to be the poor soul coming into this camp unannounced.

Our new companion, O'Connor, fed his mule and his monkey, but he was more subdued than normal. Later that night, as we sat around the fire, I saw him fingering his cartouche, studying it.

"You of all people must be curious about what lies ahead," I said.

He drew a breath and casually put the cartouche and chain away. Then he looked at me. "Aye, lad, that I am. I suppose if God had forced a choice, I might have been tempted to take curiosity over cleverness." He paused and pushed at the fire with a stick he found lying next to him. "Curiosity is pure — no ulterior motives," he muttered without looking up. "Every great event in science or exploration began with this single element. Intelligence is not the root of knowledge or advancement, curiosity is. It is the explorer, the pioneer, and the scientist." His eyes came away from the fire then and he glanced at those around him. "Give a child intelligence, and they may or may not use it. But give them curiosity, and the world is theirs…"

The following morning, after a little breakfast and some strong coffee, we began with an examination of the mostly fossilized bones in our immediate area. Even in the light of day, it was an unsettling experience and we recognized that what we were seeing was only a minuscule amount of what had been deposited. There was an aura that lay over the whole consequence, somewhere between melancholy and evil. Centuries of droughts and floods had reduced the few remains practically to fossils, but the occasional jawbone or femur convinced us that this was a graveyard of humans. Yet perhaps *graveyard* wasn't the right word. It was all too haphazard — more like a mass dumping.

More and more we began to agree with Will's educated assumption regarding the Spanish. Perhaps a disease *had* been introduced. Insidious and subtle, it had buried its claws into the unsuspecting population and wearied it to death. By the time anyone actually realized what was happening, it was too late. Some may have made it out of the complex, in a desperate run, but my bet would be they were already far too late. They simply died somewhere in the desert — and North America lost one of its greatest archaeological treasures.

We spent the entire day working that ridge, searching for what might be an elusive entrance to another time while trying to avoid a helicopter that was also working the rim. Eddie said there were probably three or four helicopter companies that did tours of the area, so he wasn't biting his nails yet. Nonetheless, he recommended that we tuck ourselves in when we heard one.

But at the end of the day, there was no secret entrance to be found. The ancient Egyptians had eluded us, teasing us with their bones. If indeed they were their bones...

We should have been reminded that there are worse things than finding someone else's bones.

Like someone finding yours...

"Chopper One to base, Chopper One to base. We've got a visual on a group working the outer lip of the canyon on the western side, thirty plus miles from El Tovar. There are a couple of dogs and a mule with them, so they might just be prospectors."

"You sure you saw a couple of dogs, huh?"

"Yes sir, that's an affirmative.

"The boss man said to watch for dogs. What kind?"

"Big ones. Like shepherds."

We sat around the fire that evening, dusty, weary, and somewhat disappointed as the last of the sun sizzled into the horizon. All the information we had pointed to the ridge we were working. I was certain we were in the right place, and so was the Irishman, O'Connor. But there was something we were missing.

The night wind was just rising and the sands were shifting slightly, offering their lightest grains to the breeze. O'Connor was sitting by the fire sipping his coffee and staring at the rise when suddenly he exhaled hard and abruptly stood, spilling his coffee on Eddie, who produced a ripe expletive.

"By the wrinkled, virgin balls of Father O'Leary!" the Irishman shouted. "I know what happened. I know why we're not finding any bloody thing!"

That got everyone's attention.

"Look at the bloody wind!" he shouted. "Every damned night it blows from the bloody west! And it carries the sand into the walls of that rise!" He threw up his hands and swung around at all of us. "We're lookin' eight or ten feet too high on those walls. The entrance is buried in the bloody sand below us!"

All of a sudden, it was like a light bulb coming on. Over the centuries, the western winds had blown the desert sands into the bluff, gradually raising the sand height by as much as ten feet. What we didn't grasp was the colossal amount of bones that must have been left along that rise for remnants to be seen at all now. We couldn't find the entrance to the cavern because it was below us — under our feet!

"Son of a bitch!" Dax muttered quietly, coming to his feet with the revelation.

Tax and Jing looked at each other with growing, incredulous smiles, and offered a silent high-five.

Will and I just stared at each other for a moment.

"Probably another great barroom story," said my buddy.

Eddie took a moment to bring us down a notch. "Don't want to harsh your mellows but there's a couple hundred yards of ridge there. We still have to find the entrance."

At that point, Connor O'Connor stepped forward with the monkey on his shoulder. "I'm bettin' Nugget can find it."

"Why?" asked Dax, always the pragmatic one.

O'Connor offered a bitter smile. "Because the last thing a man lets go of is his gold." He waved a hand at the desert sand against the butte. "We'll find our clue there."

I had to nod in agreement. "You know, he's probably right. Even though they realized they were dying, they still stuffed their pockets with precious things. If we find gold items on the outside, the entrance to the community will be close."

"Before we all go runnin' off into the sand dunes, there's another issue or two," said Eddie, bringing us back to the present. "At the risk of harshin' your mellows, we're running low on water and supplies." He took a breath and exhaled slowly, letting that sink in. "I gotta go back and get my bird. I've been looking around, and I can probably get the Goose down on the ridge behind us that looks out over the river and the canyon. You may have to do a little clearing and it's gonna be a bit of a funky touchdown." He paused. "Another one of those 'into the wind but aimed at the edge of the canyon' gigs." Our friend offered a shrug. "Nothing I can do about it. That's the only area that's flat enough and hard enough to pull off a landing."

"You need someone to go back with you?" said Jing. "I need some meds for Cielo. He's a seabird and this dry weather has been hard on him. And you're going to need a hand with things anyway."

Tax glanced over at his sister, then turned to us. "I'll go with them."

That came as no surprise. I knew how much he really wanted to be here with us, in the middle of this gig. But his sister always came first.

The following morning we were all up and about before the sun had cleared the horizon. In a show of faith, those of us staying gave the departing team the better part of what water we had left. The truth was, we were all beginning to realize that we'd played this whole thing like amateurs, marching off into a killer desert without the proper supplies or water, all hell-bent on a treasure that no one had ever seen, built around a legend of hearsay.

Sure, if all went well, they'd be back in three days. But if it didn't, none of us would need water or gold. Like Will said, we'd been dumber, but he just couldn't remember when.

In addition, we realized we needed to knock down a few cactus and acacia trees at the rim of the canyon — the narrow strip between the edge of the Grand Canyon and the beginning of the desert, where Eddie would have to bring his bird in. Given the wind direction, Eddie was still faced with the same issue of having to get airborne before reaching the edge of the cliff, but the actual lip of the canyon was narrower here.

Connor O'Connor pulled us from our collective funk. "C'mon, gentlemen and lady," he cried. "Let's get past the bloody what ifs and get on with the issue of ancient gold!" Then he offered an expression by the Florida Keys' most acclaimed treasure hunter, Mel Fisher. "Today's the day!"

After a meager breakfast, we watched our friend and family march off into the desert. Then, those who remained packed some gear. O'Connor put Nugget on his shoulder. There was Dax, the Irishman, my partner Will, and me, as well as Shadow and Smoke. Quite a team…

The first thing we did upon reaching the ridge was spend a miserable, hot hour clearing a better landing place for Eddie. It wasn't much, but Eddie had seen worse. Then we returned to the edge of the ridge where it met the desert sands. It was then that O'Connor spoke to the monkey in that strange, almost melodic language, and the simian chittered back. It was all too reminiscent of a stroll through that lunatic asylum our Irish friend had mentioned earlier.

"Let's take a walk along this sand-hammered ridge and see what happens," the old miner said, adjusting his hat and his monkey. "Today could be the day..."

But two hours and three hundred slow and deliberate yards later, we still hadn't sensed a breach. We stopped for a sip of water, plopping down on the hot sand near the middle of the sandstone ridge, the morning sun still at our backs. Nugget hopped off the Irishman's shoulder and sat for a moment — not as much concerned about the two dogs any longer, who were exploring on their own, but always within calling distance. If anything, he seemed to have developed a sort of cautious disdain for them.

I was about to suggest that we extend our search just a little farther north when Nugget began to mutter softly. I swear, it was like someone talking to himself. Slowly, the monkey moved away from his companion and down the ridge. Then he began to dig in the sand with his hands — not frantically but deliberately. At first, he was chattering to himself, but as he became more excited, he began turning to O'Connor and extending the one-sided conversation. As we all moved over and gathered around our little friend, the simian became more intent. Suddenly, he paused and began to tug something from the dirty sand. It was a skeletal hand and forearm. It was very old — so old that it had petrified. But the interesting part was the two gold rings on the bent, crooked fingers. They were large and heavy — so much so that ego may well have surpassed comfort.

Very carefully, with soothing words, O'Connor took the withered, bony hand from Nugget and eased back to sit in the sand. We watched quietly. Engraved on the rings were Egyptian symbols. The Irishman slowly slipped the rings off the disintegrating finger bones and studied them while we all waited impatiently.

"One ring has the symbol of the god Isis," whispered our friend. "The other has the symbol of Osiris." He sighed heavily. "Old

Egyptian gods…"

Dax took off his cowboy hat and wiped his forehead with the back of his arm. He turned to us, eyes alight. "Here's to old Seth…" he whispered reverently.

I looked over to Will, to celebrate the moment, but my friend was on his knees digging something from the warm sand. Just moments later, he pulled out the better part of a skull. It was old — *really* old. But the heat and the lack of water had preserved it. That wasn't the best part. On the right side of the jaw, one of the molars had been rebuilt with gold, showing a great degree of sophistication.

"Egyptian dental reconstruction work, from primitive bridges and cavity filling to tooth replacement and repair, goes back at least 4,000 years," said O'Connor. He offered a slight grin. "We're here, my friends. We're in the right place. I bloody well know it."

I couldn't help but sense the voice of our old Jamaican Rastaman friend, Rufus. *"Sometimes da gods, dey get impatient and dey throw you a bone…"*

"Literally…" I muttered. I looked up at my friends, and suddenly I was filled with an almost celestial insight. "I think the entrance is here," I said. "Right here."

Inside of a miserable hour of digging, we discovered a neatly cut six-foot by five-foot cave entrance in the sandstone. After two more hours of wretched, sweaty, but incredibly exciting labor, we had cleared it enough to enter the bowels of the granite and sandstone hillside. A rock staircase led downward, then leveled out. We realized that we were probably the first humans to enter here in well over 500 years. More importantly, we could well be the first modern people to witness the last of a remarkable, indigenous society over 3,000 years old.

It was humbling and more exciting than anything I could remember. Will said that it even beat "first-time, back-seat car sex."

I was withholding judgment. I remembered that being pretty damned good…

O'Connor told us both to shut up — that we were in the presence of "bloody history being made."

We got out our flashlights and lit the two gas lanterns we carried. Then we all slipped on protective, filtered facemasks that our Irishman produced. The possibility of bad gasses in a situation like this always existed. I eased out a breath and stared at my partner. I could see the fire and excitement in his eyes.

"This is what we do it all for, isn't it?" I said.

He offered a knowing smile under his mask. "Fill your life with adventures, not things, and have stories to tell…"

I grinned. "Let's go, Frodo."

CHAPTER THIRTEEN

The next few hours were nothing like I had expected and everything I dreamed they would be. In our previous adventures, Will and I found ourselves in the presence of remarkable antiquities from time to time, but for its sheer "slap-you-in-the-face" phenomenon, nothing compared to this.

We wound down a large, eight-by-ten-foot-high tunnel on a well-worn path once apparently lit by oil torches on the walls. As the passageway began to widen out and became part of a cavern, we passed what appeared to be huge, rounded granaries, built from a cement of sorts.

We quickly moved into the primary cavern itself, which was at least a half-mile in circumference, with passages branching off into the darkness here and there. I realized immediately that this was a remarkable society, to be sure, and the center cavern was the focus of the city. Most interesting — hell, beyond belief — was a now dry waterway/canal that led from the sealed entrance in the exterior wall of the canyon to the inside of the city. But that was nothing compared to the incredible, ancient Egyptian sailing ship in perpetual dry dock above the interior canal.

"It's like something right out of a Charlton Heston movie," whispered Will, in absolute awe.

O'Connor looked at us. "We've found it! We've bloody well found it!" He offered that cagey grin of his. "Lord, we're gonna piss off a bloody lot of historians and social theorists!"

The ship was an absolutely incredible archaeological find, but the wood it was constructed from, after all these years, was impossibly fragile. It had apparently been covered with a clear pine resin to preserve it. Nonetheless, the whole thing just got better. This was obviously an industrious, certainly prepared and capable people. We found copper tools and stores of weapons (swords, knives, shields, bows, and arrows) in armories, and sophisticated implements were abundant. Some of the tools, and particularly the weapons, seemed to be made of an amalgam of copper and some other silver-gray metal, which was in evidence around the smelting areas, giving them a more resilient, tougher finish.

There were artesian wells strategically placed throughout the hub, and in many of the small cave/homes and businesses were fine copper and gold vases, silver ornaments and utensils, and remarkable glassware consisting of vases and plates. This was a highly advanced civilization that appeared to have spokes that extended well into the interior of the canyon walls.

One of the oddities I noticed, however, was that here and there on the floor, and in deteriorating baskets and urns along the walls, were the oddest stones — similar to what we call cat's eyes — and almost every stone had the image of a face carved into it and what appeared to be a name in hieroglyphics. My first thought was that the images might have been of people who had died of the plague — miniature memorials of sorts. Almost anything was possible in this "Alice in Wonderland" spectacle.

During this whole time, our animals were equally fascinated. The dogs wandered ahead of us, just into the light of our lanterns, scouting, cautiously exploring, but captured by this new environment as well. (Although I think they also sensed the magnitude of failure here.) O'Connor's monkey was continually moving about, though not far from his human companion, jabbering to himself and picking up and examining objects.

The part of the puzzle I had wondered about (what did this underground society use for light?) gradually came together as we moved into the primary cavern system. I started to notice large, narrow holes in the ceilings, enclosed and protected by a system of tight metal grating obviously designed to prevent unwanted creatures from entering but not stopping the sunlight. Under each grate was a huge, burnished copper shield of sorts, set at a 120-degree angle — all designed in a slight concave fashion that reflected onto another, opposite shield against the interior walls, creating a "bounce" of the sunlight. In addition, mounted to the shields were copper ducts that caught and fed exterior rainwater coming through the openings, and funneled it into concrete-like channels along the interior walls. The surface holes had long since filled in with debris and dirt, and for all intents and purposes had disappeared hundreds of years ago, but it wasn't hard to envision the system of light they, at one time, created while catching the majority of rainwater and carrying it to large cisterns inside. The multifaceted light and water design was extraordinary, to say the least. But I was also reminded that, in the times that this operated as a city, there was a huge opening in the east side of the cavern walls, abutting the river, which added the direct light of the ascending sun every day.

The place was beyond huge. It was indeed a city, with a central hub that branched out into four corridors. There were what appeared to be trading and shopping areas. There were small amphitheaters and military training facilities and barracks, and what could only be called residential areas, all strategically placed around artesian wells. There were smelting rooms with residual copper, silver, and gold still in evidence — all cut from the sandstone walls. Just the archaeological items alone made this one of the greatest finds of modern times, not to mention the gold and silver. Then there were the statues — perfect replicas here and there of what was probably their kings and their leaders, offering snapshot images of the people.

This was not a small group of castaways, nor an indigenous Indian settlement. This was, without a doubt, a transposed group of people from an advanced Egyptian society. It was extraordinary and mind-numbing. This was a find that would, without question, challenge opinions of transmigration and its timeframes on our planet. It would likely raise questions about the genetics of what were considered indigenous Indian tribes, question land-bridge theories on early Indian migration, and perhaps challenge the original nature of Central American cultures.

As Will said, "This whips up a nasty freaking stew for dyed-in-the-wool historians and New World culture-based gurus."

The people's hieroglyphics were everywhere — on the walls, on the stone floors and deteriorating wood tables, in the passageways, and on metal and papyrus-like scrolls and tablets. In addition, there were magnificent statues representing a timeline that seemed to start with the pure homogenous Egyptian, but eventually morphed into a powerful and intelligent Southwestern desert culture with Middle Eastern roots.

O'Connor was capable of deciphering some of the hieroglyphics, on about the same level as a four-year-old relating to Shakespeare, but it gave us some insight into this incredible society.

Unfortunately, there was an obvious dark side as well, and had we not possessed the knowledge of the expedition of **Captain García**

López de Cárdenas under the orders of Coronado, and their brief, probably disastrous meeting with three strange Indians near what is now the Grand Canyon, we would not have understood the pall of disaster that hung in the air and in the corridors after all these years. We wouldn't have been able to fathom how the shroud of death came to surround this seemingly magnificent society.

For all its beauty, artistry, and intellectual advancement, this was a culture that had its feet kicked out from underneath it. The deeper we moved into the city, the more the vestiges of death spread. There were buildings filled with linen-wrapped bodies and half-finished sarcophagi. I remembered the first two explorers to this area, Kincaid and Jordan, remarking in their notes about the unusual number of linen-wrapped mummies filling rooms, and incomplete sarcophagi stacked against the walls in the cave they found. And for a moment, I was reminded of their notes regarding all the strange cat's-eye stones everywhere with the faces carved into them. I guessed that they were an inexpensive barter with the gods for the poor — to remember their loved ones in passage... There was something about the cat's eyes that left me more than just intrigued...but I couldn't grasp what, or why.

We continued wandering through the honeycombed complex as if we were sharing a dream. It was an experience of the extraordinary and the iniquitous, filling me with equal parts of wonder and sorrow. Near the end, it appeared the few souls who were left no longer had the strength or the desire to cart bodies out to the desert, so they simply began piling them up in rooms within the caverns. I was reminded of the explorers Kincaid and Jordan speaking of the foul, dead odor coming from certain rooms. The smell and the horror of death never left the walls...

As we began our trek back to the opening near the desert, Dax looked around and sighed — a strange thing for him. "Probably a few survived," he said as he shook his head sadly. "There are always a few that seem immune for some reason. They were the ones who walled-up the entrances, hoping to contain the disease they had no understanding of, hoping to preserve their memories." He glanced around at us. "And damned if they didn't..."

"The few survivors probably banded together and lived in a nomadic fashion," Will continued. "Eventually, I imagine they were absorbed by the existing tribes." He sighed. "And all this was forgotten. It fits in perfectly with the Hopi legend of their people coming from the bowels of the earth."

"Come on, me philosophers," said O'Connor. "We're losing sunlight. Time to return to the real world."

At the end of the day, when we finally stepped out into the cleansing twilight of the desert and sucked in the warm, fresh air, we were humbled and awestruck. We had just been given the privilege of slipping back in time to witness something that no other living human beings had ever witnessed. It was both incredible and heartbreaking. Modern man, motivated by his greed and empowered by his diseases, had once again decimated one of the flowering cultures of the early Western world. It was enough to make you cry.

CHAPTER FOURTEEN

"The question now is, what do we do with what we've found?" muttered Will, as we sat outside the cave entrance with our animals, sucking in some fresh air and attempting to digest the magnitude of this experience.

"I think the real question is, how do we stay alive while we try to prove we found what we've found?" said Dax. "It didn't work well for Kincaid and Jordan in 1909, and it sure didn't work for my buddy, Seth."

O'Connor nodded. "Right you are there, lad. Remember, we're in a national park. If we were to tell the world we found this tomorrow, the following day this entire area would be declared off-limits by the Smithsonian and the National Park Service, and the following day we'd all have strangely disappeared."

Dax looked over at our Irish friend. "Ahhh, at least you have an astute understanding of our government and the issues."

"I'm going to tell you, lad, what I think of your government," said O'Connor. "A bloody spaceship full of bloody little green men could land on the White House lawn today, and tomorrow the newspaper headlines would read, 'Weather Balloon Crashes on President's Lawn.'"

Will turned to me. "I like this guy. He gets it."

"The best chance we have is to get some relics out of that cavern," I said. "Physical proof. Ultimately, what we have to decide is, are we mercenaries looking for wealth, or do we want to augment history?"

"I got all the money I need," replied O'Connor. "I want to be remembered as the man who changed America's Southwestern history."

"One of the men," I corrected dryly.

The Irishman shrugged. "Aye, okay. One of the men…"

"All right, moving ahead," said Will. "By midday tomorrow, Eddie and his team should be back here with the Goose — if all went well." He tapped the two-way radio on his hip. "These are useless until they get over those hills and come back into range. So, what I would suggest is, we spend a portion of tomorrow morning bringing out a few items of proof. I'm not sure who we can trust, and I don't think going to a newspaper is the right thing just yet. If this hit the streets tomorrow, there'd be a thousand treasure hunters in this canyon by noontime."

"There's me pilot as well," said O'Connor. "He's a fine man — been with me for years. We can trust him and he's got me bird in Tusayan."

"We haven't got anything that'll reach him," I said.

"I did have," replied O'Connor. "But I took a spill down a ravine three days ago and damaged the bloody transmitter on me radio." He sighed. "It was a heavy bugger, so I left it..."

"Okay," Will said, glancing at the faltering sun as it hewed out a groove in the crests of the distant mountains. "There isn't much we can do tonight so let's go back to camp. First thing tomorrow morning, we'll bring out a handful of impressive but portable items and hide the entrance as best we can."

The following day, my companions and I were up with the sun. We fed the animals, grabbed a little breakfast, and were on our way. We worked down the ridge to the hidden entrance and opened the cave just enough to slip inside. Back into ancient history...back down the rabbit hole, just like Alice...

We had just finished pulling out a handful of distinctly convincing artifacts from the cavern, including an extraordinary bronze sword forged with the mystery metal we found in the smelting rooms, and three thin, engraved, golden tablets that O'Connor found mounted at the foot of one of the larger pharaoh-like statues in the central cavern. Will and I added a couple of extraordinary wine goblets and a little glassware, a small bag of gold coins we found (showing an Egyptian ship on one side and a significant leader on the other), and a few of the strange, engraved, yellow cat's-eye rocks. In addition, the team had taken several rolls of film of the interior. The lighting was, of course, poor — just flashlights and lanterns. Nonetheless, I had no doubt those photos would rock historians. We were disguising the entrance to the cavern with rocks and sand, and a handful of mesquite and catclaw acacia branches, when we heard the Goose. (Those big twin radials have a distinctive hum, even at a distance.)

"It's Eddie and the team," I cried. "Right on time!"

Earlier the previous day, we had taken an hour to clear a runway for Eddie on the plain at the edge of the canyon. It wasn't much, and he was still forced to come in aiming at the gaping canyon that was 6,000 feet deep, but the wind was up and as always, he needed a "nose into the wind" landing, given the terrible terrain.

The landing proved to be nip and tuck, even for a veteran like Eddie. Once again, I thought the plane was going to run right off the cliff but somehow, in the last few seconds, he brought it under control.

I exhaled the breath I'd been holding as Eddie turned his bird around and brought it back toward us at the junction of sandstone canyon rock and the desert. I noticed that our pilot had run duct tape over his N-numbers on the tail of his plane. I just smiled. It was the old smuggler coming out in him. I doubted we needed that, but who knew?

Will, whose sense of preservation always seemed to run higher than most, had suggested we bring all our gear with us from the camp, so we wouldn't have to waste time going back, then return to the makeshift landing field. It was a wise thought. The only fly in the pudding was O'Connor's mule. We weren't going to get her into the aircraft. Besides, she would over-gross us. So, our Irishman reluctantly released the tethers on his friend. He put his arms around the animal's neck in an unabashed moment of affection, whispering in the old mule's ear, then set her loose, promising to come back for her. It was a hard thing to do but if there was one creature out of our whole party that could survive here, it was the mule.

By the time the props stopped spinning, Tax and Jing had the cabin door open. It was a brief but spirited reunion, which became even more intense when we told them we'd found the underground city.

Eddie and the kids couldn't wait, so we had to show them a few things from the duffle bags in the shade of the Goose's wing. It was madness for a few minutes, and we couldn't answer their questions fast enough.

Unfortunately, the joyous reunion was interrupted by the distant thump of helicopter blades. A large copter was coming up over the nearby hills, maybe a mile or two out. As it got closer, Dax tilted his head.

"Sounds like a Bell 407," he muttered. (His time in Vietnam had bought him an understanding.) "But it's got civilian markings."

"We need to be on our way, lads," O'Connor said ominously. "Those people are not our bloody friends, that much I'll guarantee ya."

Eddie was already headed back into the plane and the cockpit to fire up the engines.

While we were gathering gear, dogs, and monkeys, and tossing everything into the Goose, the all-gray copter sat down in the desert not 200 yards behind us. The cabin door slid open and a handful of unpleasant-looking folks quickly exited. They were dressed in military fashion but there were no proper insignias, designations, branches, or rank.

From the exterior speaker on its belly, a voice bellowed, "You are trespassing on government property. Stand down and step away from your aircraft! I repeat, step away from your aircraft and raise your hands."

"Yeah, right," Dax said. "I'm pretty sure that's the same mistake Kincaid and Jordan made the better part of a century ago."

I called to Eddie through the fuselage door. "Can you get us out of here? I mean, do you have enough runway from here?"

Eddie glanced out in front of him, then shook his head, his one gallant eye well beyond concerned. "It's not just the distance, which is short, before we go over the cliff. It's the weight and the lousy damned strip. We're gonna be near grossed." He exhaled hard. "And when we run out of strip, there's the freakin' canyon..."

"I thought you said you could jump this old girl off the edge and you'd have 6,000 feet to get her flying."

Eddie scratched his chin nervously. "Yeah, well, that's the theory..." He shrugged again. "It sounds better when you've had a couple beers."

The guy with the bullhorn was shouting again about our surrender.

"Screw it!" growled our old pilot, jerking a thumb at the new arrivals. "I sure as hell ain't going with them." Then he got that typical Crazy Eddie grin — somewhere between clever and demented. "Besides, it'll make a great barroom story...for the ones who survive..."

O'Connor had to smile. "I like this man," he cried. "He's got bloody elephant balls!"

The folks with the bullhorn brought us back to reality. A squad of four men was cautiously moving toward us, weapons at the ready.

We didn't need any more convincing. A moment later, everyone was in the plane — Tax and Jing (with Cielo) were seated in the last two seats. Will and Dax were in the seats behind the cabin wall. I was flying co-pilot (for what that was worth), and the dogs were hunkered down in the aisle next to O'Connor, who was having to make do with a backpack as a seat and a terrified monkey as a pillow. Crazy Eddie, who was about to earn his name again no matter what, was pushing the throttles forward. We were about to dance with the devil one more time...

As we jigged and jagged and bounced our way toward the cliffs of the freaking Grand Canyon, well over-grossed, I found myself thinking that we might have finally outrun our luck. We didn't seem to be anywhere near takeoff speed and the ridge was coming up fast. I was thinking that this was probably the worst airstrip in America, when I heard the popping sounds.

There were holes appearing in the fuselage, letting in streams of morning sun.

"The sons of bitches are shooting at us!" I announced incredulously to no one in particular.

"No joke, Cinderella," replied Eddie, his face an amalgam of fear and exhilaration as he fought the controls. (And I couldn't tell which one was winning.) One thing was for sure...the edge of that cliff was coming up way too fast.

Moments later, Eddied cried out, pulling back on the flight controls, and we sailed off the precipice with the engines screaming. For a second or two, I felt the wings buy some lift from the relative wind, but it was short-lived. We simply never reached takeoff speed. I felt the plane falter and start to slide in the air. I knew intrinsically that in a second or two we would stall and roll. Death was irrevocably here — decisive and inescapable.

I turned back and looked at my friend in the seat behind the pilot's seat. Will stared at me for a moment. I could see the pure terror in his eyes. His fingers were clutching the armrests with a helpless tenacity — permanently indenting them. *Not that it mattered*... But at that moment he looked at me and in those few seconds that our eyes held, I watched a calmness fall over him. The terror drifted away and in its place was some sort of understanding — an amalgam of affection and acceptance.

He smiled. "See you at the bar on the island," he whispered over the roar of our failing plane.

I was about to reply in kind, about the accommodating girls, the free drinks, and the jukebox, when suddenly Eddie did the only thing he could think of. It was a last-minute Hail Mary — the absolute rock-hard quintessence of courage and desperation. He mashed the throttles into the wall, then slammed the controls full-forward, forcing the nose of the plane into a pure, near-right angle dive. As the canyon floor, 6,000 feet below, rushed up at us, I know I was screaming. Hell, everyone was screaming. Even Eddie was screaming.

Then suddenly, out of all the chaos, I felt the plane begin to respond to the dive. The control surfaces began to do what they were designed to do (even though I was sure at any moment the wings were going to rip away from the fuselage). We were flying... a little...albeit straight down at rivet-popping speed, and Eddie, our remarkable, impossibly clever pilot, was gradually pulling back on the yoke. Not too much, but just enough to gain some control, while carefully working the throttle to see what the old girl could stand.

This was all good news. The bad news was, the floor of the canyon, and the river below, were coming up way too fast. But Eddie gradually began easing up the nose of the aircraft, without tearing off any valuable pieces with the inertia. It was a slow process at first, but that was okay. We were alive and we were flying, not crashing. Eddie's exceptional engines had the speed edge over the helicopter's, and before our nemeses figured out that we weren't dead, we were ten miles downriver and snaking along the twists and turns like a winged toboggan. None of us felt safe about returning to the Flagstaff airport. It was obvious that we were already on somebody's list. O'Connor recommended we head for the Grand Canyon National Park Airport, just a few miles south of the town of Tusayan. It was where he kept his Piper PA-30 twin-engine Comanche.

O'Connor had Eddie tune to the frequency the Irishman always used to contact his friend, Bradley Filmore, but there was no answer. I'd already come to realize that for all his blustering about being a tough guy, O'Connor had a good heart, and I could see the worry in the man's eyes when we couldn't reach his friend.

Once we had landed and disembarked, O'Connor tried Bradley Filmore again, without luck, so he called the police. He received bad news. Bradley had been found in an alley on the edge of town yesterday. He'd been shot twice in the chest. But it also appeared as though he had been tortured to some degree. There were butane torch burns on his body in several places.

We had to physically restrain the Irishman for a few moments. He wanted blood, and damned if I didn't understand. It was obvious that somebody was putting this puzzle together and was starting to take out some of the pieces. If we were going to survive, we needed to keep a low profile.

CHAPTER FIFTEEN

The tall, thin, blue-eyed man sat behind his desk, back straight, eyes distant, a single forefinger stroking his thin mustache. He occupied a particular, if not challenging position in this rather well-known institution. "Status quo." Simply put, that was his job. Actually, it had been his grandfather's job before it became his father's. Now it was his, and an important role it was. While he and his lineage represented a constant overview of sorts, their real job was to assure peace of mind — to maintain a status quo, if you would. Business, philosophy, and faith should have some balance. No, actually they *required* balance for the peace of mind of the masses. He wasn't just protecting "the Institution," he was ensuring "a social sanity."

His long fingers formed a temple under his chin and he stared off distantly. The Brooks Brothers suit he wore was carefully cut but it added nothing to his personality. Oddly out of place was his long, sparse blond hair, and his wide mustache that drooped from one side to the other above his disdainful mouth.

Professor Baal was of an odd lineage. His father was full-blooded Egyptian, but the man had met and married a blond, blue-eyed American while doing graduate studies in America. Baal carried his father's passion for ancient Egypt, but he had inherited the pale complexion and blond hair of his mother. It was an odd combination that pleased Baal little. However, he spent a good deal of time in his "real" homeland, and he missed the dry sands and the warm air of Egypt. But most of all, he missed the culture — particularly the ancient culture of the land.

Baal shook his head, drawing himself back to the present. There was much to do. Of course, he wasn't expected to do this all by himself. He had access to government "teams" throughout the country for the more dynamic situations — inventions or discoveries that would interfere too greatly with commerce, industry, or theological status quos.

He sighed. Now, here he was, reliving a situation his great-grandfather had dealt with nearly a hundred years ago. The news was, these people had perhaps stumbled upon an extension of an earlier "find" in the Grand Canyon. Apparently, his Special Teams had bungled this in a couple of places. Now, these people had not only survived what should have been another simple "disappearance in the canyon," they were actively searching for an answer to the death of two friends. And now there was the possibility of another 1909 "Egyptian hysteria" breakout.

He frowned, brows arched menacingly. It was what it was, and it certainly wasn't the first time he'd dealt with this sort of situation. But umbrage always made the perfect nest for error. Let them make the mistakes. He would remain calm.

Like his father said, "Bury your enemies deep..."

He could work with that.

We found a small hangar for Eddie's Goose at the Grand Canyon National Airport, outside Tusayan, then rented a large, eight-passenger van. We took four rooms at a nondescript motel on the edge of town. Will and I shared one with Shadow. Dax shared a room with his dog and the Irishman, who was still in a funk at the loss of his friend; and Eddie found one for himself. Tax and Jing shared another, with, of course, Cielo. As our new friend O'Connor was fond of saying, it was like the "bloody circus coming to town."

When night fell, we snuck the relics into our quarters, guarding them like ancient souls, for they were the last voice of a remarkable civilization.

We found a copy of the local newspaper. It carried a small article about the killing of the Irishman's friend, but there was no evidence that the investigation was going anywhere. O'Connor was beside himself. He wanted blood but he didn't know who to cut. There was no question now that somebody with heavy connections was after us.

"I think the best thing to do is get the proof we're carrying in the plane to someone of significant power — someone we can trust," I said as we gathered around a table at the back of the motel restaurant's nearly empty dining room that evening. "Or we could do what Kincaid and Jordan did — find a big newspaper and give the story to them, complete with photos."

"Yeah," muttered Will sarcastically. "That worked really well for those boys, didn't it?"

"Besides," said O'Connor, "you do that, and the following day you've got a thousand treasure hunters in the Grand Canyon." He huffed out a sigh. "I'll tell you how that works. In no time at all, somebody finds our cave. In just hours past that, there'll be a free-for-all that even the bad guys can't control, and everything of historical value in that cavern will be lost."

"Would it really be lost?" I asked. "Maybe that's the best way to ensure the survival of this tale." I held out my hands. "Think about it. Maybe 500 people with relics of an ancient community, showing them to everyone they know, seeking answers, lending them to museums, selling them..." I glanced around. "And being invited to tell their 'treasure-hunting story' to the world, on radio and television shows..."

O'Connor got a cagey look in his eyes and smiled. "You know, he's right. This is not about us owning that treasure. It's about the truth! It's about the fact that they existed — that Egyptians traveled across the world long before anyone else and made their home here, and that probably the features and genetics of the peoples in this area are gleaned from these incredible explorers. The feat itself is enormous. Who knows what influences they left when you open your eyes to their existence?"

At that point, Tax weighed in, offering some sound advice for a youngster in the adventure of a lifetime. "We brought out a few golden tablets that were mounted at the foot of the largest pharaoh-like statue in the central cavern, very near to the incredible Egyptian ship. I'm betting that those may hold the answers — they may be the historical threads that bind this whole affair. Before we go dancing off this cliff, maybe we could find somebody —"

"I know someone," interrupted O'Connor. "Damned fine idea, lad," he said, holding up a forefinger. "If we knew more about what we had, we'd know how to deal with it." Before anyone could interject, he continued. "My friend...my pilot, Bradley..."

He paused and drew a breath. Even the name left a wound.

"Bradley had a sister who worked for the college here in Tusayan. That's why we ended up here and chose this airport as a base of operations. It was also Tanya, his sister, who contacted us originally about the legend of a lost city in the canyon and the wild tale about the explorers, Kincaid and Jordan..." He took a breath and continued. "She works for the language department of the college. It just so happens that she has a poor but workable understanding of ancient Egyptian hieroglyphics. It's her thing. We wouldn't by any means get it all, but we might get the gist of those tablets."

"Works for me," said Jing. "Going off half-cocked is a sure way to shoot yourself in the foot."

"I think there's plenty enough people lookin' to shoot us as it is, girl," muttered Dax. "But most of them would think we'd be as mad as a box of frogs to stay here. It's the last thing they'd expect." He shrugged and looked around at everyone. "Besides, I owe it to my buddy, Seth, who started us on this trail. I'm not cuttin' and runnin'."

Eddie held up a finger. "But you know, it might be good to have those rapscallions think we did cut and run…"

The following day, a man stood at a pay phone outside a small restaurant in the Grand Canyon National Airport. "Yes sir, yes sir, I know. But they got in their plane and flew away this morning before we had a chance to hit them." He paused for a moment and listened. "Yes sir, it looked like all of them. Word from the tower is that they were headed for Dallas. That's all I know at this point. Yes sir, of course, sir. We'll stay on it, and yes…I understand exactly what you want…"

The tall, thin, blue-eyed man in the bowels of the Smithsonian hung up the phone and leaned back in his chair, a single forefinger stroking his narrow mustache. He needed to resolve this now, before it got out of hand. *Like that damned Roswell thing in New Mexico…* He hated personal appearances but sometimes you just couldn't rely on the field players. Besides, he was good at "wet business."

It was true, we all did get on the plane, with the dogs and the hawk and the monkey. (*Christ! It really was a circus.*) And Eddie took us out on a southwest course toward Dallas. But at about sixty-five miles southwest of the Grand Canyon National Airport, he dropped into a small airfield outside the nondescript town of Cameron. There we rented another van, and while Eddie stayed behind to guard his investment and our getaway vehicle, the rest of us headed back to Tusayan and the college, and O'Connor's friend in the language department.

As we drove along in silence, watching the desert roll silently past us, Tax, upfront with Jing, turned on the radio. *Maybe a little music would lighten the atmosphere.* For the next fifteen minutes, we listened to Country Rock and that seemed to work. Our mood lightened a little. A disc jockey by the name of Jason Cotter came on to tell about a new restaurant in town, and I saw Dax turn his head and stare at the radio for a moment.

"Jason Cotter..." he said incredulously. "Well, I'll be damned. I know that guy well. We went to high school together." Dax exhaled and continued, talking as much to himself as anyone. "He wanted to be a bronco rider, like me." He smiled. "I was just getting recognized in rodeo back then. Jason was sort of inspired by my moderate success and he did some rodeo work for a while. But I remember he had the opportunity in his high school senior summer to work at a radio station. He was quick with words, well read, and he could be snot-nosed funny when he wanted to. He called it 'moving the world,' and on many occasions, it was just that."

Our friend paused, then smiled again. "The truth is, he really was a better radio host than a bronc rider..." Dax blew out a breath in distant reminiscence. "He just wanted to be a part of the world. He wanted to laugh with people, argue with them, enlighten them, and entertain them. And so, he eventually became a disk jockey/radio talk show host at a local station." Dax straightened up in his seat. "It wasn't long before Jason's laid-back, humorous but clever style of banter made him one of the favorites on the airwaves in the region."

He paused again. "KARK in Flagstaff! Evidently, he's moved up well." He drew a breath. "You know, I think inside every entertainment host of any sort is the desire to be part of something significant — to be present at an apex of an experience that's powerful and unique, and maybe be remembered for it." He shrugged and glanced around at us in the van. "You know what I mean — one of those significant moments that grows into a collective public memory. We all secretly want to be remembered for something..."

When we returned to Tusayan, we quietly began our search for the college and the next piece of our puzzle.

Tanya, the late Bradley Filmore's sister, was a slight, bespectacled redhead in her early forties. She was better looking that I would have expected for the head of a language department on the second floor of the Arts Building. She wore stylish glasses that accented her bright-blue eyes, and was dressed in slacks and an attractive blouse. She seemed capable, but she was taken back when the whole crew came marching in.

Tanya's eyes darkened when we offered our condolences regarding her brother but she came back when we began to speak of golden tablets and possible Egyptian script. Of course, she wanted to know where they came from. We, of course, told her that was above her pay grade. She accepted that. Just the opportunity to decipher this ancient (and possibly historically valuable) information was a huge thrill.

"I am by no means an expert on Egyptian writings," she explained immediately as we all gathered around. "But that language is one of my hobbies, if you will, and for some reason, it just…comes to me…" She shook her head, somewhat embarrassed. "So I may be able to help you."

She did indeed help, and at the end of an hour, we had been rocked one more time by this incredible discovery. The tablets we had found were a brief history of the journey of two ships that left Memphis, Egypt, in 1207 BC at the decree of Merneptah, the 13th son of Ramesses and the fourth Pharaoh of the 19th Dynasty of Ancient Egypt — almost 3,000 years ago.

The odyssey was greatly condensed, as these tablets were designed to present only a minimal history, mostly to confirm that the journey had actually happened. As Tanya relayed the story as best she could, she came to a part and slowed, then reread it herself.

"There is only one ship here now because the other was lost." She took a breath and continued. "They had followed the coastline of their landlocked sea, what would have been the Mediterranean, then sailed out into a great ocean — 'waters without end' they called it. They sailed west, into the sun, as had been commanded by Pharaoh, and days turned into weeks. They were starving and almost out of water. The only thing that saved them to that point was the incessant rain, which provided drinking water. Then finally, they came upon another land. It ran as far as the eye could see in either direction, with huge mountains in the distance and monstrous forests to the very edge of the water. They decided to attempt an inland anchorage, but disaster struck." She paused and glanced around at us. "As they entered a bay, one of the ships hit a reef and tore a hole in its hull. The other ship, the captain's vessel, was forced to hold back from the bay and the survivors of the foundering ship were forced to swim for shore or grab what they could and float in."

Tanya paused again, lost to the adventure she was recalling.

"It was a tragic time. Most of those aboard the slowly sinking ship were able to make shore and they managed to salvage much of their tools, equipment, and weapons, but they were ultimately abandoned as the second ship was forced to go on, for this was not the place that Pharaoh Merneptah had commanded them to search for — the land that he had seen in his dreams..."

Will, ever the historian, cut in. "Given the route they had taken, and the time at sea, it sounds like they made the eastern coast of the U.S. — what would become South Carolina, or North Carolina perhaps." He paused. "It's apparent that the majority of the Egyptians survived the shipwreck." He held up a finger. "Now here's where this gets really interesting. That area, along with Georgia, Alabama, and Tennessee, came to be the home of the Cherokee Indians." He paused again. "And here's why that's interesting. No one has ever been able to figure out why, but when tested, the Cherokee Indians have intensely high DNA markers for native Egyptians and Mesopotamians." My friend took a breath. He was on a roll. "The level of haplogroup T in Cherokee blood is 26.9 percent — almost the equivalent of full Egyptians — and their pure facial features are primarily Semitic, not Native American." Will eased out a breath. "There was a blending of races! Damned if this doesn't explain a lot."

Will stopped, slightly abashed by his outbreak. "Sorry," he said to Tanya. "Didn't mean to digress."

She continued. "Eventually, the last ship found a safe place to harbor and refreshed water and food supplies. Many of the people on board were anxious for the journey to end but Pharaoh

Merneptah had seen a vision of an area like Egypt — with a large waterway like the Nile to traverse, where there were 'the sands of Egypt and the huge cliffs of Memphis, and a rich land to cultivate by the water.' So they moved on." Tanya read for a few moments to get a handle, then continued to narrate. "Finally, they came to a commanding curve in the continent before them and a huge bay that led to the north. They sailed north, as their Pharaoh had seen, and shortly thereafter they entered a canyon that held a magnificent river, and they followed it into a pleasant land of mountains and valleys, and fertile soils."

Will shrugged. "It ain't that way now, but indeed, I would hazard a guess that she could be describing the Grand Canyon and its rivers pretty well, a few thousand years ago." He paused for a moment and exhaled pensively. "What it really sounds like to me is that they came into the interior of what would eventually be America via the Rio Grande in the Gulf of Mexico, then probably picked up the Little Colorado, which led to the Colorado River." He glanced around at us. "It's the only thing that makes sense."

O'Connor still carried a wound with him at the loss of his friend, and seeing Bradley's sister had triggered it again. While we spoke with Tanya for a few final moments, the Irishman said his good-byes and excused himself.

When finally Will and I were leaving, I heard O'Connor's voice from the stone steps below. It was barely a whisper of a verse that he offered, and it was intended for no one but himself and his grief, but I heard it softly floating in the breeze.

> *The Garden of Eden has vanished, they say.*
> *But I know the lie of it still;*
> *Just turn to the left at the bridge of Finea,*
> *and stop halfway down to Cootehill.*
> *Tis there that you will find it,*
> *when fortune has come to yer call.*
> *Oh, the grass it is green around Ballyjamesduff,*
> *and the sea is over it all.*

CHAPTER SIXTEEN

"I'm very sorry, Professor Baal," said the voice on the phone. "The Grand Canyon National Airport tower lost their airplane about fifty miles out, and we're still not seeing anything on radar. At your request, we have the Phoenix Team headed that way."

"I think this could be a ruse," replied the tall man, staring out the window of his upstairs office in the Institution. "I think it's possible they're still there. I'll be on the ground in four hours. Check the local motels within a thirty-mile radius. We're looking for a group of six or seven people. They may have large dogs with them." He paused. "I want a rendezvous with the team at the Grand Canyon National Airport at 1800 hours. You good on that?"

"Yes, sir. That's an affirmative."

We all gathered together in one room back at the motel. It was crowded, what with the animals, the hawk, and the rest of us, but it was necessary. The people chasing us had tortured O'Connor's friend, which meant they knew what we were after, if they didn't before. There was a serious hunt on, and we were the fox.

"I don't think they've found it yet," I said, glancing around at everyone. "But if they can cut us off at the pass, and if they can kill us before we get much of that treasure out of there, they can contain this."

"Nothing to see here, folks," muttered Will. "Just keep walking..."

"I'm beginning to think like Dax," I added, nodding at the big cowboy sitting in the corner of the room, his huge dog at his feet, and my Shadow next to him. "I don't think we can save this treasure or this incredible find by ourselves. Whoever runs this status quo show has put a lot of people in the dirt before us — anyone who got in the way of conventional thought, from seventy-mile-per-gallon carburetors, and light bulbs that never need to be replaced, to inconvenient history." I paused. "We have to beat them to the punch. Before they kill us..."

"You're right on, Dad," said Tax with a remarkable sense of courage.

105

Dad... I couldn't remember being prouder.

"This is no longer about simply saving the treasure of a particular group of people, said Tax. "This is about exposing the truth and saving history." My son turned to Dax. "How well do you trust this radio personality of yours — this Jason Cotter?"

"I don't know," replied the big cowboy. "It's been a long time since I've seen him."

"Find him," said Tax adamantly. "Find him tonight. Give him the news story of a lifetime. We need to defuse the need to kill us."

O'Connor looked around at all of us. His monkey sat hunched on the back of his chair, pensively eating an apple. "As much as it pains me sense of greed, the boy is right. If there's no bloody treasure — if the world knows about the ancient Egyptian civilization in the bloody middle of America — then there's no one interested in us anymore."

My buddy, Will, chuckled humorlessly. "You're dead on, so to speak..." He paused and his eyes got that devious look that I knew so well. "But we need to do a couple of things first. We've got to get the photos developed that we took at the cavern, right away."

The rest of us agreed in unison.

Will continued. "Here's how I see this. We need to make up press packages with a brief story of what this is about, and a handful of good photos in each one. Then we need to deliver those to the newspapers in the area tomorrow, *after* they've already printed their daily papers so they can't jump the gun on us." He held up a hand. "And with the express understanding that they give us the day to get back to that site and recover anything we think is precious to the world, because within twenty-four hours, anyone in the Southwest who owns a metal detector is gonna be there." Will couldn't help but grin. "And our find will have made history before anyone can rewrite it."

"But we have to go back first," I said. "The scrolls, the etchings, anything that can be deciphered that we didn't get photos of, we have to save. They're the social and scientific precedence here." I looked over at Dax. "Then your radio host buddy will release this affair on the airwaves the same time it comes out in the papers." I drew a breath and glanced around the room.

The fire in Jing's eyes was clear and bright. She carried a

righteousness in her breast that made this all-important to her. "We need to get those photos printed ASAP," she said, as she sat in an armchair. She had hooded her hawk and left him in her and Tax's room to keep him calm. "And find me a typewriter and I'll write up a brief history on this for the newspapers — without names." She took a breath. "I refuse to let this civilization be lost to secret, buried archives because it doesn't satisfy an organization's or even a government's sense of social or historical propriety."

O'Connor was smiling. But it was a feral smile because he could see some justice here for his lost friend.

I couldn't help but grin. "We might just pull this off..."

Dax rose from his seat. "If you'll excuse me, I'm gonna see if I can find a radio personality." He exhaled heavily. "Damned guy better be around. I'm about to make him famous." He had suddenly realized how huge this was. "You folks need to get your gear together, check your weapons and your ammo. One way or another, the next forty-eight hours will mark your lives."

It was strange but the air in the room changed when Dax said that. It wasn't exactly an ominous feeling, but it was close. We knew that we were on someone's short list, and whether we liked it or not, this game could only have one set of winners. Jing sensed it and simply moved over to her father's side. Will put his arm around her. Tax looked at me, his eyes saying things that a young man doesn't express easily.

I understood.

Even Shadow picked up on the vibration and slid over to my side, gently rubbing against me.

Without further ado, Dax was out the door, Smoke trailing behind him.

Will opened his carryall and found the film containers, then turned to his daughter. "Com'on, hon, let's go find a twenty-four-hour photo lab and a typewriter. It's gonna be a long night."

O'Connor, who was sharing a room with Dax, stood and stretched. "It's been another excitin' day, lads and lasses, and I'm fair puggled from it all. I'm gonna slip out to the wee store of convenience around the corner and grab meself a beer or six, then get a little sleep."

The rest of us retired to our respective rooms, or chores, or our overactive imaginations…

———————

While Professor Aaron Baal's aircraft landed at the Grand Canyon National Airport and he met with his Central Team at a quickly established command center, Will and Jing found a one-hour photo shop in a late-night pharmacy and had the film processed. The photos took their breath away — and they had been there.

Dax got the address for KARK Radio in Flagstaff, had the motel front desk find him a car rental, and was on his way in half an hour. As luck would have it, Jason Cotter was working the evening shift at the station that night.

As Rufus would say, *"Sometimes, for no good reason, the gods smile on you."*

Dax found his way past the precocious front desk manager at the radio station. Most of the time, just watching Dax growl out a few words was sufficient to change a person's attitude. Needless to say, Jason was taken aback. He was more than surprised when Dax gave him a rundown on the exclusive story he was offering.

"You know, if it was anyone but you, partner, I would already have security escorting you out," said the somewhat befuddled radio host. "And even with you telling me this, I'm going to have to ask, did you miss your meds today?"

Dax chuckled. "No sir, I'm good. No meds of any kind." He paused. "I'm telling you, this is your chance at the story of a lifetime. This is the broadcast you'll be remembered for fifty years from now. Besides, you'll be able to get an early morning paper the day after tomorrow, before the sun comes up, and see the story there — before you air the tale I give you tonight. The difference is, I'm giving you an exclusive interview now. I'm even going to give you directions on how to find the cave, so you can tell others. But you have to wait until the day after tomorrow to air it." Dax paused. "Because we need some time on site before anyone else shows up."

Jason Cotter stared at his cowboy buddy. "If you're wrong, or lying, or making this shit up, I'm gonna be out of a freaking job. Hell, I'll be out of the broadcasting profession."

Dax just stared at him.

Cotter sighed heavily. "Okay, okay, let me hook up my recorder."

While Dax was relating his story, Professor Aaron Baal and his people were setting up to shake down the small town of Tusayan.

The following morning, when we gathered for breakfast, we discovered that O'Connor was missing. Dax shrugged nervously, which was out of character.

"The last time I saw the Irishman, I had gotten back from my interview and was getting ready for bed. He dropped off his monkey — said he was gonna walk down the road to the convenience store, about a quarter-mile away, to get more beer." He shrugged, looking around at us, somewhere between ugly guilty and hating himself. "I fell asleep and slept through...I just figured he had come back and gone to bed."

It got worse.

We learned from our talkative waitress that an "unknown federal agency" had hit five of the seven hotels and motels in town last night, searching for "persons of interest" in a national security issue.

But they missed us.

"Righteousness is nice," Will said. "But I'll take blind luck every time..." Then he paused. "But I'm not sure about our buddy, O'Connor..."

That morning, Tax and Jing took Dax's rental car and distributed an "information packet" and photographs to the managing editor of the newspaper in Tusayan. From there, they headed down to Flagstaff and the major newspaper there, hitting near ninety miles an hour most of the way.

The editors were, of course, skeptical at first, but Jing had done a masterful piece of writing. She presented a brief but poignant story about the journey of two ships that had left Memphis, Egypt, in 1207 BC at the command of the fourth Pharaoh of the 19th Dynasty of Ancient Egypt, almost 3,000 years ago. She explained how the remarkable ancient Egyptian expedition had settled in the Grand Canyon, complete with their extraordinarily rich society, and their poignant ending in disease and death. She even included O'Connor's basic set of directions to the site: *Take Hermit Road out of Grand National Park and follow it to West Rim Trail, up to Pima Point. From there, you have to find the old mining road that leads to Cathedral Stairs. Watch for the huge pine tree struck by lightning — the turn is there. The road after that becomes more like a path that leads to Ninetyfour Mile Creek on the Colorado River.*

The landmark that made it all work, really, was the huge tower-like ridge to the west that had a red, sandstone line running through it horizontally. That was just about impossible to miss. The cave entrance to the city was in the small rise off the Grand Canyon's back rim, facing the desert and the huge red sandstone strata, about a half-mile away.

It was relatively easy to find if you followed directions. By air it was a cinch — all you had to do was find the huge, red sandstone strata and move your eyes north across the desert to the outer canyon rim. Additionally, we had decided to place a red flag at the entrance of the cave.

Although the story was initially met with great skepticism, as the editors read the information Jing had written, then stared in awe and incredulousness at the remarkable photos of a lost society, they started to come around. If there was any doubt, it was dispelled instantly when Jing pulled one of the small but weighty golden tablets from the briefcase she carried. It shouted authenticity like nothing else could. The newspapers agreed to no early releases, amazed that we didn't want any monetary return. The story would come out the following morning.

Dax called his radio buddy and confirmed the directions to the Egyptian cave that Jing had written.

Jason eased out a sigh of fatal commitment. "Okay, sure. What the hell, the worst they can do is fire me…"

The hope and the plan were that we might draw out a few hardy souls who would not only validate our find, but enter the cave, find the lost city, and take stuff home with them. At that point, it would be damned near impossible for any "institution" to deny the discovery. At least, that was the hope.

By mid-afternoon, Tax and Jing were back from the newspapers and had tied up with the rest of us, including Dax. We had already packed our van and moved out of the motel. Tax explained that the newspaper articles wouldn't be given front-page coverage — it was too risky. It could be an elaborate ruse, but it was too good to pass on completely, so most of the editors put it in Current Events/Outdoors. That was better than nothing...

Things seemed to be falling into place for the moment. But I suppose I could have been reminded of a quote by our old Rastaman buddy, Rufus: *"The gods, mon, they rarely give you what you want. Where's de entertainment in that?"*

CHAPTER SEVENTEEN

Professor Baal listened as his people explained what they knew and what they didn't. The latter was more voluminous but the men did have one lead — one "tangible asset."

It looked like a group of people had shown up at the Best Night's Sleep motel near the edge of town. Somehow, the professor's team had missed that one last night. By the time he had a crew there in the morning, the targets were gone. But in the process of the sweep the night before, they had picked up a big Irish fellow near a convenience store about a half-mile from the motel. The guy fit the description of one of the people of interest. They took him back to their base of operations near the airport and locked him up. But with all that was going on, the fellow was forgotten about until morning.

Baal angrily swept back his willowy hair with one hand then skewered the man in front of him with a look. "You got this guy last night and you're just telling me about him? Take him to the basement and prep him. I'll be there directly."

An hour later, O'Connor sat in a hard-backed wooden chair under the glare of a harsh white bulb. His hands were tied behind his back, the knots tight enough to have long since cut off his circulation. He could taste the blood in his mouth from an earlier, brief introduction.

The tall, svelte man in the suit, who seemed clearly out of place, leaned into the Irishman again. "We've got photos of you coming into the Grand Canyon National Park Airport with your friends. Like they say in the movies, we can do this the easy way or the hard way."

O'Connor looked up at him and shook some of the sweat and blood from his face. "I'm Irish, mate. We're bloody well used to this — from the invading Romans and the righteous bloody English, to the bloody Germans and their Nazis." He struggled for a grin. "It's almost a national sport…"

The tall man studied O'Connor for a moment, then blew out a breath. "He's right. I know the type. He'll be dead before we know anything worthwhile. We'll need drugs for this one. He's tough, like the old miner…" The fellow paused for a moment, his eyes lighting with a sadistic gleam. "Your pilot friend was nowhere near as tough." The man paused, holding O'Connor's stare, the corner of his mouth lifting in a small, malevolent smile. "He screamed like a child. Over and over again..."

Baal saw a flicker of pain in the fellow's eyes but it was soon masked by a searing enmity.

"What's your name?" asked the Irishman, staring at his tormentor with almost inhuman control.

Baal shrugged, seeing no harm in answering at this point. The man in front of him had only a short time to live. "Aaron Baal. Professor Aaron Baal." He paused. "Does that make you feel better?"

"Aye, aye, it bloody well does," hissed O'Connor, offering an old Irish curse. "I'm gonna be waiting for ya in hell, mate...with a baseball bat." The Irishman's eyes went cold and hard as agates. "And I'm gonna beat you to death with that bat, once a day, every day...*forever*..."

Even the stalwart Professor Baal blanched at the vehemence in that curse. He turned to one of his men to get away from the Irishman's glare. "Get the drug kit. Let's pump him up and see what he really knows."

Baal's underling glanced at the battered Irishman. "He's in pretty bad shape. You might kill him."

The Institution's high priest glared at the fellow and brought up his hands, palms out. "Do I look like I care?"

But about a half hour into it all, Baal got a phone call. One of his few "superiors" in Washington had received word regarding a newspaper article that was to be a special edition of the Flagstaff, Arizona paper the following day. (The Institution's fingers were long and in many a pie...) The superior wanted to be "on site" from here forward — especially when this discovery was breached and viewed. This was too big to be left to "security."

While Baal's blood boiled at his organization for reining him in like a dog, it may have been a blessing. His frustration with the Irishman's intransigence might well have had him killing the fool before the night was out. When he finally recovered and his face returned to its normal pale indifference, he turned to his second in command.

"Get the helicopter ready. I want it on standby for the next twenty hours. You understand?"

O'Connor, as battered as he was, smiled. He knew exactly what had happened. He shook his head to clear it and stared at Baal. "Don't ya just hate it when ya come in second?"

Aaron Baal offered a brief glare. "The game's not over yet."

———————————

We had given up our motel room and were on the run now, trying to stay alive until tomorrow, when the newspaper articles were released and Dax's broadcaster friend did his thing. Five adults, two dogs, a hawk and a monkey, all in one van — I'd have gladly paid a hundred bucks for a cot in a tool shed.

We ended up buying some sleeping bags and camping gear, and Will found a country road that led to a small recreation area on the fringes of a pretty little lake just south of the Grand Canyon National Park. It wasn't luxurious but no one was shooting at us. Yet...

I huffed and glanced around warily. "Now I know how they felt at the Alamo."

"Don't get comfortable," growled Dax. "We gotta head back to the strip in Cameron and get the Goose and Eddie. We need to be getting out of here and setting up in the canyon, for visitors..."

Jing had released her hawk; there was no point in keeping him caged. A short time later, that remarkable bird returned and dropped not one, but two plump quail on the ground in front of his mistress.

"That's just about the most amazing damned thing I've ever seen," muttered Will. "He fetches well. Can he sit up and bark?"

As the sun melted into the western mountains, Jing dressed the birds and put them on a spit. Tax heated up a couple of cans of beans, and we ate, mostly in silence. No one was really that hungry.

Dax glanced around at all of us. "There's no percentage in being back at the cave in the canyon too early. One, that will just advertise where it is; and two, I'd bet dollars to donuts they've got somebody watching it. I don't want us taken by surprise while we're sleeping."

There was no argument.

"Let's be on the road by daylight tomorrow," our big friend continued. "We'll head south and pick up Eddie and the Goose, then move into the Canyon and set up for visitors."

Well before ten the following day we had driven back to the little town of Cameron, returned our van, picked up our plane, and were in the air, headed at the mountains in the distance — now six adults, two dogs, a hawk, and a monkey.

"This is gonna be interesting," said Eddie, next to me in the cockpit.

He had no idea...

When we reached the canyon, Eddie brought the Goose in the same way we'd gone out — across the flat rim between the desert and the deep, empty void of the vast canyon. But coming in, we didn't need anywhere near as much strip as going out. So, after touchdown, he turned the plane around and brought it back to the side that led into the desert and was nearest to the entrance of the cavern. We unloaded our gear and our weapons. All bets were off on what we could expect today.

Inside of an hour, we had the entrance to the cavern dug out once more — a wide enough pathway for two men to walk in side by side. Tax planted red surveyor flags on both sides.

"This is not a scavenger hunt," he said, looking at all of us. "We want a handful of people to find this."

"If anyone shows up," replied Dax. "On Sundays around here, folks are mostly nursing hangovers and going to church. Digging holes in the desert probably isn't real high on their list of entertainment."

Will, our historian, stepped forward and exhaled, looking around at us, suddenly serious. "Don't take this event too lightly," he said. "Today, we are preserving ancient history and making American history. If this goes just halfway like we've planned, teachers will tell this story to their students. History books will record it, and probably years from now, a few grandfathers will sit by the fireplace and tell their grandkids about how they were part of a remarkable damned tale, however inconvenient."

I don't know why, but at that moment, a shiver passed through me and I recalled a saying by Rufus. *"History, mon. Anyone who reads history understands it always come with consequences —*

somebody always getting da short end of da damn stick. Sometimes even da heroes..."

Just then, as if Mother Nature was emphasizing the expression, the ground began to tremble. Once again, just like the other day, there was that deep, abiding movement within the heart of the canyon — not harsh, but heavy, yet almost malevolent. It stopped within seconds, but Mother Nature had made her point. She was in control, not us.

Later that morning Dax, Will, and I were taking inventory on supplies and weapons at the cavern, not really knowing what to expect, if anything, when we heard a helicopter. I looked around. The monkey perked up and gibbered uncomfortably. Tax, Eddie, and Jing had gone back to the Goose for supplies. Jing's hawk was in the air, doing what hawks do. The dogs were exploring in the cavern. They, too, found the history of smells and tastes fascinating — which probably touched the core of their nature.

As we studied the horizon, we spotted a large helicopter coming up over the distant southwestern rise. It looked exactly like the one we had seen the other day.

A few moments later, the copter landed about a hundred yards out from the entrance of the cavern and two men exited. Then they turned and dragged out a third — O'Connor! God, he looked terrible! His face was black and blue, eyes puffed closed, and he could barely stand, even with help. His white shirt was covered with blood. I felt my fingers closing on my rifle, but at that moment, I felt Dax's steadying hand.

"Wait, my friend. Timing is everything. First, let's find out what they want."

It didn't take long. The pilot pulled the blades back to a soft, steady rotation and someone began to communicate using his microphone and the outside speaker on the chopper.

"You see the fifty-foot-high mesa a hundred yards to the west of you? Leave your weapons here and make your way over there, to the base, and we'll negotiate."

"I'm not leaving my weapons anywhere," Eddie snorted, starting to bring up his gun.

But the man holding O'Connor put his pistol to O'Connor's head. Two more men armed with M16s stepped out of the chopper.

"We can do this where you win a little, or we can do it where you lose everything," shouted the guy holding O'Connor. "We don't need you or your friend. We just want possession of what you have."

"Yeah," said Eddie. "And I bet you've got a bridge you want to sell me."

"We don't have any choice," huffed Dax. "We've got to try to save him."

I stepped forward and shouted, "Okay, okay! We'll do it. We'll move to the cliff."

It was about that time I started to hear a distant hum, sort of like a wasp's nest, but deeper and more metallic. I glanced around. It wasn't the helicopter but it persisted.

The chopper lifted off, moved across toward the mesa, and landed on the flat top at the edge. About that time, Shadow and Smoke emerged from the cavern. We were at a disadvantage here, and we didn't need any distractions, so I tied the boys to a tree near the entrance of the cave. Five minutes later, we had walked to the base of the cliff. Needless to say, it wasn't the best of situations.

"We're like freaking geese staring up at the rain," added Eddie angrily. "This ain't gonna end well."

The man apparently in charge — a tall, willowy fellow with thin blond hair, wearing a gray summer suit — stood at the edge of the cliff, staring down at us. There was an arrogance and a complete lack of conscience in that narrow face and those blue eyes. He surveyed us for a moment, then motioned to the people in the chopper. A big guy dragged O'Connor out. Our friend could barely stand and I couldn't find a place on him that wasn't bloody.

As locked into this bizarre happening as I was, I could still hear that hum in the distance but now it was more like a dull roar coming from the west.

The thin guy motioned to his heavy friend, and together they pulled O'Connor forward to the precipice. "Here's the situation," he called, his voice raspy yet silken. "You're going to leave now. You're going to get in your plane and fly away and never come back. And for that, we'll give you your man."

I started to argue, but in response, he and his friend dragged O'Connor to the very edge of the cliff. "This is not negotiable, friend," the man said.

Our Irish buddy seemed lost to misery, eyes barely focused, shoes dragging in the dirt as they pulled him a little farther forward, his feet almost over the lip of the cliff. O'Connor teetered and the pale guy eased him back a touch and patted him paternally. The guy was enjoying this. It wasn't about negotiation — he was pleasuring himself. I suddenly realized that it didn't matter what we did. He was going to kill our friend.

I also realized that the strange noise in the air was suddenly familiar. Yeah, for a guy who had owned light aircraft and dune buggies, it was damned familiar.

At that moment, a flimsy-looking, high-winged, two-seat ultralight aircraft came sliding over the crest behind the cliff and roared over the heads of the two men holding O'Connor. The high-winged plane continued downward, losing altitude rapidly, as it aimed for the desert sand at the mouth of the cave.

The plane hit the earth hard and bounced, then came down rough a second time, spinning to an abrupt halt in the sand. The engine stopped. But the all-encompassing, distant roar hadn't changed. Actually, strangely enough, it just morphed to a slightly deeper pitch. Two fellows stumbled from the ultralight with shovels and metal detectors, apparently not at all vexed by their minor crash, moving with unerring accuracy toward the red flags and the hole in the now not-so-secret cavern.

At this point, we were all engrossed in the show — those of us below, as well as the two men holding our mortally battered friend at the top of the cliff. Absolutely no one was ready for what happened next.

While the spooky pale guy and his friend were distracted for a second, our remarkable friend Connor O'Connor suddenly straightened up and turned as best he could. "Can you blighters fly?" he burbled to his captors through broken teeth. Before they could begin to formulate an answer, he suddenly grabbed both men by the fronts of their shirts with those huge, ham-like hands, and dragged them off the hundred-foot cliff with him.

We all stood there, mouths agape, eyes wide in horror and disbelief, as our Irishman and the big bodyguard tumbled off the edge, the guard screaming, his arms flailing. By the purest of luck, the strange-looking pale man somehow broke O'Connor's grip and as he tumbled, he managed to grab the withered branch of a dying Joshua tree sticking out from the side of the cliff just a few feet below the crest. The branch, against all that's holy and good, held. But I remember, and I will remember as long as I live, watching the Irishman's face as he turned and fell. It was an amalgam of pride and courage. There was no fear there — not a goddamned dime's worth. As he tumbled, he looked at me. He looked right into my eyes. And he smiled...

The guard hit the solid sandstone hard. A breath later he was gone, eyes wide, staring upwards with the surprise of death, his blood painting the yellow-brown rock below. My friend fell soundlessly and bounced once on the solid rock, then lay still. We rushed over to him. I fell to my knees and pulled him up into my arms.

There wasn't much left of O'Connor. He looked like he'd been put through a meat grinder, and in the end, they had obviously used drugs to get what they wanted. He lay in my arms, eyes wide, his focus fading as we all gathered around. The Irishman choked and spit up blood.

"I guess they bloody well killed me, mates," he groaned painfully, eyes growing distant. "I'd always envisioned a heart attack in the arms of a talented hooker..." Our Irish friend coughed again for a moment, then eased out a sigh and looked up at us, his face softening. "I'm gonna have to go now..." he whispered, trying futilely to inhale through crushed ribs. "Home to Ballyjamesduff..."

O'Connor saw the look of angst in my face and offered a small smile as he drew a final breath. "Tis a small step, my friend, to the sweet clover on the other side..."

Then, with the last of his strength, he grabbed my arm. "Take care of me boy, Nugget, aye? Find him a good home where he can come across something shiny on occasion..."

I nodded but before I could answer, his eyes softened, and with a final, almost peaceful exhale, our friend settled in my arms.

Connor O'Connor was off to the sea mists and the green hills of home...

I closed his eyes, then wiped my cheeks, which had somehow become wet. I turned to Dax and Will. In the background, we could hear the strange roar of a hundred shrill engines growing stronger all the time.

Suddenly, above us, the tall, thin guy began yelling. He was still hanging on to the branch that was growing out of the side of the cliff a hundred feet above us. His people were frantically reaching down, grasping at him, trying to pull him up. By the time we had straightened up and I found my weapon, they were already dragging the fellow over the lip.

It didn't matter. I wasn't going to forget that man's face.

But as it was, there were other issues of concern. That sound I had been hearing had grown almost deafening. We all turned and looked to the west. I couldn't believe my eyes. There had to be nearly a hundred four-wheelers, dune buggies, and desert bikes coming through the pass at Ninetyfour Mile Creek and spreading out across the desert — the heart of Arizona's amateur treasure hunters and dedicated gold diggers. It looked like something out of a *Mad Max* movie. Our articles in the papers had awakened the passion of the past and the pure, unadulterated imagination and spirit in the hearts of those who still lived for the thrill of history and shiny metal.

I turned and looked at my friends. "This may not have worked out exactly the way we planned it, but by the time this day is done, there will be no way that anyone can say that this most unique civilization didn't exist."

Long before midday, the news people from a half-dozen stations had shown up. The Arizona National Guard was being called in to protect what was now being deemed "an incredible state and national treasure." Fortunately, the State Police had already arrived but they were behind the curve a little, and a solid collection of very definitive items was already on its way out of the canyon on the backs of four-wheelers, dirt bikes, and dune buggies. Between the relics and the thousands of photos taken, both inside and out, no one would ever be able to deny the existence of this find.

We played it innocent, having spoken with the State officials who were moving in, setting up barriers, running people off, and confiscating what artifacts they could get their hands on. We explained that it was not our intention to remove anything — that we had just wanted the find to become public knowledge. *What they didn't know wouldn't hurt us.* Eddie had already hidden our precious collection, including the golden tablets with their remarkable history, in a few of his secret places on the Goose.

When things quieted down that afternoon, we buried our friend, Connor (whose body we had hidden from the authorities), on a hillside by the mesa. We threw the other man's body in a ravine. Finally, as we quietly loaded our equipment into Eddie's Goose (after having him back up far enough so that takeoff into the canyon wouldn't be such a heart-stopper), we felt pretty good about ourselves — more content than in quite some time. Yes, we had buried a friend here — a fine Irishman that not a one of us would ever forget. But we had given our country a truth that could be added to the history books. Maybe even more importantly, we had opened the eyes of the public in general to the possibilities of ancient travelers and unique societies that helped the world we know to grow.

Toward late afternoon, as it started to cool off, we began preparing an evening camp near the Goose. Will and I were warming some canned stew. Tax was sitting with his sister in the shade of an old sandstone outcropping. Jing was brushing down the feathers of her hawk, who had grown remarkably comfortable in this strange environment. The dogs were sprawled in the shade next to Dax, and Eddie was checking the oil in his engines.

At that moment, a weathered old prospector came ambling into the edges of the firelight. He asked if he might share our fire and perhaps a meal, and of course, we said yes. Lord, he was the perfect picture of a "searcher" — an old ragged hat, weathered blue jeans and boots, a sweat-stained khaki shirt — and he pulled a mule behind him. When I got a good look at the animal, I couldn't believe my eyes. "Saluda..." I whispered. "It's Saluda!"

The mule brayed softly in greeting and I was astounded at the kindness of the gods. *Our Irish buddy would be so pleased...*

Will glanced up from the fire and paused, an incredulous look on his face. "I'll be damned," he whispered. "It *is* Saluda!"

"Is she yours?" asked the fellow. I found her in the desert the other day."

"No, no," Will replied. My partner exhaled sadly. "He belonged to an old friend of ours...who would be pleased to see that she has found a home, so to speak…"

It was incredible but it got better. At that moment, Nugget came wandering out from under the Goose. He took a look at the old man and Saluda. The monkey chittered cautiously, but he was obviously pleased. Slowly, Nugget ambled over to the mule and chattered a greeting, then he came over to the fire and sat down next to the miner. The monkey cocked his head and jabbered at the fellow again.

The prospector looked at us, a little taken aback by a simian in the desert. Nonetheless, Nugget cautiously eased up next to the man. The prospector smiled and stroked the little fellow's back. He fellow looked at us. "Is he yours?"

I shook my head. "No, not exactly. He belonged to a friend of ours, but he's gone…"

"I've always wanted a monkey…" the old fellow muttered to no one in particular.

"Well, in that case, now you've got one," said Will. "His name is Nugget."

"What's that all about?" the miner asked. "The strange chatter…"

"I think it's Gaelic, my friend," I said with a smile. "You'll just have to learn it as you go." I paused and drew a breath. "But if I could give you just a little advice, I would tell you, learn to pay attention to that little fellow — where he goes and what he says…"

Will couldn't help but smile from across the fire. "I suspect he might just make you a rich man."

About an hour later, the old prospector thanked us for sharing a meal with him, then stood, gathered his gear, and grabbed the rope to the mule. As he turned to head out, he looked at the monkey and cocked his head. "Would ya like ta come, little one?"

Nugget got up, offered a gracious acceptance in "monkey," then scooted over, jumped up on Saluda's back, and settled in comfortably on the pack's goods. The old miner shook his head and smiled. As they strolled off into the growing evening, and the setting sun silhouetted them like characters in an old Western movie, I couldn't help but hear the voice of our old Irish friend, echoing off the sand and the stone…

The Garden of Eden has vanished, they say.
But I know the lie of it still;
Just turn to the left at the bridge of Finea,
and stop halfway down to Cootehill.
Tis there that you will find it,
when fortune has come to yer call.
Oh, the grass it is green around Ballyjamesduff,
and the sea is over it all.

CHAPTER EIGHTEEN

The night before, we had decided not to discuss any plans until morning. We were all worn out and shell-shocked by O'Connor's death. We would wait until the following day, when our heads were clearer and our sense of revenge had cooled.

The truth was, the revenge in us didn't cool much at all, but in the light of day, after a fairly good night's sleep, we realized the depth of the quicksand we were in. We had taken on a government agency — which one, we weren't exactly sure, but pretty much all our money was on someone with connections to the Smithsonian. (The helicopter that had brought the men in yesterday had a symbol on the fuselage — an "S and an "I" enclosed by a circle.)

We needed to be careful. We needed to get out of there and return to someplace we trusted, where we could put our backs to the wall while we made some decisions. Every one of us wanted blood but we wanted it to be someone else's on the ground this time.

I was reminded of a quote by our Rastaman buddy, Rufus. *"Insight, mon, is what you get when you survive your own stupidity."*

We couldn't afford to be dumb and still play in this league.

We said good-bye to the officials who had been watching us like hawks. With Eddie's extraordinary hiding places, they hadn't managed to find a single relic in our aircraft and they couldn't prove that we had actually done anything wrong (other than find an ancient citadel in the side of the Grand Canyon and put the location in the newspaper, which wasn't actually against the law).

Eddie backed his bird up to the maximum distance he could buy for takeoff over the cliffs of the canyon, and things went a hell of a lot smoother than the first time. A few minutes later, we were in the air and winding down through the canyon walls, not *falling* into the canyon. I could feel that old sense of euphoria sweep across the cabin — that tangible amalgam of intrepidity, arrogance, and deep gratitude that Eddie called "the spirit of the homebound gambler." Yes, we were headed home. We had done it again — rolled the dice, beaten the odds, and we were still alive.

Well, most of us...

But whether we liked it or not, we knew this game was far from over. There were some heavy choices to make. Like Dax put it, "Now do we become the gazelle or the lion?"

The trip home was uneventful — a carbon copy of the journey over. We refueled again at Nick Crow's place just outside the Pearl River Wildlife Management area in Louisiana. Nick had questions and there was no way we could deny our old smuggler buddy. We told him the story and showed him a few...*things*.

"Jesus Christ," he hissed as we sat around the dinner table.

Nick had dismissed all his employees for the day. He was taking no chances.

"You guys hit the fortune-hunter's lottery! What a damned story!"

And it was. Maybe for the first time, I saw this whole thing from the outside. This wasn't about the gold or the silver or the wealth. We were making history.

"You're going to find your names in historical dissertations. College professors will tell their students about you."

But Eddie brought the euphoria down a notch. "Yeah, sure. If we live long enough."

"Well, technically, you'd still be in the dissertations," said Nick with a wry smile. "But the dead part would be a bit of a bummer..."

The following morning, we were on our way again, "shooting the pond" as smugglers called a run across the Gulf of Mexico. Unfortunately, when we landed in Key West, we discovered our moderate fame had preceded us. Apparently, a couple of the Arizona State people who grilled us had later let our names slip to the press. Reporters from Florida Keys newspapers and a couple from the mainland were waiting for us.

"I smell an institution from Washington D.C.," growled Eddie.

Dax nodded. "Yeah. They realize they lost the opportunity to be subtle with us. So they changed their plan. Now they don't have to worry about where we are. The press will take care of that for them. Then they can pick the time and place."

In the end, we realized that there was no point in packing up and running again. If the bad guys were going to come for us, they would find us wherever we were, regardless. I had Tax come stay with me, at least for a couple of weeks. We hired a little extra security to watch the house at night (friends of Travis and Cody — people with Vietnam histories who could become shadows, with instruments of destruction).

Dax refused any protection. I expected nothing less. But at least he had Smoke, a fine-tuned intuition, and guns.

Will refused to leave his shrimp boat/houseboat on Stock Island, so Jing went to stay with him. Will did hire an old biker acquaintance of ours from the early days to watch the place at night. His name was Little Mike — long black hair; one really fierce-looking eye, the other gazing upward, glazed and indifferent; ice-pick acne; tattoos everywhere; and roughly six-and-a-half-feet tall. He was a person who gave the enemy — any enemy — pause...

Eddie practically lived at his bar. He felt safe there and it provided at least a modicum of safety in numbers.

Anyway, after a nervous first week, we found we were all still alive. That was a good sign. Maybe the creepy guy from the D.C. "Institution" had decided to cut his losses and fade to gray. Really, the truth was, the last thing he and his bosses needed was any more light on their business. It made sense.

———————————

Professor Aaron Baal sat at the desk in his office. He was not a happy man. He'd been beaten at his own game. He'd lost a member of his team and the entire event in Arizona had made newspapers across the nation. There was no way to put the cat back in the bag regarding this remarkable but troublesome find. The people at the top in the Institution were very unhappy. There were individuals of historical, clerical, and genealogical positions who weren't pleased with the idea of having to rewrite history in any fashion. One of them told him, "It's all like a line of dominos — you knock one over..."

Baal swept back his flaxen hair with a slender hand, then pushed aside the papers on his desk and exhaled heavily. He needed to clean this up. It wasn't as if he didn't know where they were, but anything really messy was likely to come back on him because too many people knew about this. *These folks need to just disappear, quietly and completely — at least the ringleaders.* He paused for a moment and scrolled back in his brain. Who could he use to remove a few of these people without making large waves? Suddenly, he stopped and smiled. *The Griffins! Of course, the Griffins!* They were highly professional, as deadly as vipers, and totally discreet. They were very selective in their clientele but there were few in the "dark industries" who didn't recommend them.

Baal smiled wickedly. *Revenge is good for the soul. It's cleansing.* He pulled a special address book from a secret drawer in his desk and paged through it.

The following day, Baal managed to reach the Griffins. A meeting place was arranged that was agreeable to both parties. There, a price was agreed upon but Baal noticed a glance between the two hitters when the names of the targets were given. Nonetheless, the money was right, the deal was settled, and a down payment was made.

Baal was happy but he was even more pleased to be out of that motel room and away from those deadly, strange people. The Griffins were one of a kind. Once they took a contract, the victims might as well just shoot themselves. From that moment on, they were dead people walking.

The situation brought back a brief memory jab about that damned Irishman he had killed. There were moments when Baal remembered the Irish curse about a baseball bat and the man killing him in hell every day. He was an Egyptian and he understood curses. He involuntarily shivered.

CHAPTER NINETEEN

Two weeks had passed since our return. The reporters had given up on us. Old news is no news. Def Leppard was doing a concert in Key West this weekend (they called it a benefit concert but I wasn't sure who it benefited, other than people who drank heavily and smoked pot), and there were a couple of special elections taking place in the city, so these items had the news people's attention. Things were quieting down. The kids had moved back to their duplex in Summerland. Tax found a gym with a fairly strong martial arts crew — a place where he could continue to "tune himself." He also bought an "end-all-to-beat-all" dirt bike and was getting into racing in Homestead. Tax wasn't a bells-and-whistles type of guy. He didn't care about pretty. He wanted hot and scary fast, and he was already getting noticed.

Jing spent a good portion of her days with her hawk. I swear, after watching them work together in hunts, it was like they read each other's minds. It was both eerie and remarkable. Jing had trained Cielo to identify hand signals — and I mean *subtle* hand signals. She was training that bird like you would a Doberman — she could command an attack or a retreat with the slightest of movements. Most remarkably, the hawk had grown to like the touch of his mistress — not just like, but delight in her caress. It was a damned strange, beautiful thing…

Dax had taken his horse up to Homestead for a small rodeo. When we spoke, I could see he was getting "itchy" again. He mentioned there was a big, six-day rodeo outside Dallas in two weeks that he was considering.

Eddie was just Eddie, back at his bar, trying to remember enough stories to live up to his reputation.

Will and I had dismissed our "security" and were beginning to see things with cautious optimism. There was an article in the *Miami Herald* regarding the "amazing find" in the Grand Canyon, so the word was definitely out.

One day, Will called me from his houseboat. "Well, Tonto, it looks like our work is finished here. Time to ride off into the sunset. Or sit back and watch the sunset."

I shrugged, staring out the window at the bight. "Yeah, I hope you're right. I mean, there's not much point in killing the messenger now…is there?"

One afternoon shortly thereafter, Will and I decided to tie up and head into Marathon for a night of "drinks and strange." Even though it was late summer, Key West seemed a little crowded for our taste. But then, we remembered the early seventies, when it was like something out of a Tom Corcoran novel.

Will picked me up in his Mustang convertible. It was a good car for cruising. Shadow wasn't happy about it but I left him at home to watch things for us.

We bounced around quite a bit that night, neither of us discovering the girl of our dreams, until finally, we found ourselves outside the Overseas Liquors and Lounge. Will pulled in and we clambered out of the car. (Both of us were well into the spirit of things by now.) But about a half hour after my buddy and I entered the bar, a dark sedan pulled into the parking lot. There were two men inside — fairly big fellows dressed a little too Miami in slacks, white shirts, and light jackets. The driver had backed the car into a position that allowed them a view of the bar entrance.

"This should be an easy ten grand," said the larger of the two, in the driver's seat, as he rolled down the windows. The fellow shook his head. "You gotta ask yourself, why would a genetics professor at a major university want these two assholes killed?"

His partner shrugged indifferently and lit a cigarette. "The story I got from the guy who hired us was that this professor dude was pissed about something — some damned thing that was going to possibly change his tenure — and he was going to have to rewrite some paper about a Siberian land bridge, whatever the hell that is, and he could well lose his mark in history." The fellow paused and drew a breath. "And he wanted somebody to pay for it."

"A serious prick for a college professor…" his partner muttered, then he eased out a breath. "Probably just a bullshit cover, anyway. They all lie when they hire us — names, places, reasons… What the hell, doesn't matter to me. Pay me cash and I'll do my job. I don't judge 'em. I just shoot 'em."

But about that time, a Lincoln Town Car turned into the parking lot. There were two people inside — what appeared to be quite attractive women, a redhead and a blond. They pulled in, windows down, and backed up into the space to the left of the fellows in the sedan.

"Hi, boys," said the blond in the driver's seat as she turned off the ignition and leaned over.

The tawny redhead in the passenger's seat opened her door and eased out, smoothing down her short skirt and putting a cigarette to her lips. "You have a light?" she asked the guy at the wheel of the other car.

The two men passed a hurried glance. There wasn't much they could do. The driver jerked a lighter from his pocket and was offering it upward but in the process, he displayed the butt of a pistol in his shoulder holster.

Will and I were just stumbling out of the bar. The last two drinks had dropped us over the edge of sobriety and we were feeling no pain — and a pizza was sounding pretty good. But Will had dropped his keys coming out of the bar entrance and we were kneeling drunkenly, trying to focus with all the finesse of two walleyed monkeys.

The guys in the sedan threw another glance at each other, then out at us, then back to the girls.

"Yeah, I know, I know, you need us to leave you alone so you can kill those two idiots," said the redhead. "But that's not likely to happen." She brought up a hand that held a silenced .22 caliber automatic. "I'll make you a deal. You leave now and you get to fight another day…"

There was a moment of electric silence. Sometimes testosterone can be more of an enemy than a friend…

The guy at the wheel went for his gun. The girl shot the driver twice in the head. As he slumped forward, eyes filled with the cold surprise of death, she leaned in and shot his partner three times.

As it turned out, the girls' "employer" had warned them that there might be other people looking to earn money on this job. Their employer had a personal interest in this. He wanted to be the one who brought about the "untimely passing" of the marks.

No kill, no money.

Finally, I found the keys in the loose marl rock a couple feet from the doorway of the lounge. We were really quite proud of ourselves that we found them at all. My buddy and I had just staggered to upright positions when we looked up and there, moving toward us from the cars, were two women.

My God! Of all people! Margo and Kendra. Margo and Kendra! Damn!

That took us back a few years. I winced. Not all of those memories were that good, actually. Panama, Jamaica, Florida — it seemed to be a collage of very high adventure; exotic, mind-boggling sex; and lots of people trying to kill us. And here they were again. Pretty spooky. But damn, they were both looking really good...

Kendra (who was my lady at one time) still had that heavy mane of soft blond hair, a slightly prominent nose, and those wide, emerald-green eyes. Margo, Will's former lady, was graced with long caramel hair (which she had tied up in a ponytail sometimes for play or work), beautiful pale-blue eyes, and a wide, sensuous mouth. They were dressed in white pants, sandals, and soft, almost transparent blouses. No bras...

I read Will's face. "Don't let your dick do your thinking here, buddy," I whispered harshly. "You need to remember... I'm betting they're still doing what they do best...whacking people."

Will glanced at me. "They wouldn't...you don't think..." He held out his hands. "Not us..."

I couldn't get any more conjecture out before the girls were in our arms. *Damn! Damn! Kendra felt good.* It swept me back in time and almost made me forget who they were. *Almost.* Kendra and I had lasted for about four months after our Caribbean/Central American adventure a few years back. She wasn't a bad person. Okay, she wasn't exactly a good person either. While we were together, she and her sister were still tying up occasionally to do "hits for pocket money."

It was just, I guess, that I liked a little danger and excitement. But shooting strangers for fun and money was out of my entertainment league.

Margo had her tongue so far down Will's throat, she was tickling his Adam's apple. It didn't seem to bother my snockered buddy. He was lost to fresh, drunken decadence. He, of all people, should have remembered who/what he had in his arms. Truthfully, Margo could only be described as a ruthless, conscienceless nymphomaniac who had chased him across several countries either trying to kill him or screw him unconscious — whichever happened to be most appropriate at the time. The last time he had seen her, a couple of years back, she was boarding an airplane at Miami International, headed for Costa Rica with our old buddy, Sundance, of all people.

Kendra finally tempered her enthusiasm and pulled back, staring at me. "I've missed you…" she whispered.

"I've missed you too," I said, a little out of breath. "Damn, what a coincidence! You and Margo…here…"

"Yes, isn't it?" my lady friend said with a smile.

"How…why…are you here?" I asked cautiously.

She offered a small shrug. "Oh, you know, a little vacation. We've been working too hard. We thought it might be nice to see the Keys again." She glanced out at the moon, which was Halloween orange and nearly full, then turned to me and smiled. "What wonderful, nearly impossible luck…"

The arrival of our old friends had sobered Will and me somewhat, and we all decided to go out for a late dinner.

"Who knows where this will take us," murmured Margo, as she slipped her arm around Will.

We all knew where it was going to take us, but no one was arguing… And there would have been more nagging concerns regarding this coincidence if we hadn't been so drunk.

Kendra offered to drive. Will and I were still well lit. It seemed like a good idea. As my friend and I crawled into the ladies' rental — a Lincoln Town Car — the girls drew back slightly before reaching the car.

Margo touched Kendra's elbow and whispered out the side of her mouth, "Remember, you can play with your food all you want, but in the end, you still have to eat it."

Kendra nodded reluctantly.

It was an interesting night, to say the least. The food at the restaurant was excellent. (But then, the drunker you are, the better the food is. That's a universal truism.) The liquor was excellent and the conversation — that which I can remember — was stimulating. Margo was particularly enlightening regarding what she planned to do to/with Will. Toward the end, my partner was beginning to get that "sacrificial chicken" look, even with all the alcohol.

Yeah, it was quite a night...

Eventually, through it all — beyond the booze, the food, and the sex — back in the blurry caverns of my mind, there was a single, persistent, and certainly annoying thought. Somewhere along the line — I think when the girls had gone to the restroom — I leaned over and whispered into Will's ear (a little accidental spittle running down my chin and onto the shoulder of my friend's shirt) and asked as quietly as I could, "You don' thi-think these two are... *working...do you?*"

The problem was, even in my inebriated state I realized that some people lack mooring — to ideas, principles, and even to other people. Mooring helps most of us find equilibrium. It doesn't mean we can't move vertically or laterally, but like a boat line at a dock, it keeps us from drifting away. Kendra and Margo were both a few yards short on mooring...

Will shook his head in that loose-necked, drunk fashion. "Nah, man. They love us. They've always loved us..."

CHAPTER TWENTY

Remarkably enough, the next morning, Will and I were still alive in our own rooms with our respective ladies and our respective, massive hangovers. I hurt so bad I was thinking about asking Kendra to kill me. There was still a part of me that said I might just get my wish. They were a lot like cats — they liked to play with their food...

But there was something else. Something that outweighed all the romance and suspense that surrounded us.

I had experienced the dream again...

The dream... The dream that took me back thousands of years to another time and another place. I could see the cavern in the Arizona desert again. I was inside, and the early morning sun was lighting the interior through the monstrous opening facing the river. My black hair was long, almost to my shoulders. My clothes were different but comfortable — a belted white shift, leather sandals on my feet, and a gold chain about my neck. I was someone of importance — not so much a warrior but perhaps something like a priest. And I saw the cat's eyes again — almost everywhere I looked. Then, suddenly, I was walking along one of the deeper corridors. I came upon a mural of a cat's face on a wall in a small room off to the side of a main corridor. And I suddenly realized...

It all came flooding back in a stunning epiphany. I found myself split between two worlds, bound to a history before Egypt existed, and I realized exactly what had taken place so long ago. *The Anunnaki! The Egyptian pharaoh, Merneptah, and his fascination with the Anunnaki — the ancient race from the stars and their secrets written into the Sumerian cuneiforms.*

I found myself walking down a hallway or an enclosed passageway. The huge cat's-eye relief on the wall...a clever disguise...but I remembered. I pushed the third claw of the right foot and the flawlessly hidden stone door with the mural on it opened. A path led inward, into a chamber filled with large, sealed jars and papyrus scrolls. And I knew, without question, what those perfectly preserved jars held. It was a gift from a distant race to the hierarchy of Egypt, later passed along by a benevolent leader to brave explorers headed for a new world — the elixir of compliance, the glue of conformity for a society, the matrix of an overwhelming desire to be "part of." Just a little in the water supply on a regular basis...

But at that point, I was drawn back through a swirling vortex, awakened by the fervent administrations of Kendra. Her head was in my naked lap, making the ardent sounds of a young, feeding cat. It was certainly pleasing, but damn, I had to get to Will. I had to tell him what the gods had given me while I slept...

I offered Kendra a flimsy excuse about needing to speak with Will about our animals being left unattended. I promised to be right back. She reluctantly agreed. I could see the need for sleep in her eyes. I threw on some clothes and headed out. As I reached the lobby of the motel and passed the restaurant, I saw Will, alone, at a table in the back. When I walked up, he barely noticed me. My friend seemed almost comatose, elbows on the table, wrinkled clothes, hands wrapped around his coffee cup, eyes bleary. He jerked slightly as I sat down, then relaxed when he saw it was me.

"Are you okay?" I asked tentatively.

My buddy sighed heavily, still staring ahead, eyes as red as stop signs, hands shaking. "I forgot," he whispered. "It has been a while and I forgot. The woman doesn't leave you alone for a minute. There's always something she's doing to you, or wanting you to do...things that would make a sailor cringe...eight, nine straight hours." He shook his head. "Man, it's just heavy lifting, constantly. No breaks, no liquid, no food. It's like being attacked by a horny anaconda or a troop of sex-crazed simians." He sighed again. "I never even made it to the bathroom. Every time I tried to get up, she grabbed me and dragged me back down." My friend shook his head again, embarrassed. "I peed in the bed and it didn't matter to her. In fact, I think she liked it."

Again he offered an exhausted sigh. Then he grabbed my arm. "Also, when she thought I was asleep, she got up and made a quick phone call. I didn't get it all, but I did hear her whisper, 'Yeah, we have them...' Then she paused and replied, 'Yeah, yeah, I know...'"

I empathized with my partner and his disconcerting news. Man, I was really regretting not having brought that little truth-telling magic rock I had found in the Venezuelan jungle a few months ago.

It would have saved a lot of guessing. But it was locked in my bank safety deposit box in Key West.

Nonetheless, I had big things in my head — things that I had discovered via a wild dream; things that might change the world, one way or another…if they were real and if we stayed alive…

"You have your wallet?" I asked.

Will checked his hip, then nodded.

"Okay, we gotta get out of here," I hissed. "Now!"

We knew that our nemesis, Professor Baal, had big connections and that he had people deep in our archaeological find in Arizona. I was certain they were stealing things and taking things apart, even as I considered the thought. What in God's name would happen if they found the hidden room with the containers of mind-altering/society-altering powder from what might well be an ancient Anunnaki formula? Assuming there really were containers and it wasn't some alcohol/sex stress-related nightmare… The greatest uneasiness came with the knowledge that if I didn't act, and it *was* real, and that formula could be duplicated, I might well be responsible for changing the world for the worse. No one should have the wherewithal to change the mindset of mankind.

We found our car and raced out of Marathon, flying across the old bridges that spanned the distance back to my place on Big Pine. From there, I called everyone — Dax, Jing, Tax, and Eddie. I didn't contact Travis and Cody or Arturio yet…but I hadn't ruled it out. I wanted to talk with the original team first. While we waited for everyone to arrive, my buddy and I managed something to eat and grabbed a couple cups of coffee each. Even with the caffeine and food, poor old Will was just coming around.

Finally, three hours after Will and I returned to Big Pine, we had the gang assembled in my living room. Even the dogs, Shadow and Smoke, were there, spread out on the floor but not far from each other.

Jing had even brought Cielo, now a constant companion she hardly ever had to hood anymore. The creature had truly become more like a dog than a hawk, and seemed to possess a broad intellect not generally attributed to birds.

I had already given Will the "Reader's Digest" version of my dream and the historian in him was able to fill in some of the gaps.

The excitement of this "discovery," if that's what we could call it, brought him back to life. Once we had everyone seated in my living room, I let Will have the floor because much of this was his forte.

My buddy glanced around at everyone, then began.

"For thousands of years, mankind has tossed around speculation and theories regarding an ancient race called the Anunnaki. This particular race was the deity pantheon of the ancient Sumerians, and there are a number of historical architects who believe the Anunnaki may have been the fathers of mankind on this planet." Will paused and drew a breath. "I want you to consider for a moment one of the primary elements that makes societies great. It's passion — the single-minded desire to serve your country and your people. In essence, it's the selfless coalition of minds that makes a society rise to greatness."

My friend took a breath. He was on a roll.

"All this 'collective consciousness' really equals is a surrender of self, to a degree, and a passive compliance." He held up a finger. "Now, I'm not talking about surrendering to the iron glove of communism or the heart-and-soul, life-and-death worship of a godhead, like the ancient and even modern Chinese and Japanese, but more of a pure, unadulterated yearning to...*serve*. Like the Marines — the overwhelming desire to be 'part of the good.'" Will looked around at us. "That altruism exists somewhere in the folds of man's intellect and emotion, but it's generally overwhelmed by narcissism and selfishness — especially in our societies today."

Will took another breath. "But what if you had a formula that you could put into the water of a community, or a state, or a country, which made people passionate about their work, eager about getting things done, interested in serving others, and doing the greater good, more than anything else?"

My friend paused again and smiled. "What if you could make jealous, self-centered, arrogant man considerably more driven for and obsessed with 'the hive?'"

"We'd be like ants or bees, with big brains..." I said. But I also realized that the old saying about "too much of a good thing" applied here. "On the other hand, would man lose his objectivity, and eventually become like a slave?"

"Don't know for sure," said Will. "But it appears that possibly there was an ancient race of people called the Anunnaki who may have applied a similar process. The Anunnaki are generally recognized as a bona fide culture by most ancient civilization historians. However, they have been most thoroughly studied by the Russian researcher and best-selling author, Zecharia Sitchin. Unfortunately, it seems most of the academics dismiss his work as pseudoscience." My friend smiled. "There's a lot of jealousy in the business of being intuitive, and a lot of times, if it's a new idea and it ain't their idea, it ain't real. Sitchin's critics couldn't translate a Sumerian cuneiform if their lives depended on it, but they don't accept what he's done." Will shrugged. "I guess the kicker is, the Anunnaki are considered by some early earth historians to be quite possibly an extraterrestrial race that came to this planet well over a hundred thousand years ago, in order to mine gold here."

The room got quiet. My friend again took a breath. "Of course, this concept lacks mainstream acceptance but the person who tells this story best is Zecharia Sitchin. This guy is, evidently, one of the few people in the world who can accurately translate the extraordinarily ancient Sumerian cuneiform tablets that have been found in the Middle East." Will eased out a dramatic breath. "These tablets specifically tell of 'a people from the stars' called the Anunnaki."

That statement caught everyone's attention.

Will glanced around, then continued. "Sitchin claims that when it became too difficult for the Anunnaki to do the mining work themselves, they genetically created races on this planet to mine the gold, which was not as readily available on their planet but was as essential for them as it is for us, in the manufacture of modern technology and life-support elements. Sitchin adds that, as they moved along, the Anunnaki created a variety of races, trying to find the most productive, then perhaps genetically tweaked some of what they had already created, adding a desire to serve and to be accepted — to make the process easier. There is some speculation that the Anunnaki may have later used a long-term chemical-based 'encouragement' that could be added to the indigenous people's water or sprayed in the air to get the same, continuous result — keeping such tight-knit, but hard-working communities peaceful and focused. I think it's entirely possible that there was a unique formula designed by the Anunnaki and eventually passed down to perhaps the Sumerian priests, and in the end, maybe conveyed to certain Egyptian hierarchies." My friend paused. "And I think it's possible that it was included with the Egyptian explorers who came to the Grand Canyon, to create cohesion and increase their chances of survival in a new and dangerous land."

That sucked the air from the room.

"And what are you basing all this on?" asked Dax.

"A dream I had," I said. "Actually, two dreams..."

Dax huffed dismissively. "Dreams, huh? You've been smoking that wacky stuff again, haven't you?"

I held out my hands. "I could be wrong. But what if this formula actually exists? What if it's hidden in the cavern we found in the Grand Canyon?" I paused. "I know that this Professor Baal is looking for something, and I know he's an ancient cultures/Egyptian historical enthusiast. This wasn't— *this isn't* — just about the relics of ancient explorers. My guess is he knows something about this 'ability to influence.'" I drew a breath. "All I can tell you is, I have seen this in two dreams — and it was as real as anything I've ever experienced. I think someone, somewhere beyond my pay grade, is trying to prevent this extraordinary element from falling into the wrong hands." I stared at Dax, then glanced around at the others. "How would it feel to be remembered as the people who gave a man like Professor Aaron Baal a power like this?"

Will picked up from the pause. "What you have to remember here is, what the Anunnaki were doing. They were making their subjects as responsive as possible to the needs of 'the hive.' But they weren't necessarily concerned about the well-being of their subjects. Merneptah, the pharaoh who sent these early Egyptians from the cavern on their journey, was known for his penchant for ancient secrets and potions. I think it's possible he gave the leaders of this exploration/migration this ancient secret — the power to 'influence society' — because that small group of people would need an edge if they were to survive." He paused. "But here is where the worm turns. Do we...does *anyone*...have the right to change the nature of man, individually or collectively? When you get right down to it, I don't think so. The idea of 'the greater good for all' always inevitably seems to get bent into 'the greater good for *some'* — especially in situations like this." Again he paused. "I think the Anunnaki were playing god, and I think we have to be careful we don't do the same."

"All I know," I said quietly, "is that I have seen in my dreams a hidden room in the stone walls of that cavern, where there are sealed jars, and scrolls…"

"Damn, that's far out," Eddie muttered incredulously. "But I gotta admit, think about the potential, man, for misuse with something like this in a freakin' rapscallion society like ours."

"I'll tell you what this is," said Jing, who had been quiet through most of this. "It's a complete disaster for free thought. It's like salt — you use it sparingly and it's wonderful, but you use too much and it destroys the meal." She brought up her hands, palms out. "And when have you ever known man to have a sense of dignity or unselfishness when it comes to power?"

Even the pragmatic Dax shook his head doubtfully. "And you put something like this in the hands of a scoundrel like Professor Aaron Baal…"

CHAPTER TWENTY-ONE

Professor Baal was sitting in his upstairs office when one of his people knocked, then entered. Baal put down the report he was reading. "What is it?"

The large fellow drew a breath. "Apparently, there was a team taken out last night. In Florida — the Florida Keys..."

That brought Baal up. "Taken out? Dead?"

The fellow nodded. "We don't know who did it but it was clean. Professional. It's just a guess but it looks like they may have gotten in the way of...of someone else."

Baal cursed vehemently, totally out of character. "I told them to stay out of it and observe from a distance," he hissed, staring at the ceiling. "By the weeping eyes of Isis, what did they not understand about the word 'dangerous'?" The professor brought himself to his feet. "Send someone for the bodies, now. We don't want any more attention than necessary." He exhaled angrily. "The bloody damned fools! We not only lost two good men but now we're blind down there."

"We picked up a report on lodging this morning," said the man in front of him. "From a local motel. But now, there's no telling where the targets are."

Baal nodded, somewhat mollified. So, at least the Griffins had reported in — an unexpected blessing. But there was no way to second-guess them. That was like trying to capture smoke. He sighed angrily. "All right," he said. "We'll wait to hear from our people. In the meantime, get me a plane ready. I've sorted things out here as much as I can. It's Allah's will now. I want to get back to the site."

And indeed he did. He had teams using ultrasound devices, subtly trying to locate any hidden cavities in the cavern. From all the information he had bought, borrowed, or stolen over the years — including ancient Egyptian scrolls, precious cuneiform tablets from the Sumerians, and in particular, the writings of the mysterious Anunnaki — everything indicated that an integral piece of the power and control that the hierarchies of these ancient societies had exercised was missing. This superintendence, this unique discipline, seemed to rise from an external, induced source. He'd had dreams.

Strange dreams. And sometimes he could almost see the answer. A potion, or something similar, that could bend the will of the masses — and it always came from a dark cavern and in a single image — the eyes of a cat...

He smiled. He didn't want to control the world. That was way too much work. He just wanted to own a piece of it. Cairo would be nice, for a start...

————————

As we all sat around the living room, still struggling with uncertainty and its consequences, Dax eased out an uncomfortable sigh. "I think we got to go back," he growled. "My daddy always said, 'Don't dig up more snakes than you can kill.' And that's a good motto. And I can tell you right now, I don't really want to go back." He exhaled heavily and aimed a forefinger at me. "And all we're going on is the drunken dreams of this particular scoundrel, who is either just as dumb as freshly piled shit or as brave as the first man who ate an oyster." Our friend paused and drew a breath. "But if something like this exists, and we don't go back and try to find it, and that murdering bastard finds it first..." He shook his head, eyes down. "Well, I'd have to buy an old pickup and ride it off a cliff just to make myself okay."

We realized that we would have to approach this differently than we had on our last visit. There were no real roads into or out of the cavern site. Everyone was coming in and out via helicopter as the authorities were now policing the area. On top of that, there were Grand Canyon park rangers assigned to the immediate area now, especially any access trails. Beyond the rangers, there were a number of prominent individuals from different historical agencies and universities who had been called in to examine the find, and I was damned sure that we could absolutely count on Professor Baal and his gang of thugs being mixed into that pudding as well. None of these people would be happy to see us. We couldn't exactly ride in and we couldn't land the Goose without really drawing attention, so, ultimately, we decided to just "drop in" for a visit.

Eddie had dug through his charts and discovered an old mining airstrip — basically a flattish piece of ground — about three miles from the cavern. It was, apparently, still used for emergency access on occasion by park officials (when tourists did stupid things and needed to be airlifted out). The park had several of those throughout the canyon. The plan was, we'd land there (hopefully) and hike to our destination. Eddie would stay with the plane and wait for word.

If we needed to get out in a hurry, Dax had come up with an emergency backup plan. Our cowboy friend normally seemed to have both feet planted firmly on the ground, and generally, he offered sound advice. But this time...

"Are you nuts?" hissed Will. "Did you forget to take your meds again?"

There was a stunned silence as we glanced around at each other.

"You want us to jump off the walls of the Grand Canyon — at night?"

"It's only a backup plan," said Dax, fairly unperturbed, "if Eddie can't land where we came in before. You know, if the situation gets too hot for him to come in safely. And besides, it could be early morning by then." Dax took a breath. "Everyone here has parachuting experience. It's a huge coincidence but it's true." He turned to Will and me. "You guys have done quite a bit of jumping, if any of your stories are true. Tax and Jing have told me about attending a jumping school in Barbados and jumping off the mountain cliffs there." Dax paused. "And the government trained me well for Southeast Asia."

He looked about, hoping for positive feedback. It wasn't happening yet.

"Look, it may sound like I'm a few pickles short of a barrel —"

"You got that right," Will cried. "You're as mad as a box of frogs. We could get thrown against that monstrous freaking wall on the way down."

"Not much chance," our big friend replied. "The canyon curves there, providing plenty of gravel beach along the river to land on, where Eddie and the Goose will be waiting. You've got a 6,000-foot fall, which is more time than you could possibly need to get a chute open, and the prevailing winds should pull us out and away from the walls. Probably..."

"There's that spooky word, *probably*," I replied cautiously.

My son looked at his sister and words passed. They smiled slightly. They were already freaking gamblers by nature.

"It would be a hell of a story," Tax said with a grin.

"No question he's from your loins," Will moaned, realizing we were about to get outvoted. And we were...

"Remember, it's just a backup plan," Dax offered in consolation.

"Yeah," I muttered. "That's what they said at the Alamo."

Out of the blue, Jing straightened up and said, "I'm bringing my hawk. He's a lot less trouble than a dog and he can take care of himself if any of this goes sideways." She looked around and drew a breath. "Besides, he's more aggressive and possessive than a Rottweiler. He did just fine on the last trip and he's twice as well-trained now."

I could see that look in her eyes. There wasn't much point in arguing with her.

We decided to take the day to organize equipment and supplies, then head out in Eddie's Goose the following morning. There were a few things we would need — several official National Park uniforms, parachutes for all, weapons, food, and other miscellaneous articles of survival, but the one thing we hadn't decided on was how to handle the possibility of finding what this nearly mindless escapade was all about. It was going to be a busy day.

Still, the nagging question on all our minds was, what if we actually found what we were looking for? What if there actually was a substance that could alter the mindset of mankind, making him more dedicated and almost myopically focused on the betterment of "the hive." And then there was the huge, sixty-four-thousand-dollar question: Who decides what's best for the hive?

Admittedly, it was a pretty impromptu if not shaky situation, with the possibility that confusion might well be our epitaph. But the good news was, I had another dream that night. Actually, maybe it wasn't such great news...

There I was again, in the cavern — later in time, maybe only a thousand years ago. But as I wandered about, still one of the people — dressed in a darker-colored shift (similar to before but obviously a different soul now), there had been a subtle change since the time I had last visited. Whereas in my last visit, the people seemed to be relatively content and seemingly healthy, moving about with a purpose, there seemed to be a slight change in the "hum of the hive" this time. Again, it was subtle. There was still a sense of prosperity to some degree. Few people seemed hungry or set aside. (Although I suppose all societies have souls who seem to be almost genetically opposed to work. America is certainly subject to that). Nonetheless, while the feeling of general prosperity still existed, there was a difference in the way the people moved. There was the slightest of shadows in their eyes. It wasn't a look of oppression necessarily, but a sense of purpose without the passion I had seen before in my earlier dream. It was odd, but my first thought was that of the drug addicts I had met (because no one lived in South Florida without knowing someone who had slipped off the tracks of life due to the lure of illicit substances). There was lethargy in their eyes, even when they smiled.

Watching the people move from place to place, I realized that the desire to perform for the hive still existed, but it was like they were exhausted. Were they being over-used or over-medicated — or both — in order to maintain a satisfactory level of production for the leadership? I was reminded of the Pony Express riders, who rode their horses into the ground from station to station on their routes. Those proud, dedicated animals did their master's bidding willingly, but many were driven into the dirt in the process, dying with the light of affection and purpose still in their eyes.

That's what the scene before me looked like. Too damned much of a good thing…or a good thing gone wrong…

When I told my friends what I had seen, there was a distinct moment or two of silence and speculation.

Will sighed heavily and glanced around at us. "Generally, only a few end up with 'the greater good.'"

"Because in the end, the creature that is man is just a selfish bastard," muttered Dax.

CHAPTER TWENTY-TWO

Speaking of selfish people who had a fondness for weapons...

Will had returned to his live-aboard shrimp boat in Key West. He needed to gather some personal stuff, his travel diary, and a gun or two before returning to my place for the night. After loading everything, he decided to grab a quick shower. It would probably be his last for the next few days, at the very least.

Will locked the doors on the boat and checked the windows, then stripped down and stepped into the pleasant, steamy stall. He was just beginning to relax, eyes closed, leaning against the far wall of the small shower, just letting the water beat on him, when he realized there was no soap in the dish. Will sighed, turned, and slid back the curtain — and screamed.

There was Margo, buck naked, holding the soap. My friend instinctively threw himself back, hammering his head on the metal washcloth rack. He was bleeding, dizzy, and terrified, all at once. After all, this was a woman who once chased him over several countries alternately trying to kill him or screw him to death (the end result being much the same). "I...I...Margo! Sorry I just took off...there was an emergen—"

"It's okay," said Margo with a slippery sensuousness, somewhere between angry and horny. (But then she was always somewhere between angry and horny...) "I'll let you make it up to me."

An hour and a half later, Will felt more used than the condom machine at a "Girls to Go" nightclub. So, while Margo was in the john, Will quietly grabbed his clothes and the small bag of "to-go" essentials he'd gathered earlier. Then he squeezed out the bedroom window, leapt lightly from the boat to the dock, and was gone like a beaten dog.

After a few minutes, Margo heard Will's car screech out of the marl parking lot. She exhaled, somewhere between anger and acceptance. There was no point in becoming too attached. Like her bastard stepfather used to say, "It's okay to have a chicken for a pet. But that only works until you get hungry..."

It really didn't bother her that Will had gotten away. He and his friends were up to something — something big. The bug they had placed in Kansas's home had produced some really interesting information. She and her sister might as well play out this hand.

Kendra watched me from her car, at the western end of Big Pine Key, as I helped the others load equipment into my pickup at the house. Finally, she sat down her binoculars and sighed. There was no good time right now to do what she'd been hired for, and she wasn't in a hurry anyway. The arrogant Smithsonian guy could jump up and down all he wanted. This was her gig and she would pick the time and place. The skinny bastard acted like God's own messenger. He needed to be careful. Kendra smiled but it wasn't pretty. Death could be so arbitrary and totally indifferent to one's opinion of themselves.

Late that evening, Margo and Kendra slipped onto the airfield in Key West and hid a long-range bug on Eddie's Goose. They had become intrigued with what was going on. And besides, they weren't done playing with their food.

And so it was that the following morning, the remnants of the Hole in the Coral Wall Gang, along with a handful of new recruits, gathered themselves for an uncertain quest. The plan was to save the world from past and present challenges, and the skullduggery of the eminent Smithsonian bastard, Professor Aaron Baal.

But then I was reminded of our old friend, Rufus, and what he thought about preconceived ideas... *"Plans — dey like butterflies, mon. Dey don' never fly straight and everything want to smash, bash, or eat 'em."*

Just before we left, I took Smoke and Shadow over to my neighbor — the attractive but attentive blond who lived next door. She had a chain-link fence, so the guys could stay out as much as they wanted, and I knew she would take good care of them. Dax and I weren't happy about leaving them, and God knows, the boys were well aware that we were packing for a trip and it seriously disappointed them that they weren't going. But it was just too complicated an affair and we needed the freedom of movement if things went sideways. Besides, Dax told me that Smoke hated jumping out of airplanes. I didn't ask...

We tied up briefly with our buddy, Bobby Branch, on Cudjoe

Key. He supplied us with a handful of special "instruments of destruction." Specifically, a few grenades, silencers for our AR14s and newest pistols, and a couple of AT4 anti-tank weapons, which were basically small shoulder-launched missiles with a grenade on the pointy end. Just aim and pull the trigger — perfect for simple folks like Will and me. But Branch also made sure we had several handheld military radios, which we had found so important in the past when things got "scattered." In addition, when we gave him the "Reader's Digest" version of where we were headed, he went back to his office and returned ten minutes later with some marvelously official-looking documents for our trip.

When we were done, Will looked at me. "I don't say this very often," he said, "but that damned guy is better at 'amazing bullshit' than I am."

While we were preparing to depart, our Egyptian nemesis was landing at the airport outside Tusayan, where we had stayed earlier. From there, Baal was picked up by a helicopter and taken to the cavern site. Within an hour, the professor had met with his people at the hidden city — those who were using ultrasound devices in an attempt to discover hidden cavities in the interior walls of the cavern. They had discovered a small chamber near what the explorers had come to call "the upper echelon quarters." There were items there of some wealth and historical value, but nothing along the lines of what Baal had instructed them to seek out.

Professor Baal was being afforded some priority because of his connection with the Smithsonian and his Egyptian historical knowledge, but he knew that time was running out. There were too many people working the dig now, and sooner or later, someone would stumble onto the place that he intuitively knew existed.

While all this was taking place, the Hole in the Coral Wall Gang was once again lumbering across the Gulf of Mexico. Eddie took us into New Orleans for fuel, and an hour later, we were in the air again. After we got underway, I spelled my old friend at the controls. About five hours beyond that, we refueled in Albuquerque, and about an hour later, we were dropping into the airport at Flagstaff. There was no value in landing at Tusayan and advertising we were back. Flagstaff was far enough away and busy enough to provide us a degree of anonymity. We rented a van, spent the night in a motel, organized our gear, checked our weapons, and studied the plan one more time.

Thanks to our "official" friends in Key West, we all had state park uniforms. The identifying patches were for the Florida Keys but if one wasn't paying too much attention, we could probably slide under the radar. Or we could have Will bullshit the curious until they were dizzy. Each of us would carry a small, two-way radio. Big weapons would be too obvious and were out of the question, but everyone going into the cavern would have a pistol and a couple of magazines.

Kendra and Margo were now also aware of the prize in this affair, thanks to the bug they had hidden in my home. They knew what the game was now, and where it was being played. The whole situation was really more than they wanted to deal with — they were more "hands-on, direct persons." But the girls realized that if they could stay close enough to the primary parties in this affair, they would undoubtedly find a course to their benefit. So they packed a couple of bags with clothing and weapons, drove up to the mainland, and chartered a light twin at Tamiami Airport. A day later, they landed at the Flagstaff Pulliam Airport, where they bought a map of the Grand Canyon, rented a car, and drove up to Tusayan. Also, thanks to the bug in my home, the girls had a working knowledge of our thoughts on Professor Baal and his people, and the cavern...

The sexually charged, conscience-challenged duo was very good at discerning information, in one fashion or another. And hell, everybody in the bloody town wanted to tell what they knew about the whole cavern thing. By the end of the day, the Griffins had a pretty good handle on who the players were and exactly where this new historical dig was located. Unfortunately, the ladies had asked just enough questions to catch the attention of Professor Baal's people. With the descriptions, it didn't take Baal long to figure out who they were. But the ever-suspicious professor had to ask himself, *Why didn't they take out their targets in the Keys, when they had the perfect opportunity?* That made him nervous and he had a policy — most anything that made him nervous, disappeared. It seemed brutal but it had kept him alive over the years. And ironically, it had often been the Griffins he used to expedite matters. Nonetheless, he would wait a little longer. Patience is the hunter's friend... They still might do his work for him.

We knew, or at least I knew (from the intriguing but disturbing dreams I'd been having) that there was something in that cavern that had the potential to move the human creature; to emotionally and mentally drive mankind in a subtle fashion. (Or maybe not so subtly...) I could sense it. I knew that this was not a fantasy. But most of all, I was certain that we stood at a crossroads here. I couldn't make myself feel good about this possible panacea for laziness or noncompliance in society. It was like Crazy Eddie said. "If God would have wanted us to be ants, man, he would have given us them wiggly antennae and more legs."

I also knew my friends were gambling their lives on this whimsical notion of mine. We were really rolling the dice all the way around — all on the words written on some flat Sumerian tablets over four thousand years ago by a race few people knew anything about.

But through it all, I just couldn't shake the reality of my dreams and the feeling of uneasiness. I knew I had to get into that cavern. Soon...

The following day, as we gathered our gear and loaded into Eddie's Goose at the airport in Flagstaff, the earth trembled slightly beneath our feet for a good ten seconds. (It seemed a lot longer, given what was happening.) We all looked at each other.

"Don't go getting yourselves in a twit," muttered the unshakable Dax. "Doesn't mean anything. Old Seth used to tell me, 'It's just Mother Nature wiggling her ass and settling in a little.' We're in a quake region. Happens all the time around here."

"Seems to be happening a lot now," Tax said uncomfortably. He glanced over at his sister.

Jing stood there, that huge hawk on her arm. I swear it was the largest osprey I'd ever seen. Her eyes darted around as she stroked the bird's back, calming him, but that was it. She was a tough person to rattle.

Will looked at me, and his eyebrows did that little dance of concern. I just shrugged. There was nothing we could do about it. I knew we were about to step into it again with both feet. The only thing I could think of were random lines from a Shakespeare play about the battle of Harfleur:

Once more into the breach, dear friends, once more...

Stiffen the sinews, summon up the blood
Disguise fair nature with hard-favour'd rage...

Once more into the breach, dear friends, once more...

CHAPTER TWENTY-THREE

Professor Baal was having breakfast when one of his people interrupted him, saying the Grumman Goose and its occupants had just departed from Pulliam International in Flagstaff. There was no flight plan. That was okay with Baal. He knew where they were going. He asked about the other issue he had — the two hit women who hadn't yet done what they were supposed to.

The fellow nodded cautiously. "Yes sir, we're staying on that." The man paused. "We're at your discretion. However you want that to fall..."

Eddie and I had studied the area map well and the little dirt airstrip three miles northwest of the cavern was still our best bet. From there, it was a straight hike through high desert that shouldn't take us more than two hours. The trick was to show up about dusk, when the activities for the day were closing down. Maybe we could sneak into the cavern, or maybe Will could double-talk us in with our fake patches and documents.

The flight was a piece of cake. Eddie found the tiny dirt strip without a problem. As it turned out, the only security they had on the entrance (the same entrance we had originally dug out) was a couple of local sheriff's deputies. In the first week after the discovery, they had arrested enough people to pretty much discourage unofficial visitors. Will performed a marvelously confusing but convincing verbal dance about us being sent in by the State Department to determine any correlation between the apparent Egyptians in this project and the ancient Mayans. The guy took all of three seconds to look at Will's "official" identification papers. He did offer a questioning look at the osprey on Jing's arm.

Will's daughter stared at the man and said, "He senses bad gasses, like a miner's parakeet, only better."

Apparently mollified, the fellow turned to our duffle bags (which contained weapons, parachutes, and various instruments of detection and destruction) and offered another questioning eye.

Will waved a hand at the gear bags and shrugged. "Sure, help yourself. But the radioactive-detecting equipment in there is still a little...*hot*...from our last assignment in Chernobyl." He shrugged. "For some reason, we're supposed to test here, as well." He shrugged indifferently again. "If you've had your shots, you should be okay. Besides, you guys have probably had all the kids you're planning on having, right?"

One minute later, we were on our way into the cavern, our bags untouched...

We had seen it before but it still took our breath away. The huge statues were still in place, and the ship, of course, was still there. In addition, the archaeological people had installed generators and electric lighting in some of the more accessible areas. But there was one most remarkable difference. The powers-to-be had knocked out the ancient, hastily constructed back wall that faced the Grand Canyon and the river below, returning the cavern to how it was originally designed thousands of years ago. The moon was rising, coming up off the far canyon rim, and it shone brilliantly through the huge opening and into the citadel, illuminating the structures, statues, and passageways. It was stunning. And for a fraction of a minute, I could envision how it was before — a small, exceptional metropolis, a shining extension of Egypt in the middle of nowhere. It was truly a remarkable spectacle of accomplishment and courage.

Will nudged me from my reverie. "C'mon, amigo, we've got places to be and things to do, and a story, of some sort, to tell."

Indeed, I was certain there was a story here. But would we find it? I knew from my dreams that I was looking for a room set back off of a corridor, and in that room was the image of an ancient cat in the position of a sphinx. Still, when I looked around at the size of the cavern, and the possibilities, it seemed like a daunting challenge.

As Professor Baal quickly gathered his team, Kendra and Margo watched from the sidelines. There was really no percentage in going into the ancient citadel in the canyon cliffs. It might be better just to wait and see who walked out of the cavern. They had decided that neither of them was particularly interested in this formula of ancient knowledge. That was way too much work. They had a contract they had taken, and the right thing to do, for their reputation, was to buck up and finish that. The problem was, they *liked* the people they were supposed to kill and *disliked* the guy who had hired them.

Oh well, business was business.

Margo had noticed a dark-colored sedan that seemed to be suspiciously close at times during the day. She mentioned it to Kendra. Her sister nodded.

"We're either being monitored or targeted by that asshole. I don't like either one," Margo said.

"Maybe we're shooting the wrong people," Kendra muttered.

While the main cavern was fairly well lit now, the illumination beyond that was still spotty. There were teams running wiring from generators but it would be days before all that was completed. The best we could do was turn on our lanterns and act as inconspicuous as possible. We knew that the citadel was established in a pattern like the spokes of a half-wheel. There was a hub around the original opening to the canyon which, thousands of years ago, led to the river, and about five spokes ran out into the cliff behind it. There was, of course, the large, circular central cavern, where we had originally come in via one of the spokes, which served as a marketplace and a business community. But all of this was too open to have housed such an essential component as the room for "devotion to community — truth, balance, and harmony…" Those were the words I kept hearing. And I still kept seeing a cat.

All the while, Will kept trying to reach Eddie on his handheld radio, just for the security of knowing that we could. But he couldn't quite get through. My friend said he could just barely hear a distant, scratchy reply. Not good…

Adding to "not good," about that time there was another slight tremor as we worked our way deeper into the interior of the underground city. Needless to say, being stuck in the bowels of a mountain at the time added a whole new dimension of discontent.

At this point, we had just come to the end of another spoke, its entrance to the outside world blocked by the dirt and debris of a thousand years, and were slowly working our way back out to the hub. We were already fairly sure that only one of the spokes in this enormous underground wheel was now open to the desert — the one we had originally uncovered. It appeared that all the others were still sealed by time, tremors, rock, and dirt.

It was about then, when we were all growing a little discouraged and somewhat overwhelmed by the task before us, that the gods threw us a small bone. When we finally reached the hub again and had made our way to the next darkened spoke/tunnel in the wheel, I saw the carved relief of a cat's face on one side of the entrance. It wasn't large — maybe a foot in diameter. But it was there. I called to my friends and showed them. We needed a sign at this point, and this was better than nothing.

It was a remarkably well-carved hallway. Like the others, the walls were nearly smooth and there were rooms along both sides. But this wing appeared as if it might have been a storage facility for the more wealthy. The interiors of the rooms weren't quite as finished and there were items of general life in many — furniture, artwork, etc. We checked each cubicle as we moved along the tunnel.

We were beginning to grow weary of this process when we came to a room that was considerably smaller than the others. It was nearly empty with the exception of a few carved chairs and empty wooden boxes with their lids thrown open — nothing of value and nothing anyone would pause about. But as we turned to leave, I stopped and stared at the bottom of the back wall, which was fairly well hidden from sight.

Will studied me. He could see that look in my eyes. He'd seen it before.

The mists were swirling around me, opening up, just as in my dream. Slowly, I walked back to the wall and knelt. I grabbed a rather large but empty trunk, and suddenly, Will was there next to me, dragging it away from the wall. We paused and everyone stared in anticipation as I brushed away the dirt and dust from the old stone with my hand. As I did, the face of a cat appeared, its body in a sphinx position, exactly like the one at the mouth of the tunnel wall. It was small, perhaps two feet in height, but there it was. I remembered, from my recent research, that the image I was seeing was referred to as "Bast," and was an Egyptian goddess worshipped in the form of a cat. She was the daughter of Ra, the sun god, and was the deity of a significant cult in ancient Memphis — of all places...

I smiled and placed my hand on the third claw of the right foot of the cat, then pushed.

Nothing happened.

"Damn, that was disappointing, Houdini," muttered Will sarcastically.

I couldn't blame him. We were all worn out — stressed well past comfortable endurance. We'd been on the run for days now, battered by the elements, chased by an arrogant sociopath, and challenged by a relentless desert. I guess we had all reached the end of our rope.

I shrugged and rose to my feet. "It was worth a try," I said.

We all turned and were in the process of filing out of the small room when there was a distinct creaking sound.

The two-foot-wide block that held the image of the cat began to slide forward. I realized that it was set on primitive rollers of a sort — very well designed and disguised. While it was twenty-four inches wide, it was only eight inches deep. The block was still remarkably heavy but somewhat maneuverable. Will and I grasped it and slid it to the side as our friends watched in open-mouthed silence.

There was a distinct pause, somewhere between anxious and unnerved, then I grabbed my flashlight, bent down, and shined it inside. The dust that had lain for centuries, stirred by our efforts and caught by my light, swirled in the still air like the currents of a river. Bent at an uncomfortable angle, with just my head inside the entrance, I realized it was a fairly sizeable room — perhaps fifteen feet square. What I noticed immediately were the jars, similar to Roman or Greek amphora. There were shelves throughout the entire room on which sat rows of perfectly formed, identical jars, oven-glazed to a perfect sheen. All of them were about a foot high and perhaps four inches wide. They narrowed at the mouth and appeared to be secured with cork or balsa plugs, then covered in a sealing wax that ran over the top and down the sides of the jars. My immediate guess was perhaps a hundred jars. There was no question what they were. I knew intellectually and intuitively, from my dream. They were the river of good and bad for mankind. I felt a shiver run down my spine. *Just a little in the water occasionally...* But my attention was also drawn to one corner, where there appeared to be neatly stacked rows of ancient scrolls.

"The mother lode..." whispered Will reverently. "We found it." And indeed, it appeared we had. I found myself equally intrigued and terrified. But the scrolls... My God, the stories those scrolls could tell! The truths they could offer and the questions they could answer. I couldn't help myself. I wiggled into the room, moved over, and gently pulled the first one out of its slot. It was terribly brittle but I knew it could be treated. *Lord, what a find!* I knelt and shuffled the scroll back out to Will, who was watching me from the small entrance, shining his flashlight inside for me.

Dax brought us around as he called, "C'mon gentlemen, don't keep us in suspense out here."

Reluctantly, I wriggled my way back out and explained our find. It was beyond extraordinary and our friends were as stunned as we were. Via the light of our lanterns, each one had to have a look at the room and the scroll I had retrieved.

We had killed a good deal of time in this whole process. I wanted to be out of there long before any sign of daylight and the influx of authorities. But I couldn't help myself — I had to crawl back into the chamber and secure a couple more of the scrolls. The first one I had taken was right off the top. However, when I went back in, I pulled one from the middle and one from near the bottom, to hopefully provide some perspective. But at that point, I was inexorably drawn to the containers — the epitome of serenity at a price. I stepped over and picked one up...

Once we had our finds safely wrapped inside heavy plastic bags and tucked into the duffle bags Will and I had brought, we were on our way out. We'd pushed our luck to the limit as it was.

But right at that point, deep underground, a fire-hardened, antediluvian geological plate was stretching its ancient sinews, slowly grinding loose from the bonds that had held it for over a million years. The last of its tenuous grip was slipping.

As we stood in the tunnel that led back to the cavern, we all felt it. This was not the inconsequential nudge from nature we had experienced recently. As the floor shook and gave slightly, we were dusted by loose dirt and gravel from a bouncing ceiling, and could hear the ancient rock around us cracking like gunshots. I realized that this was Mother Nature waking up. And she was pissed...

CHAPTER TWENTY-FOUR

In the next minute, we were moving briskly down the tunnel, headed for the central cavern. If we could slide out the way we came in, we would be on the solid earth of the high canyon. From there, a quarter-mile farther inland to the solidarity of the desert strata, and we would probably be safe — if there was a serious problem. But there was nearly constant movement around us now, and a weird crackling sound. We could see places where the ceiling of the tunnel had collapsed slightly, creating piles of rock we had to circumvent.

While we stumbled along in the blinding dust, I tried to reach Eddie. I wanted him in the air. But there was no reply.

We were three-quarters of the way out of the tunnel, coming around the bend that would put us into the main cavern, when we were hit by another punch from Mother Nature. The walls of the passageway literally shook, and this time, chunks of the heavy sandstone ceiling came tumbling down around us. Dax took a piece of rock on the shoulder and it knocked him to the ground. The rest of us were covered with dust and dirt. For the first time, Cielo was showing real distress, screeching wildly and circling around us. Jing kept calling to her hawk, trying to calm him, but for the moment, it wasn't working.

As Will helped Dax to his feet, the cowboy shook his head, then turned to all of us. "Get your parachutes out of your duffle bags and get them on," he growled.

There was no hesitation from anyone. He swung around to me. I could see blood running down the side of his head.

"Try to get Eddie on the horn and tell him to get in motion. We need him, now!"

I immediately did as my friend asked. But there was still no reply. I realized now that we might have overplayed our hand. There was a good chance that no broadcast from our VHF radio was going to get out of this cavern.

By some miracle, Jing had finally managed to call Cielo down and bring him under control. Will and I settled into our chute straps, tightened down, and grabbed our duffle bags. Tax moved over to Jing and helped get her chute secured while she held her hawk. Then he quickly slipped on his. They looked at each other, intuitively realizing that this had suddenly become far more than they had bargained for. But in the thick of it all, their eyes locked and a touch of a smile made it to their lips.

"Beats detective work on a one-horse island anytime," said Tax.

"Hoorah, little brother," Jing said with a grin.

"Hey, I was only born five minutes later than you," Tax replied. His sister shrugged. "It is what it is…"

Will and I watched the exchange. My buddy and I looked at each other.

"I've probably been prouder," said Will, "but I can't remember when."

Another rumble took us from our reverie. More dust and gravel came raining down.

"Time to go, Tonto," I said.

Will looked at me, then shook a finger. "How many times do I have to tell you? You, Tonto…me, the Lone Ranger."

Dax dusted himself off, backhanded the blood from his forehead, and glanced around at all of us. "Check your parachute straps. Tighten them down!" he said.

Again, no one hesitated.

A few minutes later, we could see the dim glow of artificial lights ahead in the main cavern but we hadn't gone another fifty yards when, suddenly, we were almost blinded by high-powered flashlights coming at us. As we adjusted somewhat to the glare, I could see a number of men gathered around a tall, thin man with stringy, yellowish hair. Aaron Baal! Beside him stood an equally tall man, but this guy was big and heavily built. He was dressed in Army fatigues and jungle boots. The man had a shaved head and carried what appeared to be a heavy-caliber "hog leg" revolver in a shoulder holster.

They were maybe seventy-five yards away. There was a very pregnant pause.

"Well, did you find it?" shouted Baal.

"Find what?" asked Dax, stepping forward.

Baal ignored him as he stared at the duffle bag I now carried in my hand. Half of one of the ancient scrolls had become displaced in the struggle through the cave and was sticking out, advertising our success.

The professor never even waited for my denial. "I told them you would figure it out," he called. "That you could find it."

The big man next to Baal stepped forward several paces. "Give it to us and we won't have to kill you," he shouted over the rumbling in the background.

Dax suddenly straightened up and stepped forward. He motioned the rest of us back, then pushed up the brim of his cowboy hat and exhaled, almost unconsciously brushing the pistol in his holster. "You're gonna have to get through me first, amigo, before you start punching holes in anyone else." He paused, took a few more steps forward, and stared at the man. "Are you up for that, mister?"

There was dead silence. The challenge was clear and while Baal may have had a gunman or two on his team, not many of them were really all that willing to die for him. They much preferred the way it was playing out here. There was a fifty-fifty chance that no one else would get shot.

I stood there, watching in awe. I couldn't believe any of this. It was like something out of an old Western. I glanced at Will, whose eyebrows went up slightly in question. At that point, Tax glanced at his sister and a message passed in their eyes. As Jing casually removed the hood off of Cielo and whispered to him, Dax slipped his pistol from his belt. I felt like I was in the middle of the OK Corral.

Before anyone else could make a decision, Baal's gunman pulled his pistol and fired. I swear, at that moment, everything seemed to go into slow motion. The bullet ripped through Dax's shirtsleeve, grazing his arm. The big Texan drew his gun and fired twice. One of those rounds struck his opponent's leg, but it didn't stop the man, who fired twice more. We all watched as Dax's hat flew off his head, the victim of a solid hit. The two men just stood there, like statues, seemingly oblivious to the death they were throwing at each other. I can't remember ever seeing anything like it, before or since...

Strangely enough, no one else had fired a shot and somehow, it hadn't deteriorated into a free-for-all. In fact, the professor's men had actually shifted back, recognizing the mano-a-mano thing that was taking place here.

The whole damned affair was straight from the streets of Tombstone a hundred years ago. Again, I'd never experienced anything even close to this situation and I'll use that as an excuse for not reacting, but there was a distinct sense about this that said neither man wanted any interference. This was their fight, the ultimate contest of courage, and it was to be lost or won on the honor of the challenge. Like a rite of passage.

If it had taken place at the reasonable distance of twenty or thirty feet, as about ninety percent of gunfights do, it would have been over pretty quickly, but sixty or seventy yards is a lot of ground when the other guy is trying to kill you too.

The two of them stood there, not dogging or dancing, but set in stone. Both of them had realized that they had come to the moment where death had its hand on their shoulder and they just didn't give a damn. Only one of them was going to walk away from this.

Suddenly, as if on cue, they were moving in at each other. The big man in the distance fired two more rounds and Dax flinched as a bullet grazed his hip. But our friend got off two quick shots himself, one of which hit Baal's man in the shoulder.

In one of the most amazing combat scenarios I had ever seen, the men were still stumbling toward each other, firing once more without great effect, then reloading their revolvers as they moved. If this wasn't enough, the walls in the cavern had begun to shake again, and everyone could sense and hear a deep grinding — a monstrous moan by Mother Nature as the stone of the cavern floor began to tremble. That primordial tectonic plate below us had finally given way, and the ancient earth that it had held in place was imploding. The cavern was beginning to collapse.

Then there was the gunfight…

The only thing that changed the game was a gamble by Dax. Bleeding in two places, all the rounds in his pistol expended, and barely able to keep on his feet on the trembling earth, he could see his opponent still coming at him while reloading his pistol. The man was ahead of him on the reload. There was no way he'd manage to get a handful of bullets into his weapon before the guy killed him. For just a moment then, I saw my friend turn and look at me. He offered a strange smile and I knew we were about to lose him…

Dax's opponent was bringing up that big pistol. I was raising my gun — to hell with the mano-a-mano bullshit. I was going to kill the guy. But at the last minute, instead of trying to completely reload his revolver, Dax punched out the spent cartridges with a quick push of the ejector rod and dropped one single bullet into a cylinder chamber.

At that same moment, Jing pointed at the big fellow and yelled something, then threw her hawk into the air. I don't recall what she said, but it was a game-changer. The man got off a shot but the huge hawk swooping in past him threw off his aim.

As his opponent's last shot whizzed by his ear, Dax snap-closed the cylinder on his revolver with a practiced flip of the wrist, brought the gun up, and fired.

The fellow in front of him was a millisecond away from pulling the trigger on his own weapon once more when the lone bullet from Dax's gun struck him on the forehead.

Somewhere I heard Rufus saying, *"Sometimes da gods, dey get bored and dey make little miracles, just for entertainment…"*

That was the good news. The bad news was, the cavern was coming apart.

CHAPTER TWENTY-FIVE

With the death of Baal's champion and the apparent imminent collapse of the cavern, it pretty much became an "every man for himself" thing. That's certainly how our nemesis, the professor, saw it. In seconds, he and his people were scrambling back toward the hub in the cavern, lost to the dust and confusion.

In a flash, we were all around Dax, supporting him and checking his wounds. Our gun-fighting hero had a sizable cut on his forehead where he'd been hit by falling debris earlier, and in-and-out damage to the flesh on his hip and the ball of his shoulder. None of these were life-threatening, yet together they represented enough trauma and blood loss to easily subdue the average person. But then, our cowboy buddy wasn't exactly the average person.

After impatiently waiting while we took two minutes to staunch his bleeding, Dax pulled himself to his feet. "Time to get the hell out of here," he barked. "Time to make a jump…"

"Sonabitch must be related to King Kong," muttered Will, with an amalgam of pride and respect.

The cavern was coming apart at the seams. Baal and the last of his people had disappeared up one of the tunnels that led toward the outside and the high desert. I figured, with all the earthquake damage in the last fifteen minutes, that was a pipe dream. This was a major earthquake. Survival was built around one thing — getting the hell out of there.

I could see the enormous opening of the cavern just ahead, facing the canyon and the river, hewn by God and finished by a race long lost. That was our goal in this terrifying contest. As we neared the huge breech, a nearly full moon was casting eerie, yellow-green hues across that truly "grand" canyon.

The cavern was imploding around us. The great walls that had been carved by Mother Nature and man were crumbling. The noise was deafening and the dust was swirling about in suffocating waves. Just when I was damned near exhausted, and surrender seemed an inevitable option, Tax suddenly had my arm, forcing me along, shouting encouragement to me and the others. Ahead, I could see that Jing had found her dad. Somewhere above us, I heard Cielo cry out.

The great maw of the cavern was coming up fast. I could just make out the last stars in a blue-black morning sky. I wanted to tell Tax how proud I was of him — how amazed I was at what he had become (with the lousy genes of a self-centered adventurer and an amorous meerkat of a mother), but at that moment, we were at the lip of the huge cleft. The nearly endless cliffs and the river below stretched out like the blue-gray painting of a deranged Van Gogh. I could hear Dax, ever the hero, bringing up the rear, shouting encouragement, last man out as always.

I don't really remember leaping but I know I did. I do recall the wind in my face and the dark, winding river below coming up at me with remarkable speed and clarity. I don't recall pulling my ripcord, but I did feel the jerk of the chute as it blossomed. I think I peed my pants somewhere along the line in that dark and frightening chimera.

The last thing I remember clearly, before being lost to the immediate challenges of flaring out and touching down on the huge gravel beach that abutted the winding river, was glancing up and seeing my companions' parachutes silhouetted against the moon above me. I could see Jing's remarkable hawk, huge wings distended in a tight glide, working a circle around his mistress, watching and protecting her as she glided downward. We should all possess such loyalty...

And I suddenly thought of my Irish friend, Connor O'Connor, who would have said that we looked like a "bloody bevy of Mary Poppins lookalikes all floating down on their flippin' umbrellas."

It was a strange time for retrospect, but I realized I missed that bloody Irishman.

I was snapped back to brutal reality as, in the distance, upriver, the cavern mouth crumbled inwards and the cliffs that had protected their ancient secret for so long imploded, cascading down in a huge conglomerate of rock, dust, and lost history. The slightest of bitter smiles touched my lips. Given that god-awful destruction, there wasn't a chance in hell that the arrogant bastard, Professor Aaron Baal, had made it out of there alive.

Somehow, we all managed to land on the large, half-mile curve of gravel beach that Crazy Eddie had shown us on his charts a few days earlier, about a mile south of the now-disintegrated cavern. As we shined our flashlights into the darkness, calling out, trying to find each other as the earth trembled beneath our feet, we slowly, gratefully, gathered.

For the next half hour we collected our gear as best we could. The great canyon around us was still trembling with aftershocks but it appeared that the largest portion of the collapse was over. With the moon as a lantern, we could see that the very walls of the Grand Canyon had come tumbling down in numerous places. I couldn't help but wonder how the area towns and cities had fared. During much of that time, I also found myself wondering what had happened to our pilot and his Goose...

But right about that time, as if the gods had heard me, I sensed a distant drone. It was faint, and at first, I thought it might be my imagination. I shrugged. At this point, all we had was hope. I lost the sound for a few moments, then there it was again, echoing off the battered walls of the canyon, growing stronger.

Moments later, Crazy Eddie and his magnificent bird came soaring around the far bend. I couldn't remember a more consoling sight. In minutes, Eddie had his plane on the river, then pulled into a rough sand cove near us. We all stumbled over like a scene from *The Living Dead* — and indeed, we weren't too far from that.

In the end, it was little more than a miracle. We had all made it down safely. There were a few cuts and bruises from contact with the rough canyon exterior, and our champion, Dax, needed some specific first aid and some downtime, but as my old flight instructor used to say, "Any landing you walk away from..."

In addition, and equally as miraculous, was the fact that I had somehow held on to my duffle bag during the jump from the cliff and the landing in the gravel by the river. All its precious contents were still intact.

By sunrise, we had gathered the gear we could salvage and were loading aboard the Goose. Eddie had explained that he'd lost radio contact with us shortly after the first major portion of the quake — probably a combination of atmospheric and geological conditions. But the ground was shaking so badly, and fissures were opening around him to the point that he didn't think he could get out. The moment it slowed enough to offer him a window, he was in the air.

I couldn't wait to be in the air. I couldn't wait to make this all a memory.

We landed in Tusayan, or what was left of it. The earthquake that had torn up the Grand Canyon had seriously shaken the small town as well. Buildings were damaged and roads were buckled. The little airport had taken a hit too, but most of the damage was at one end. Given the wind direction, we were at least able to get in and find treatment for our injured, especially Dax, who was cleaned up, stitched up, and shot up with pain medicine. The motels in the area were full, accommodating displaced people and emergency personnel, so we climbed back in our aircraft and headed south to Phoenix. As Crazy Eddie so succinctly put it, it was time to get the hell out of Dodge.

———————

Margo and Kendra, who had survived the earthquake with little more than being thoroughly pissed off with a wasted trip and wasted time, also decided to get out of Dodge. It had been a mildly entertaining affair, up to the freaking earthquake. But now, whether they liked it or not, it was time to kill somebody and earn some money...

CHAPTER TWENTY-SIX

We sailed along in silence, just below and ahead of a dreary, occluded front. Most everyone was lost to their own thoughts. Eddie had the controls. I asked if I could take them for him but our old buddy was feeling too guilty about not getting to us right away, when we needed him in the canyon, and he insisted on keeping the left seat. Given the situation, I slipped back into the cabin to check on Dax, who was dealing with a lot of pain, and the kids, who seemed to have performed remarkably well through this whole affair. Finally, I checked on my buddy, Will. I sat down next to my friend and we asked each other about our minor injuries and marveled, once again, at our remarkable luck. Then, as we did so often, we slipped into conversation.

I sighed and turned to my friend. "How do you think history is going to record all this, even if we do get all our information out?"

"History," Will muttered skeptically. "She's a fickle bitch who always favors the winners…or the heroic losers." He sighed heavily. "It's not that history is really so fickle — it's more that the architects of history, both religious and academic, have always taken what they wanted and discarded the rest. They've carved the meat from the bone in many a place to preserve their precious, sometimes faulty conceptions of faith, truth, and fact. Religious and academic history is always left to the interpretations of the winners — their words and deeds emboldened and glamorized to make a point."

There was silence for a moment, then Will picked up again. He couldn't help himself.

"And truth…" he sputtered. "What a slippery, malleable word. We've carved our versions of it in stone all over the world, but wet clay would probably have been more appropriate. Religion, ego, and power are the architects of most of the 'truths' we've handed down. Unfortunately, real truth rarely survives the test of time. Things are constantly getting rewritten by whoever holds the reins of power." He paused and looked at me. "We constantly seem to be tearing down statues of people whose accomplishments no longer fit the times. With the blind arrogance of a 'now' mentality, we destroy the great yardsticks of human culture." My friend huffed out a sigh. "In the end, we'll be playing with bones in the dirt and wondering what those shattered and misshapen lumps of concrete and metal actually were."

I started to make a comment but Will was off again.

"And faith..." he said. "Without this single element, I don't think man would have made the climb to a greater collective soul. But most of our faiths simply don't believe in the ability to expand intellectually. They're terrified of that." My friend drew a breath. "Ultimately, faith isn't much more than something like a child's old blanket or the distinct smell of home — the fact that we know it's there is all that's necessary. In the end, it's perfectly okay to find your own peace with your own god, but you should never be permitted to take away someone else's 'old blanket' in the process."

After an evening in Phoenix with some good food and a solid night's sleep, we were all doing much better. We still had to "cross the pond" from New Orleans to the Keys, but we were out of the woods and we were headed home.

It was a long ride the following day, but finally, a glimpse of that curling necklace of sand, marl, and palms at the end of Florida was indeed a welcome sight. After landing, we were greeted by Customs, who took one look at all of us and decided to check things fairly well. It did them no good. Anything important (like my duffle containing the ancient scrolls) had found its way to Eddie's secret cubbyholes. I really wanted to get that duffle bag home and hidden somewhere.

It had been a long, damned hard trip. But it looked like this wild episode in our lives was coming to a close. Surely, after all this, our psychotic ex-girlfriends would just move on. (Take another contract and find someone else to kill for money, someone new to stalk, hopefully...) Hell, as far as I could tell, they thought we were dead.

The good news was, at least that bastard, Professor Aaron Baal, was history. He had to be. Not even Clark Kent and his best cape could have taken that much rock and kept on ticking.

When we were finding our cars at the airport and everyone was starting, almost reluctantly, to go in their own directions, I gave Tax and Jing huge, lingering hugs. (God, I was starting to act like a parent. It was a strange but not a necessarily bad thing.) I also asked our cowboy, Dax, if he'd like to stay with me for a while. He was stiff and in pain. But he refused, saying he needed to get his dog and make sure his horse was okay. I knew the truth. He was like an old bear. He just needed to curl up in a cave and weather the healing process.

After we picked up his boy, Smoke, at my place and made sure his pickup started, he turned to me and in his typically succinct style said, "Thanks for the adventure, amigo. You proved to be a damned fine sidekick." Then he offered a genuinely warm smile. "Long as I got a biscuit, you got half."

Finally, we'd all parted ways and the crescendo had passed. We were left with a remarkable sense of accomplishment, but I could tell there was a lingering tinge of melancholy. It was over, but it wasn't forgotten.

Like Crazy Eddie said, "It was a damned rough flight in places, but it wouldn't be a barroom tale otherwise." He smiled and offered one of his truisms. "Ya gotta remember, this whole life gig ain't about arriving safe and pretty on the other side — more like skidding in broadside, used up, worn to the nub, and shoutin' 'Damn! What a freakin' ride!'"

CHAPTER TWENTY-SEVEN

The next few days were actually sort of peaceful. The miserable bastard professor Baal was apparently dead. The news was, there were no survivors in the Grand Canyon disaster and the damage was so comprehensive (about five miles of collapsed canyon wall) that no one was likely to try to dig anyone or anything out. Ever...

It was terrific to see my boy, Shadow, again. He wouldn't leave my side. (Okay, after the first twenty-four hours he did slip over to see his girlfriend next door. But beyond that, he lived up to his name.) Still, I kept waiting for the other shoe to drop. But it didn't. Actually, we all needed some time to ourselves.

Will, our historian, did ask me during a phone call what the plans were for the papyrus scrolls we had managed to retrieve from the small room in the cavern. I told him to start looking for a good interpreter. Two days later, he called me. He'd found a fellow in Georgia — an Egyptian hieroglyphics specialist with the University of Atlanta.

I wasn't sure. We faced a quandary there. To find out more of the firsthand history of this most fascinating, if not misplaced segment of ancient Egyptians, someone else would have to know that information. The question was, how much, if any, of that information in those scrolls mentioned the possible "kumbaya" additive in the water? I wasn't happy about that.

Speaking of "kumbaya" additives, there was one other issue... When I had been alone for a few moments in that small room in the cavern (the room dedicated to the Egyptian goddess, Bast, daughter of the sun god and protector of souls), I had picked up one of the oven-glazed, foot-tall jars and, knowing full well what was in it, I put it in my bag. I knew, even as it happened, that it was a huge, dangerous mistake. I mean, what if this substance managed to find its way into the narcissistic, mercenary world we know today? But I couldn't help myself. I never looked at the action in terms of personal power, but perhaps with a knowledge that it would surely be lost otherwise. Now I found myself wondering whether it shouldn't just have been lost.

However, the scrolls were another matter.

Will and I booked flights to Atlanta and the following day, we were meeting with a short, acerbic-looking older man with graying hair and inquisitive blue eyes. He was very much the typical intellectual introvert — seemingly uncomfortable with people but anxious to get right to it. Almost too anxious. But we'd come this far…

We sat in his office as he carefully opened each scroll, and after a few minutes of airing, he sprayed them lightly with a moisturizing sealant. For the next hour, he read quietly, hardly looking up.

When he finished reading, he shook his head incredulously and sighed. Then he took a breath. "Each scroll covers the highlights of a ten-year period. But what's most remarkable is, there appeared to have been a secret society of compilers who collected this information down through the ages, each storing his scrolls in the same place." The man looked at us for a moment, then continued. "Possibly the most fascinating was the first one because it briefly covered the trials and tribulations of a new people in a strange new land. There were places and things I didn't understand, so I'm giving you a rather abridged version."

The professor took a drink of water and continued. "During this time of arrival in the canyon there were huge challenges but there was also a tremendous common hope for a new Egypt."

As he spoke, we heard, hidden in the words, the message regarding the elixir of the Anunnaki — the "pride of the common good," "the betterment of the nest," "the honor in selflessness." Without question, it had been used liberally to gently bind that new society. For the first couple hundred years, things seemed to be okay — if you were a communist. There was a good deal about "giving yourself over to the whole" and "communal mindsets."

The second scroll, from around the middle of the North American Egyptian narrative, still showed a coherent society moving forward, subduing indigenous tribes to the point of owning a good deal of the property along the Grand Canyon. But there didn't seem to be an effort to incorporate their neighbors. It appeared they preferred their pure racial autonomy. "For the better of the whole," the author said. Still, after all these years, there was that Orwellian tone to the discourse. Nonetheless, while one could still discern some "passion for the hive," there was an undercurrent now that subtly implied a weariness of sorts. It almost appeared as if they had collectively passed the peak…and there was more of a blind sense of conformity now, rather than a desire for the betterment of the whole.

"They were now a society of at least two 'hubs' then, as they called them, and a third was being sought at the time," our interpreter continued. "But while this particular author still carries some dedication to the whole, he seems to lack the enthusiasm of the earlier chronicler."

Yes, a lack of enthusiasm was probably a good term…

The last scroll was the most definitive, impacting, and somber. It seemed that even with the secret elixir of the Anunnaki (or perhaps because of it), this displaced Egyptian society had morphed into ambivalence. This particular chronicler was weary, and while you could still find the swirls of the ancient potion in his words on occasion, it seemed as if they were a people just going through the motions now. The drug had long since lost its ability to "peak" in the metabolism and had become a habit rather than an aid, and the people had become blindly obedient without that spark of "the desire to better the present" or the need to question.

Moreover, that last scroll told of the desert meeting with the Spanish conquistadors and the wholesale death that followed. It related the confusion at the beginning, when people began to break out in pustules, then fade and die, and how, at first, the people in the infected cavern escaped to the second city, only to find they had brought death with them. It soon became an indiscriminate march into the extinction of an entire society.

When our meeting was over, we realized that we had received our money's worth in this translation but we had opened a Pandora's box by trusting someone with this knowledge. In the end, Will managed to assuage a little of our concern. When we were packing up and preparing to leave, my partner suddenly garnered a sullen, almost harsh demeanor, and moved over to the man, their faces almost touching.

"What happened here today never happened," he grated. "Do you understand?" Before the startled man could answer, Will continued harshly, "We're here with you today because our last interpreter told his wife what he had read." My partner paused. "His wife had an…*accident.* Apparently, walked out in front of a speeding car and was killed." Will riveted the fellow again. "A tragic situation..."

As we headed back to the rental car, I smiled and turned to my buddy. "Your talents just continually seem to grow."

My friend chuckled. "All the world's a stage," he said, quoting Shakespeare and holding out his hands. Will grinned. "Shit, that was nothing compared to some of the distractions we pulled off in the early days."

What we couldn't have known was that the hieroglyphics specialist we'd just visited hated his wife. She was sucking his personal accounts dry with purchases of everything from designer clothes to cars. But a divorce probably wouldn't solve his problem. She was screwing his lawyer. He considered the recent threat he'd received, then shrugged. He had nothing to lose, really. He picked up the phone and made a call. The worst that could happen was he'd get paid a tidy sum for the call, and if those two guys with the scrolls found out, they would kill his wife. Gee...too bad...

By the following afternoon, we were back in the Keys. We had learned a great deal but none of it made us feel any more favorable toward that ancient concoction. It was an affirmation of how I had always felt. *There is no such thing as a good addiction.*

And I had come to a decision. The Egyptian Pandora's box hidden in the bottom of my closet had to go...

CHAPTER TWENTY-EIGHT

I don't know why I hadn't told anyone else about taking the fire-glazed jar of powdered ancient Egyptian Kool-Aid, but I hadn't. It was still in my closet.

No, wait... I knew exactly why — because taking it had been a freaking incredibly stupid thing to do on my part. Nonetheless, when we got home, after our informative trip to Atlanta, I realized I had to get rid of it. I always felt better having Will close by in sticky situations, so I sat him down in my living room and told him the story.

"Whoa shit!" my buddy hissed, staring up at the ceiling. "Stupid, stupid, stupid!" He turned to me. "God! Think about it! If that concoction was to get into the hands of...crap...just about anybody, from the Patriot Movement to the American Atheist's League! From the Catholic Church to the International Satanic Temple!" He threw up his arms. "Hell, from the communists to Jane Fonda!" Will caught himself, slapping his forehead. "Wait — that's the same thing..."

I put out a hand before this tumbled into one of his "rolls." "Yeah, yeah, you're right, okay? Now we need to figure out how to get rid of it."

Will exhaled heavily and started to calm down. "Yeah, well, if it's as concentrated as those scrolls seemed to indicate, we can't just flush it down the toilet. We'd have half of the Lower Keys stumbling around singing 'Everything is Beautiful' and praying to images of Ronald McDonald. And I don't think we can dump it in the ocean," my friend added. "No telling what that might lead to. We've got to dump it somewhere on dry land, and maybe pour something on it afterward to dilute or destroy it."

The truth was, we were probably freaking out more than was necessary. It wasn't a thousand pounds of uranium. It was just a formula that made folks enthusiastically congenial. You know, to where they loved the sound of "the hive"...

Okay...that was pretty dangerous...

I was reminded of an expression by Rufus — *"The legacy of the hasty monkey is the furry taste left in the lion's mouth."*

There was one other thing that had me just a little

uncomfortable. We hadn't heard a thing from Kendra and Margo. I was beginning to wonder whether they might have followed us into the cavern and been caught in the collapse, or if Baal might have punched their tickets just before the cavern/earthquake affair. I mean, they scared the crap out of me but I didn't necessarily want to see them dead. Just somebody else's problem... Maybe someone in, say, Argentina. Or Japan.

That afternoon, Will and I had just about decided to dig a hole and dump the powder on the high ground of Big Pine Key, when the doorbell rang. I would have expected a growl from Shadow but I remembered he was next door, visiting with our neighbor's Rottweiler.

I looked at Will and his eyebrows bounced upwards. He glanced at the door, then turned back to me. "Are you expecting someone?"

I shook my head. "No..." I got up cautiously, walked over, and opened the door. There stood a guy in a baseball cap and a nondescript, gray short-sleeved shirt, holding a clipboard.

"Hi!" he said congenially. "I'm with the electric company. We're getting some fluctuating readings in this subdivision. Can I come in and test one of your receptacles?"

I don't know why, but I was immediately skeptical. There was nothing official about what he had on and he didn't have any equipment with him. "I...I don't think so..." I said. "Not right now. How about you wear something official and come back tomorrow?"

The guy shrugged, unperturbed. Then he drew a small pistol. "How about you let me in and I don't shoot you both?"

It seemed like a reasonable request at the time, all things considered. The guy motioned us back into the living room while glancing around. He pulled the two-way radio from his hip. "Okay, I'm in."

A moment later, I could hear a vehicle pull up. Then there was the sound of people coming up the steps to the deck. The door opened and in stepped the inscrutable — and obviously somewhat difficult to snuff — Professor Aaron Baal, with two other men.

"Son of a bitch!" muttered Will, with as much bewilderment as anger.

"As you can see, I am still alive," said Baal with an ugly smile.

"How about you let me try again and we'll see if we can get it to stick," I whispered under my breath.

"Too late," said Baal. "It was, I admit, a thoroughly frightening run that night, through that collapsing tunnel, but I made it. It's my turn now to turn the tables. But first, I want the clay vase." He paused, savoring our surprise. "The one with the ancient ingredients — the secret of the Anunnaki."

Will and I both took a step back in shock and surprise. "How in the hell?" hissed Will. "How could you know?" Then the light bulb came on.

Baal saw it in our eyes. "Yes, your professor in Atlanta decided to make a deal." He held out his hands. "Trust no one, ever, and only then do you stand a chance. Now, to business." His eyes narrowed. "I will have the scrolls and I will have the vase, or I will kill you both so slowly that death will become an exquisite pleasure."

As we stood there in shock, the professor continued.

"The cipher specialist you used suspected that you possessed something. And...you talk to yourself when you are in a quandary."

It was obvious that Baal and his people had bugged the house. I had to admit it was a shrewd, anticipatory move on his part. The guy was a bastard but he was a clever bastard.

I had to ask. "What happened to Margo and Kendra?"

The man just offered a humorless smile and shrugged, but his eyes were ugly.

Margo and Kendra...gone? Dead? It was a strange damned thing but that concept found a place in the pit of my stomach and ground its high heels. I mean, I wasn't actually in love with Kendra, and to me, she and Margo had been "challenging" without a doubt. But they had been a good portion of the spicy seasoning in my life. And I found myself genuinely sorrowful.

At that moment, any congeniality Baal might have possessed fell away. He held out his hand. "The vase. Now. Last opportunity before the pain begins."

There was no use in resisting. I sighed. "It's in my bedroom closet. Bottom right, on the floor, covered with dirty laundry. The scrolls are there too."

The professor nodded to one of his men and the fellow headed down the hall. A moment later, he was back. Baal acknowledged the scrolls but he reached for the jar like it was a newborn. It was obvious, through research and intuition, even without listening to our conversations, that he knew how influential this discovery was. After a moment of gloating, he turned to his people and pointed at us.

"Bring them with us. I don't want anyone finding their bodies here." He paused. "We may just kick them out of the plane after we get underway. There'll be no bodies to find that way. And call ahead to the airport. Tell the pilot I want to be ready to depart the moment we arrive."

"That has a purely ominous ring to it," muttered Will.

I felt my stomach do a little flip-flop but I wasn't ready to give up. "Every moment you're alive is a moment you're not dead."

Having been a little busy recently, neither Will nor I knew that Jimmy Buffett had just come into town and was planning an impromptu concert at Key West's Bayview Park that evening, so everything was packed a little tighter, from the bars and restaurants to the roadways. Especially U.S. 1. Not that it made much difference for us but it explained the slow pace down the Keys.

Will and I were packed a little tight ourselves — tightly bound on the floorboards in the back of a utility van. Baal and his big bodyguard sat in the only two passenger's seats, and the other man drove. His other two companions were following us in their car. I know it had to have pained the professor to be riding in a utility van but it showed his dedication to survival. I would have been less pleased to know that Baal had his plane brought into the private hangar section of the airport, tucked away from prying eyes. There was little chance of rescue here. No one knew about us. No one would witness this. But he wasn't quite right about that...

Tax had been on his way over to our house that morning to show us his new pickup (his first "new" car) when he saw the van parked by my home. Instinct and intuition kicked in and he paused several hundred yards away, watching for a few moments. Then he saw Baal and his people shuffling us down the stairs.

Tax had immediately called Jing with his new VHF phone, then followed the van. He tried Dax but there was no answer, so he left a frantic message about following a car into Key West.

After about forty-five minutes, I could tell we were into Key West and traveling down South Roosevelt Boulevard toward the airport, just by the long, curving, left turn after reaching the island. Baal was talking about his eight-passenger Cessna 425 turboprop — a respectable aircraft with a custom sliding passenger's door from which we could be easily shoved. He was enjoying himself.

Everything seemed to be in order for him when suddenly, a pickup came barreling out of Duck Avenue and onto Roosevelt. The truck squarely struck the right front of the van as Baal's driver made an evasive turn, and both vehicles skidded to a stop. Tax's new pickup was still in the street but the van had spun and was up on the sidewalk. The front right door was thrown open in the impact and in the process *("Da gods, dey love a coincidence...")*, Professor Baal's briefcase containing the ancient container of magic dust had bounced out the door, across the adjacent sidewalk, and into a row of shrubs. Baal was incapacitated for a moment when he was slammed into the window frame and didn't see this happen.

CHAPTER TWENTY-NINE

While we're mentioning timing and fate, there was one other curious act playing out in this little theater of life.

Buffett's concerts always drew a solid, modern crowd, but there was always that old hippie element as well. One of those was Willie Benjamin, commonly known as "Lost Willie." A true hippie by every sense of the word, Willie had found the sixties when he was seventeen and never left them. He had wandered across the southern U.S. for over thirty years, working when he had to but mostly searching for the next concert and the next high. He smoked a lot of pot. Actually, as long as he had it, he was using it.

Willie just happened to be camping out under the hedge in the back of the house next to our accident, which woke him up. The oddest damned thing was, he'd just come around from the loud bang when he saw this briefcase come bouncing across the sidewalk right at him. It slid under the hedge and stopped right in front of his bleary, still-struggling-to-focus eyes.

He figured it was a dream. He had lots of dreams about pot being magically delivered to him. He cautiously grabbed the handle (it didn't disappear or turn into a snake — all that was good) and pulled it through the hedge.

Just before the accident, Tax had left another frantic message for Dax, telling him he suspected Baal was headed for the airport and a private plane. His sister had obviously been trapped in the god-awful traffic and he needed to keep the professor from getting away. He couldn't just start shooting. How exactly do you explain trying to shoot an official of one of the largest historical institutions in the United States?

The professor and his people were thoroughly hammered by the impact but unfortunately, it hadn't seriously damaged the van. The quick-thinking driver was already yelling about closing the doors while grinding the starter. In a moment, the vehicle was backing up.

In the impact, Tax had blown a front tire. He could change the tire but he was out of the chase and the van was getting away.

It took the professor a couple of minutes to come around. They were turning into the section of the airport for private aircraft when he suddenly noticed his briefcase was gone. He turned white and screamed.

Regardless of the risk, Baal and his people returned to the site of the accident. The pickup had limped away and the police were just arriving. Baal had the driver park a couple of blocks down the road. He got out and hurriedly returned to the scene but the briefcase was gone, as if it had disappeared in a puff of magician's smoke. The professor wanted to scream, to hammer on something or kill someone. But in the end he knew — he unequivocally knew — the vase was gone.

Lost Willie found a quiet place in a small neighborhood park a few blocks away. He squatted down by an empty merry-go-round and opened the case. At first he was pretty disappointed — just some old, rolled-up papers in a weird language, which he tossed in the dumpster, and a vase of some sort. It took a little doing but he managed to twist the old cork top off of the jar. He sniffed the contents. It smelled ancient but it had the smell of, and carried the consistency of, ground herb. He poured a little in his hand and took a whiff of it, then put a little on his tongue. It didn't taste bad — musty but not bad, so he got out his trusty "papers" and rolled himself a small spliff.

In just a few minutes, he found himself "lightly lifted" — sort of on the edge of a groovy, soft high. The odd part was, he felt... nice... Like in the old sixties songs, Simon and Garfunkel's "Feelin' Groovy" and The Monkees' "Daydream Believer." He didn't quite understand it but he felt like he wanted to do something...good... You know, man? Something for "the whole"...

Normally, he would have sold this stash to the highest bidder he could find, then taken the cash and run, but somehow he felt more like sharing it than selling it. He wanted everyone to feel this "connection to the center." He wanted everyone to get this strange but cool "attachment to the whole world." So...Lost Willie took some of the last of his precious change, walked to the closest store, and bought several boxes of small plastic bags. It took him an hour, under the shade of the Australian pines by the playground, but he packaged up about a hundred nickel bags. He knew these would get shared several times over at the Jimmy Buffett concert this afternoon, and probably for several days to come. It was a great gift to give, man. It made him feel...cool...good... It connected him. It was groovy.

The good news was, Baal had not only lost his scrolls but his ancient Egyptian Kool-Aid as well. The bad news was, Will and I were still in the back of a van that was once again limping toward the hangar where Professor Baal had his plane. It was very likely that we would be in the air directly, and not too long after that, my friend and I would be fish food after an exhilarating fall from the professor's aircraft.

A few moments later, Baal's van eased to a stop.

"This is not good," said Will. "This is where the Lone Ranger is supposed to show up."

He was right on both accounts but there was no sign of a big guy in a cowboy hat wearing a thin, black mask.

In less than a minute, Baal's two men had pulled us out of the van, dragged us over, and unceremoniously pushed us into the cabin of the big twin-engine plane. The other two of his men, who were already aboard, pulled us in.

They didn't even bother with seats for us. They just left us in the aisle. What the hell did a seat matter? It was going to be a short flight for us anyway.

Baal came over and knelt beside us before taking his seat. There was a gleam of victory and viciousness in his eyes. "You have cost me much over the last week or so," he whispered. The professor smiled but there was no humor to be found. Actually, there was an image of distraction and anxiety. Like a man on the edge. "But, he who laughs last..." he muttered.

"We're ready to roll at your order, sir," said the pilot from the cockpit. "Tower has given us clearance."

A minute later, the professor had taken his seat. He was a seriously bitter soul. Not only had he lost the scrolls and the incredible Egyptian formula, but he had been beaten at every turn by a handful of commoners. Bloody treasure-hunting mercenaries! The damage control would be challenging at best. The anger of failure was seeping into his bloodstream, overriding common sense and caution. His hands were shaking. The only compensation he would have at this point would be watching these two tumble out the side door at five thousand feet.

We were moving away from the hangar toward the taxiway. Will shuffled himself around on the floor next to me, to where we could see each other's faces.

"I think this is it, ol' buddy," he said, as the pilot swung the plane onto the taxiway and headed for the threshold of the runway. "Could be that we're fresh out of magic dust…"

The big twin came around briskly at the threshold, did a quick run-up, and immediately requested and received clearance for takeoff. This was it. Once we were in the air, we were dead. Baal's pilot pushed his throttles forward and the big twin responded lithely. We were picking up speed. In twenty seconds or so, we would be airborne — and Will and I would be history.

I was about to reply when we heard a randy expletive from the pilot.

"Son of a bitch," he blurted.

Suddenly, the tower came back on the radio. "Cessna N422SL, Cessna N422SL, you have a civilian vehicle on your runway! I repeat, you have a pickup truck proceeding directly at you. Please stand down and power back immediately."

The pilot, not certain what to do, and knowing the temperament of the mercurial Professor Baal, broke off with the tower and looked back toward the cabin. "Sir, we've got a pickup truck coming right at us."

Baal was already stumbling toward the cockpit. Sure enough, well in the distance but without question, there was a red pickup truck just coming out of the opposite threshold and charging down the center of the strip. He could just make out a big man standing in the bed of the truck, leaning over the cab roof. The guy was wearing a cowboy hat and he had one of those Western, lever-action rifles in his hands. The image hammered Baal with bitter recollection. *The cowboy! The damned cowboy from the cavern gunfight!*

The professor had experienced all the losses for one week that his ego and his temperament could stand. His face went hard. "Push the throttles to the damned wall!" he yelled.

"But sir!" yelled the pilot, who realized there was only a small chance...

Grabbing the pilot's shoulder hard enough to make him wince, Baal screamed again. "Get us into the air, now!"

Dax, his big upper frame braced on the roof of the pickup cab, had waited on firing, hoping just the image he and Tax presented would dissuade the pilot from takeoff. The two had tied up via their new VHF phones — something I had insisted we all have, given the recent circumstances. Dax, who had finally checked his answering machine and realized what was happening, found my son after his accident on Flagler Avenue and they had dashed for the airport in the cowboy's pickup.

But all that was small change now, as the plane and the truck raced at each other in a terminal game of chicken.

As they closed the distance, Dax realized that no one was going to give. Tax, in the driver's seat below him, clutched the wheel with the single-minded tenacity of a dying man — and maybe he was. All he knew for sure was that his dad and Will had been dragged out of the house and thrown into Baal's van back on Big Pine. Somehow, instinctively, he knew I was on that plane. At that moment, he knew if Baal got away now, I was dead. That aircraft was not going to get off the ground, even if it meant his life.

The nose of the big twin was lifting. Baal was yelling at the terrified pilot, who had the throttles to the wall and was pulling back on the controls. The stall warning was screaming and the pickup was less than a hundred yards in front of them, but the plane was beginning to rise. It looked like they were going to make it.

But at that moment, the cowboy in the truck in front of them fired three times, working the lever action on that old rifle with blurring speed. The starboard prop splintered, then disintegrated. The big Cessna started to roll precariously but the pilot threw back the throttle on the damaged engine, slammed the opposite rudder pedal, and drew off the throttle slowly on the good engine. The good news was, he'd saved an immediate roll of the aircraft and certain death for its occupants. The bad news was, they had dropped back down onto the tarmac and after a solid bounce or two, were headed right for the oncoming pickup. There was less than seventy-five yards between the two vehicles — a blink of an eye...

At that point, Tax reacted on pure instinct, throwing the truck hard to the right. As the pickup skidded away from the nose of the plane, Dax dropped into the bed. The pilot reacted by dropping flaps on the port wing to try to get it to lift a little while hitting the brakes. It worked and the wing of the Cessna raised just enough to barely scrape the roof of the cab, right where Dax had just been. The plane skidded off the runway in a sideways canter before coming to a sliding, earth-gouging halt between the east and west runways.

Will and I were bounced around but not harmed. In the silence after the crash, we were almost eyeball to eyeball on the floor.

"You okay, buddy?" I asked.

"Yeah, I think so," my friend said cautiously. Will winced a little when he moved. "Nothing that a couple of margaritas wouldn't cure."

For all intents and purposes, it looked as if Professor Baal was in serious trouble but the damned man was quick on his feet. Remarkably quick. As he undid his seatbelt, he yelled at his men.

"Get the handcuffs off of those two and get them into seats. I want things to look...normal." He paused and stared at us while speaking to his men. "If they start to say one word to the authorities about any of this, kill them. I don't care where we are — kill them! A hundred thousand dollars to the man who does it!"

It was a long afternoon, given the time with the local authorities and the FAA, and whoever else they could find to question us. The good news was, we were all alive. The professor had no opportunity to do anything to us before airport accident and rescue crews were through the doors of the plane and we were separated. The bad news was, the authorities thought that Will and I were brain damaged when we explained that Professor Aaron Baal was trying to kill us because, basically, we had some ancient Egyptian scrolls and magic dust that he wanted. When the authorities asked for proof (specifically, the magic dust or the scrolls), we couldn't produce it. They apologized to the eminent executive of one of the largest historical institutions in America and released him and his people. The FFA arrested Dax for discharging a weapon in a Federal environment, and charged Tax with malicious criminal trespass.

They were being held at the Monroe County Sheriff's Department.

Jing had finally arrived in Key West. There had been a terrible accident on U.S. Highway 1, just before Big Coppit Key, and she had been trapped for over an hour. Then she had to wait out the traffic into town.

CHAPTER THIRTY

All the while, Jimmy Buffet had come to town and done another remarkable show in the park, and Lost Willie had gone about giving ancient magic dust in nickel bags to anyone who wanted one. That magic dust, in the form of tightly rolled spliffs, probably made its way in the next few days to a quarter of Key West. Everyone who tried it just loved it and wanted to share it. We're not just talking about smokers and jokers here. This was Key West — nearly everyone smoked a little. There were city officials, real estate agents, banking clerks, teachers, college professors, a handful of police officers, nurses, doctors, cabbies, and God knows who else.

The product was ancient and it apparently had a very short half-life because of that. The sensations that probably should have lasted for the better part of a couple of months lingered for about two weeks. But during that time, Key West appeared to be under a spell of kumbaya. No one had ever seen anything like it. There seemed to be a distinct desire to glide with the flow, a sense of "serving the whole " and "working for the better good." For Key West, that was really weird. But very nice.

Ultimately, it was like Will said. In the end, no one was any smarter or any more honest or dedicated, they just didn't seem to suffer quite so much from greed and lust for control of any sort during those few short weeks. And no one understood why. Some related it to an astronomical occurrence. Some in the religious community said it was a message from God — a small miracle. Others were smart enough to relate it to that damned remarkable pot they smoked. But no one could find more of it.

Lost Willie took the last few baggies of "the good stuff" and put them in his backpack. Then he bought a bus ticket for New Orleans and he, too, was gone. But then, he was gone most of the time, even when he was here.

It took a couple of days but a good Miami attorney, along with letters of character from the Key West Police Department and the area DEA, managed to get Dax's charges reduced to reckless endangerment, for which he would serve thirty days. (Fifteen with good behavior.) He was fined five thousand dollars, which Will and I gladly paid.

Tax's charges of malicious criminal trespass were reduced to unlawful entering and he ended up with a personal apology to the judge and a thousand dollar fine. (Money well spent on my part.) Much of this largesse on the part of the judge was due to letters from friends of ours in the DEA and area law enforcement. My friends and I didn't always play by the rules but they knew we were the good guys, and they supported us when the chips were down. Our friends in authority suspected something was fishy, with Baal dragging us off like he did. But no one could prove anything.

I was greatly relieved, on one hand, but I was as nervous as hell on the other. Somehow, I just knew Professor Aaron Baal wasn't going to graciously accept defeat. It was bad enough for him that he was publically questioned regarding our "abduction," which he claimed was absolute idiocy. Ultimately, his institution, with its international standing, won out. He apologized for "the misunderstanding" with Will and me, claiming that we had been flying back with him to file a final report on the collapse of the cavern and the estimated loss of antiquities. After all, we were firsthand witnesses. He claimed that we had become rude and unruly prior to takeoff — possibly because of alcohol or drug use, which led to a mild altercation.

After installing a new prop on his plane the following day, he was gone. The eminent professor had been neglecting the duties of his office in Washington. He needed to amend that. He wasn't immune to criticism and he didn't need the negative publicity that this last incident had invited. That was the only reason Baal gave up as easily as he did.

Inside of a few days, it had all blown over. There was always something going on in Key West. It was a perpetual circus. Although, in the few moments of introspection I was allowed, I was saddened by the disappearance of Kendra and Margo. There wasn't a word from them and they hadn't done that freaky thing of just appearing out of thin air, as they did so often…just to screw with your head.

For the next few days, Will and I just tucked away in our respective haunts, trying to digest all that had happened to us. I eased back in a lawn chair, out on my deck with my boy, Shadow, who was close enough to be touching me. (He hardly let me out of his sight now.)

It had been a remarkable month or so, beginning with the bizarre tale of a dying prospector, then on to the discovery of an Egyptian city in the walls of the Grand Canyon, the scrolls, the ancient Kool-Aid, and the distinguished Professor Aaron Baal (whom we were nowhere near certain we were safe from, even now). Then there was the collapse of the cavern and the escape (which I admit was straight out of a Harrison Ford movie). That was followed by being kidnapped by Baal and the remarkable rescue by friends and family. And I couldn't help but think back to the bloody amazing Irishman, Connor O'Connor, who had helped shape so much of what had happened to us. I swear, I still felt him over my shoulder, in some of the quiet moments...

If I was to pull something truly positive from all this, it would have to be the kids, Tax and Jing. What a remarkable pair they had proven to be — bright, courageous, and authentic. Certainly more than a couple of old scoundrels like Will and I deserved. I guess, again, my only disappointment, as strange as it might sound, was the disappearance of Margo and Kendra. I suppose I could have been reminded of one of Rufus's quotes: *"Sometimes, de Gods take things away and give us a bag of perspective in return. It not always a great trade..."*

It wasn't exactly that I wanted them in my life but I would have been more content knowing that they were making someone, somewhere, nervous and crazy.

Speaking of nervous and crazy...

Oddly enough, it was the kumbaya experience in Key West that actually seemed to have caught the attention of several newspapers, — even a few dailies across the country. There was an article regarding the "strange benevolence" in one of the smaller periodicals just outside D.C. It also mentioned the survival of the head of the Smithsonian Institute in what could have been a fatal airplane crash/incident in Key West, and that he was returning immediately to Washington.

Aaron Baal sat in his relic-adorned penthouse on the periphery of Washington D.C., his anger all-consuming. He realized he was going to have to go after the two who had gotten away. They had practically beaten him at every turn, and in this last affair, which should have been a done deal, they had exposed him as no one had ever before. For the first time, he felt vulnerable. But it was a matter of pride now as much as anything.

About that same time, one of the older residents of the professor's condominium had just parked his Jaguar in the basement and was moving toward the elevator, when two ladies suddenly appeared. They were quite attractive — short skirts and tight blouses that belied all speculation regarding their remarkable figures. One had long blond hair and the other, a heavy, reddish mane. They appeared to have come from the guard/security atrium but he wasn't sure about that.

The blond asked if the fellow had a light for her cigarette while they waited for the elevator. The man did, and they struck up a simple conversation. By the time the elevator doors finally opened, they were all laughing about a story one of the girls had recounted. As all three entered the elevator, one of the girls slipped an arm through the older fellow's arm. The security guard assumed they were together. Besides, you could get yourself fired if you paid too much attention to the women (and men) entering the building.

The girls said good-bye to the older gentleman on the fifth floor and proceeded upwards.

There were two discreetly but heavily armed guards sitting in chairs outside Baal's apartment, one on each side of the door. The doors to the elevator opened and out stumbled two scantily dressed ladies. They were giggling, each holding an empty champagne glass. They teetered over and stopped in front of the surprised guards.

The blond stepped forward. "You wanna see my tits?" she drawled in a slightly inebriated fashion. Before the two men could answer, she pulled up her blouse, exposing a lovely pair of God's greatest creations.

At that point, for just a few seconds, all of the two men's attention was focused on one thing only. (Okay, two things. It wasn't their fault. It's just the way God made most men.) As the fellows ogled, open-mouthed, at Kendra, Margo pulled a silenced pistol from the base of her spine and shot them both.

They quickly rifled through the men's pockets and found a key to the front door.

Professor Aaron Baal was preparing to take a shower. He had stripped off his clothes and had on his bathrobe. Baal was running the water when the door to the bathroom opened and the girls entered.

"I know you're probably disappointed," said Margo, "but the team you sent to 'visit' us didn't fare well." She paused and offered a malicious smile. "Never send a couple of boys to do a woman's job..."

"We've been waiting for you, watching for you, ever since," said Kendra.

Baal didn't even waste time trying to deny it. "Look, I'm sorry. Okay? You were just too close to the other side. I was afraid you were going to turn. I had to do what was necessary." He held up his hands. "We can make a deal here..."

"Actually, we've made a deal here already," said Kendra. "And when we get paid, a body has to drop. That's our business motto."

"Well, there was the guy we put in the acid bath," said Margo. "He didn't exactly drop. There wasn't much more than a greasy line around the tub..."

"And there was the guy we dropped into the commercial chum machine," Kendra added offhandedly. "Not much there afterward... And there was the —"

"Okay, okay, I get it!" cried Baal, losing a lot of his machismo now, his voice moving toward pleading. "Don't. Don't do this...I have money, lots of money. You can have it..."

Margo shook her head. "Life is really about two things — money and love. But you don't have enough money to make me love you."

Kendra ignored her sister, continuing. "We've decided that you finally just couldn't stand all the duplicity and all the murders to keep your little world and your 'institution' in order. I typed you up a nice little note that explains how you just couldn't go on..." She reached into her pocket and pulled out an envelope with a clear-surgical-gloved hand and stuffed it in Baal's pocket. "C'mon, let's go out to your balcony and watch the sunset."

The professor reflexively glanced at the security camera on the porch. Kendra saw him.

"Sorry, buddy," she said. "No luck there. We've already cut the main wiring to the building's cameras."

The three of them stood on the balcony. Margo had a gun in the man's spine. Kendra was next to him, blocking any way back into the condominium. The last of the sun was burying itself in the city's skyline.

The professor exhaled. "Ladies, there must be something..."

But the eyes of the women in front of him spoke of futility.

There was an emotionally pregnant moment. The air almost crackled with electricity. Kendra could see the man's eyes changing and his body tensing. She backed up, raising her gun slightly, and her sister followed.

Professor Baal's eyes glanced at the guns again and he sighed heavily. His countenance gradually slid from electric desperation to a shrouded, prison-camp acceptance, and his shoulders slumped. "May you both rot in the pits of hell!" he hissed. Then he turned, grabbed the porch rail, and threw himself over it.

Baal was silent about halfway down. Then, as the pavement came rushing up at him, he started to scream...

"I'm impressed," muttered Margo.

"Me too," replied Kendra. "I was prepared for quite a bit of begging and whining." She sighed. "Okay, time to go, Thelma..."

Margo smiled. "You bet, Louise."

I'm fairly sure — at least, I'd like to think — that when Professor Aaron Baal reached Hell, our buddy, Connor O'Connor was waiting for him with his baseball bat...

EPILOGUE

Apparently, there had been some sort of power outage at the professor's condominium the afternoon of his death. The police were attempting to determine what had happened, but to this point, the videos during that time seemed to have been either erased or there was a recording glitch of some sort. It seemed far too convenient but the authorities had no leads.

Most of us in the Keys had a pretty good idea of what had happened but we still weren't exactly sure who did it.

Dax, our intrepid cowboy, still had almost two weeks to serve with the Monroe County Sheriff's Department, but for a guy like Dax, it wasn't a big deal. No one was going to steal his food or make him tickle their fancy. Will and I were planning a "getting out" party for him. He had saved our asses big time, more than once, over the last month or so.

My boy, Tax, had his pickup repaired and was back on the road again, working out at the local gym and doing motocross racing in Homestead. In the process, he was effortlessly managing a bevy of attractive ladies who found him impossibly attractive. (Just like his old man, I liked to think...)

Jing and her amazing hawk could be seen here and there in the Middle Keys. She was becoming a local attraction and was considering giving classes on hawking.

Our man, Crazy Eddie, pilot extraordinaire, was back to relaxing at his bar and telling stories. And Lord, he had some new ones...

Life was starting to level out. But then, like Rufus always says... *"Da gods, dey constantly in need of entertainment. We be nothing but da unsuspecting actors in da play of life."*

Less than a week after Professor Aaron Baal's unfortunate demise, Margo and Kendra showed up in the Keys, healthy, wealthy, and relatively pleased with themselves. Both Will and I were happy to see them alive and well, but it definitely complicated our lives.

When we asked them about the professor, a brief flash of the eyes passed between them, then they shrugged.

"Who's to say?" replied Margo. "A man like that has a lot of enemies."

Michael Reisig

The least Will and I could do was take them out to dinner. (Which probably meant a night of exhausting debauchery, but hey, a man's gotta do what a man's gotta do...) We settled on Louie's Backyard. With the Captain Lafitte treasure, which Will and I (and our kids) had collected earlier in the year, we could afford it.

It was a remarkably nice night, actually. The weather was perfect. The food and the wine were excellent, and Eddie had given us a really righteous doobie, which pretty much took the edge off of everything. In the end, Will and I took our respective ladies home with us — not without a good deal of apprehension, but then, we figured we owed them. Everything has a price. But somehow, I had forgotten how high the price was...

After an exhausting but not necessarily unpleasant few hours, Kendra allowed me to take a break to go to the bathroom and eat a couple of energy bars. We actually slept for about an hour after that. She was pacing me. About that time, the phone rang.

No one likes to get "middle of the night" phone calls. They are almost inevitably bad news.

I reached for the phone. Kendra was kissing the back of my neck and sliding her hand down to my groin...

It was Will. His voice was so weak I could barely understand him. "Help..." he whispered. "Help...I'm not a young man anymore. I don't think I can... She's like, somewhere between a ferret on acid and a mad Valkyrie...I can't..."

But at that moment I heard Margo's silky voice. She was whispering in Will's ear. "I could love you forever, baby..." she cooed sensuously. There was a pause and a slurping sound — I think it was Margo's tongue in my buddy's ear and on the receiver. Will moaned. I wasn't sure if it was from pleasure or misery.

"Oh, yes..." I heard Margo continue breathlessly. "I could love you forever. I mean *forever*. Or until you die..." There was a slight pause. "But that's probably going to be a long time." Another pause. "As long as you love me..."

"Help..." croaked Will. "Help..."

"You're on your own, buddy," I gasped, as Kendra found what she was looking for. Again... "Just try to survive the night. Then get the twin Cessna fueled..."

~

193

I hope you have enjoyed this novel. If you would like to be added to my mailing list (to stay apprised of new novels and to receive bimonthly updates and my newspaper columns), email me at: reisig@ipa.net

—*Michael Reisig*

And…be sure to read the rest of
Michael Reisig's best-selling

ROAD TO KEY WEST SERIES

THE ROAD TO KEY WEST

The Road to Key West is an adventurous, humorous sojourn that cavorts its way through the 1970s Caribbean, from Key West and the Bahamas to Cuba and Central America—a Caribbean brew of part-time pirates, heartless larcenists, wild women, Voodoo bokors, drug smugglers, and a wacky Jamaican soothsayer.

Kindle Book only $3.99
To Preview or Purchase this book on amazon.com, use this link:
http://www.amazon.com/dp/B004RPMYF8

BACK ON THE ROAD TO KEY WEST
The Golden Scepter—Book II

An ancient map and a lost pirate treasure, a larcenous Bahamian scoundrel with his gang of cutthroats, a wild and crazy journey into South America in search of a magical antediluvian device, and perilous, hilarious encounters with outlandish villains and zany friends will keep you locked to your seat and giggling maniacally.

Kindle Book only $3.99
To Preview or Purchase this book on amazon.com, use this link:
http://www.amazon.com/dp/B00FC9D94I

ALONG THE ROAD TO KEY WEST
The Truthmaker—Book III

Fast-paced humor and adventure with wacky pilots, quirky con men, mad villains, bold women, and a gadget to die for. Florida Keys adventurers Kansas Stamps and Will Bell find their lives turned upside down when they discover a truth device hidden in the temple of an ancient civilization. Enthralled by the virtue of personally dispensing truth and justice with this unique tool, they soon discover everyone wants what they have—from the government to the Vatican.

Kindle Book only $3.99
To Preview or Purchase this book on amazon.com, use this link:
http://www.amazon.com/dp/B00G5B3HEY

SOMEWHERE ON THE ROAD TO KEY WEST
The Emerald Cave—Book IV

The captivating diary of an amateur archaeologist sends our intrepid explorers on a journey into the heart of the Panamanian jungle in search of *La cueva de Esmeralda* (the Emerald Cave), and a lost Spanish treasure. But local brigand Tu Phat Shong and his gang of cutthroats are searching for the same treasure. If that wasn't enough, one of the Caribbean's nastiest drug lords has a score to settle with our reluctant heroes.

Kindle Book only $3.99
To Preview or Purchase this book on amazon.com, use this link:
http://www.amazon.com/dp/B00NOABMKA

DOWN THE ROAD TO KEY WEST
Pancho Villa's Gold— Book V

If you're looking for clever fun with zany characters, a and electric high adventure, this one's for you! Reisig's newest offering is guaranteed to keep you locked to your seat and slapping at the pages, while burbling up a giggle or two. In the fifth book of this series, our reluctant Caribbean heroes find themselves competing for the affections of a beautiful antiquities dealer and searching for the lost treasure of Mexico's most renowned desperado.

Kindle Book only $3.99
To Preview or Purchase this book on amazon.com, use this link:
http://www.amazon.com/dp/B01EPI6XY4

BEYOND THE ROAD TO KEY WEST
Mayan Gold— Book VI

First, the reader is drawn back over 400 years, to the magnificent Mayan empire — to the intrigue of powerful rulers, Spanish invasion, and an adventure/love story that survives the challenge of time. Moving forward several centuries, Kansas and Will stumble upon a collection of ancient writings, and the tale of a treasure that was cached by the great Mayan ruler, Nachán Can...

Kindle book only 3.99
To Preview or Purchase this book on amazon.com, use this link:
http://www.amazon.com/dp/B01M293NDP

A FAR ROAD TO KEY WEST
Emeralds and Lies — Book VII

The "Hole in the Coral Wall Gang" return to the Guatemalan jungle to retrieve the remainder of a Mayan king's incredible treasure, but in the process they find themselves engaged in a grassroots revolution, pursued by a vengeful colonel in the Guatemalan military, and immersed in the intrigue of a World War Two Nazi treasure. Then, there's the beautiful sister of a revolutionary, the golden Swiss francs, and the greatest challenge of all — *Granja Penal de Pavón* — the most terrifying prison in all of Central America.

To Preview or Purchase this book on amazon.com, use this link:
http://www.amazon.com/dp/B072VRR2VY

THE WILD ROAD TO KEY WEST
The Cave of The Stars -- Book VIII

Once again, *The Hole In The Coral Wall Gang* is wrapped in a wild adventure. Diamonds and emeralds, a lost city infused by a treasure and an ancient race, a secret cave with a timeless message, ruthless bandits, jungle Indians, and nefarious cowboys are all part of this non-stop roller coaster ride.

Did I mention the gang's new guide, Arturio — a Venezuelan outback opportunist who has a mild obsession with Russian Roulette? Or Passi, the lustful jungle witch who just can't make up her mind?

To Preview or Purchase this book on amazon.com, use this link::
www.amazon.com/dp/B078FMD5TZ

A PIRATE'S ROAD TO KEY WEST
Lafitte's Gold Book — Book IX

In the ninth novel of his best-selling "Road To Key West" series, Michael Reisig once again locks his readers into a careening odyssey of hidden fortunes, mercurial romance, conscienceless villains, and bizarre friends.

From Caracas to New Orleans, into the dark fringes of Haiti, down through the Windward Islands, then back into The Florida Keys, Kansas Stamps, Will Bell, and The Hole In The Coral Wall Gang chase a stolen Pre-Columbian treasure. Then there's the Voodoo-practicing drug boss, a vengeful Columbian Don, and a highly artful assassin. Before you can catch your breath, it all rolls together into a turbulent Key West Fantasy Fest finale.

To Preview or Purchase this book on amazon.com, use this link:
https://www.amazon.com/PIRATES-ROAD-KEY-WEST/dp/0999091476

Also, be sure to read...

CARIBBEAN GOLD
THE TREASURE OF TORTUGA

In 1668, Englishman Trevor Holte and the audacious freebooter Clevin Greymore sail from the Port of London for the West Indies. They set out in search of adventure and wealth, but the challenges they encounter are beyond their wildest dreams—the brutal Spanish, ruthless buccaneers, a pirate king, the lure of Havana, and the women, as fierce in their desires as Caribbean storms. And then, there was the gold—wealth beyond imagination. But some treasures outlive the men who bury them...

Kindle Book only $3.99
To Preview or Purchase this book on amazon.com, use this link:
http://www.amazon.com/dp/B00S8SR0WW

CARIBBEAN GOLD
THE TREASURE OF TIME

In the spring of 1980, three adventurers set out from Key West in search of a lost treasure on the Isle of Tortuga, off the coast of Haiti. Equipped with an ancient parchment and a handful of clues, they embark on a journey that carries them back across time, challenging their courage and their imaginations, presenting them with remarkable allies and pitting them against an amalgam of unrelenting enemies. In the process, they uncover far more than a treasure. They discover the power of friendship and faith, the unflagging capacity of spirit, and come to realize that some things are forever...

Kindle Book only $3.99
To Preview or Purchase this book on amazon.com, use this link:
http://www.amazon.com/dp/B00S8SR0WW

CARIBBEAN GOLD
THE TREASURE OF MARGARITA

The Treasure of Margarita spans three centuries of high adventure. Beginning in 1692, in the pirate stronghold of Port Royal, it carries the reader across the Southern Hemisphere in a collage of rip-roaring escapades. Then it soars forward five generations, into modern-day intrigue and romance in Key West and the Caribbean.

A staggering fortune of Spanish black pearls and a 300-year-old letter with a handful of clues set the course that Travis Christian and William Cody embark upon. But it's not an easy sail. Seasoned with remarkable women and bizarre villains, the adventure ricochets from one precarious situation to the next.

Kindle Book only $3.99
To Preview or Purchase this book on amazon.com, use this link:
http://www.amazon.com/dp/B00X1E2X2K

THE TRUE TALES OF THE ROAD TO KEY WEST

These tales will make you smile with wonder, remind you of the importance of loyalty and love in life, and make you laugh your ass off. I have taken my experiences, encounters, and adventures, and blended them into and around the highlights of my eight "Road To Key West" novels. Included in the package are a number of memory-jarring photos and terrific quotes, to create a humorous, insightful, walk down memory lane for new and seasoned readers.

If you haven't read any of "The Road To Key West" novels, this is the perfect place to begin. If you've read them all, you'll love these engaging, sometimes laugh-out-loud recollections.

Kindle Book only $2.99
To Preview or purchase this book on amazon.com, use this link:
https://www.amazon.com/True-Tales-Road-Key-West/dp/0999091468